Hailey ´

THE SHOALMAN CHRONICLES
BOOK 1

TONI DECKER

*Take a Picture —
it will last for Eternity*

Kira & Toni

Copyright © 2014 by Toni Decker

All rights reserved under International and Pan-American Copyright Conventions

By payment of required fees, you have been granted the *non*-exclusive, *non*-transferable right to access and read the text of this book. No part of this text may be reproduced, transmitted, downloaded, decompiled, reverse engineered, or stored in or introduced into any information storage and retrieval system, in any form or by any means, whether electronic or mechanical, now known or hereinafter invented without the express written permission of copyright owner.

Please Note

The reverse engineering, uploading, and/or distributing of this book via the internet or via any other means without the permission of the copyright owner is illegal and punishable by law. Please purchase only authorized electronic editions, and do not participate in or encourage electronic piracy of copyrighted materials. Your support of the author's rights is appreciated

No part of this book may be reproduced or transmitted in any form or by any electronic or mechanical means, including photocopying, recording or by any information storage and retrieval system, without the written permission of the publisher, except where permitted by law.

Thank you.

Interior format by The Killion Group
http://thekilliongroupinc.com

ACKNOWLEDGMENTS

There are so many people who helped make this book a reality. Without their support and sideline cheering, this book might never have been written.

To both our families for giving us the time to write this amazing story. Your patience helped make our dream real.

To our wonderful Editor, Megan McKeever: You got our story and your insightful energy inspired us to dig deeper to make it even better. We can't wait to work together on the next one.

To fellow writers and early beta readers: KD, Christi, Nancy, Anna, and Pauline. For beta reading (sometimes more than once), as well as, cheering us on the entire way along this journey. *fist bumps all around*

To Karen, for putting up with all our questions without complaint and giving us the benefit of your experience.

Special thanks goes out to our dear friend and *amazing* Cover Designer, Sharon Carpenter. You took a leap of faith with us and never stopped believing we would succeed. Your design captured our story and gave it life. As Lucien and Mandy would say, we freaking love the color red.

Lastly, to our cheering squad of family and friends, our critique peeps, and the talented people of the Maryland Romance Writers group. The support and guidance you all gave to us made such a difference. Thanks!

CHAPTER ONE

Sometimes the lengths Amanda Hayworth would go to to get a shot of the hottest band around knew no bounds. More times than she could count, it required flirting with a muscular bouncer, smoothing over his rippled ego to get the best seat in a venue. As a last resort, mentioning her father's name always helped since he owned over half of the buildings in town. Sometimes getting the right shot required little more than perfect timing.

Tonight was one of those nights that required all three plus a few skills she'd never had to use before.

After confirming *Demon Dogs* would, in fact, be practicing at Gallery this afternoon, she convinced her best friend to come with her in case she needed someone to run interference. Considering the level of secrecy her band contact kept, she wasn't sure what she might encounter showing up uninvited and determined to get the shot she so badly wanted.

In the rain, she waited for her chance. Standing in a puddle, two inches of water ruining her favorite pair of boots, with an umbrella over her head to prevent her mascara from smearing, she tried to protect the love of her life: her camera.

"The band should be here any minute," Mandy said to Kyrissa. She adjusted the plastic rain sleeve around the body of her camera. She'd withstand a hurricane as long as her camera stayed dry.

"If this rain doesn't let up, I'm not going to be here

to witness it." Kyrissa pulled her jacket tighter and the umbrella lower over their heads. "I don't care what time the band is supposed to be here, I'd rather not show up to meet my professor looking like a drowned rat."

"It's just water, Ky," Mandy mused. Kyrissa was a lot of things; patient wasn't one of them. "I want the first images of *Demon Dog's* new lead singer." The security guard assured Mandy of the band's practice time, and she wasn't moving until the group appeared.

Kyrissa stepped into a deeper puddle and splashed water up the leg of her jeans. "That's it, I'm done." She shook her rain soaked boot in the air.

Mandy refused to abandon her post just yet but she couldn't expect Kyrissa to do the same in this weather. "That's fine. I'm sorry. I didn't think it would take this long." Mandy pressed against the wall under an awning barely wide enough to keep her from getting soaked. She pulled out her phone. Raindrops fell onto the hood of her jacket. "I'll call you a cab."

"Not your fault this mysterious new singer hasn't conformed to Mandy Hayworth's time schedule," Kyrissa said chuckling. "I don't need a cab. I'll walk and see you back at the apartment whenever you give up on this insanity. But I'm taking this umbrella with me."

Before Mandy could argue, Kyrissa was halfway down the alley, a dark figure blending into the rainy afternoon. An hour later into the evening, Mandy would have refused to let Kyrissa walk alone. Not that they lived in a questionable neighborhood or dangerous part of the city, but for the better part of her twenty-two years, Mandy worried about her best friend as she would a slightly younger sister.

Mandy lifted her camera, her finger pressed down on the button, framing Kyrissa in the lens. Vibrant bands of light that didn't show to the naked eye emanated from her petite figure, filling the air around her. Color so intense it nearly whited out Kyrissa all together, showing the vibrancy she carried underneath. Mandy lowered the camera from her eye and smiled at the glow surrounding her best friend. No matter how hard Kyrissa tried to hide it, Mandy's camera could always capture her bright spirit within its frame.

Too bad not everyone possessed such luck. Most of the pictures Mandy took revealed truths many people wished she couldn't see. Men who tried to charm her were revealed as the snakes they really were by their sickly green auras. People who attempted to win her trust were too often shown as liars, their photos shrouding them in blurry shadows. And sometimes, the lies she'd been told her entire life were exposed with one single click, turning her own world upside down.

Photographing musicians was different. No matter what the performers might attempt to hide, they couldn't hide the music from the images emanating through her lens. Her pictures captured music with lights and colors. She couldn't explain why shadows appeared without a light source, or how rainbows hovered in dark rooms. Sometimes stage sets silhouetted all but one member of a band even though they all performed together under the same lights.

Mandy stopped trying to explain these anomalies years ago, unable to convince people she hadn't digitally altered the files. Denying it wasn't worth her time anymore, as long as the photos captivated the audience. That was Mandy's reward.

That's why she'd been standing in this filthy alley behind an empty club, in cooler than normal temperatures, drowning in a river created by three days of rain that wouldn't relent, not even for her. Didn't Mother Nature know who she was? A Hayworth, and daughter of the wealthiest man in all of Baltimore. A crack of thunder and an increase in the downpour answered that question. Mother Nature wasn't impressed.

When a van finally arrived, Mandy pressed herself harder against the brick wall. A figure stepped out of the vehicle into the pouring rain. He flipped the hood of his sweatshirt over his head and opened the back of the van. Slinging a guitar case over one shoulder, he moved from the back of the vehicle into the alley carrying a small amp wrapped in plastic. Hefting a box marked "Cables" and another marked "Sound Equipment", he balanced everything in one arm before kicking shut the door of the beat up van.

Mandy sighed. Just the setup crew.

Still, she couldn't help herself, or prevent her camera from acting before she instructed it not to. Snapping his picture, she didn't care that he was merely the roadie or that she couldn't see his face within the frame. The closer he got, the more she snapped, without taking her eye away from the camera.

Dark jeans that fit perfectly in all the areas that mattered. Black boots that would have accessorized a motorcycle better than they did an old van. And an unzipped hooded sweatshirt with a white t-shirt underneath couldn't hide the physique of a well-sculpted body.

Whoever he was, the guy sizzled as he walked towards her.

"No more pictures," his voice crooned through the rain.

He stood inches from her and this close, the white t-shirt, now darkened from the rain, filled her entire view. Faint tattoo lines scrolled across his chest, teasing from behind the now almost transparent fabric and called for her to get a better view. She raised her camera once more, the impulse too strong to deny.

"I said, no more pictures," he repeated covering the lens of her camera with his hand.

"Don't ever touch my camera again." Mandy flinched away from his hand. She didn't take her attention away from the camera. Partly out of embarrassment for being asked to stop taking photos, which had never happened before; partly because a second vehicle, a sleek, black SUV, pulled into the alley that could only be carrying the members of *Demon Dogs*, including their latest lead singer.

"Finally," she whispered.

The guy sighed and proceeded through the back door to Gallery.

If Mandy was completely honest, she had stopped following the *Demon Dogs* when more trouble surrounded the group than good times. Their first bassist quit after an argument over cream cheese, or at least that was the story running in the rumor mill. The original drummer parted ways when offered a spot with another band whose name was now synonymous with bestselling albums. She only featured the band on her blog because at the time, she had a soft spot for their drummer, Jay Cooley.

Why the lead singer left revolved around drug problems and ten too many times in rehab. But his replacement remained a complete mystery, one she'd like to be the first to unravel.

Three of the four members of *Demon Dogs* ran towards her, hunched in the rain. Each one as hot as the one running behind him, yet she didn't take a single picture as they approached. Two, Mandy had only seen on stage before today. The other, she knew a bit more personally than she cared to admit and had no intention of getting to know any better. She ignored the truth on her camera two times in her life, and one of those mistakes stood right in front of her.

"If it isn't my favorite little photographer." Jay leaned in close enough that the smoke from the half-lit cigarette dangling between his lips blew in her direction. He auditioned for another band a few years back, but *Spiral* catapulted to stardom without Jay, thanks in part to an article Mandy wrote about them thinking the band would include him. Regardless, the article went viral, as did *Spiral's* first single, and the combination became intoxicating for both of them. Now, an endorsement from Mandy usually convinced several music heads, and most locals, to check out a band.

"Ah, if it isn't my almost favorite drummer." Mandy winked. No doubt, Jay was rock star amazing, in more ways than one, but the layers of bullshit he hid behind were far too thick for her to ignore ever again. Not to mention the way he ran hot and cold. Images of him onstage absolutely shined, bright and clear. The moment he stepped off, he plunged into a darkness she couldn't explain any more than she could ignore.

"How'd you know we'd be practicing here this afternoon?" Jay leaned against the wall beside her, the shallow eaves barely protecting his broad shoulders from the rain. The other guys jogged past to the cover of the backdoor awning.

"You know I don't reveal my sources," Mandy said. She pointed her camera at Jay.

"I could cancel rehearsal if you're looking for a more personal show."

"Definitely not." Mandy pushed off the wall, letting her finger depress the button on her camera. When she looked at Jay on her screen, the dark circles surrounding him were even darker than she remembered, multiplied in the weeks since she'd seen him last. What she ever saw in him no longer existed.

"Putting that one on your bedside table?" Jay inched closer trying to see the image.

Mandy pulled away before he got close enough to see the haze that swallowed his form, as if the alley had taken a bite out of the air. What explanation could she give about the anomaly when it appeared as a trick of the camera or an impossible alteration?

Neither tricked nor altered, only the sad truth revealed before her very own eyes. Sometimes the truth hurt.

Creating distance between them, Mandy let the camera fall to her side. Her curiosity was so piqued she could barely stand still. "Rumor has it you've finally found a new lead singer."

"I should have guessed that's why you're here." Jay laughed.

"Any chance I'll get to meet him tonight?"

"Good luck with that." He flicked his cigarette across the alley into a puddle of water. The rain had let up just enough that a faint hiss echoed in the dank space. "He's a fucking awesome singer but he's also a fucking genius. He has a marketing plan that's going to skyrocket *Demon Dogs* right out of this town. We're planning a re-launch that'll blow this local scene to pieces."

Mandy was aware of the rumors about the lead singer's voice. The few people who had heard him claimed angels wept when he sang and she was prepared to find out if those rumors were true. She even had a few tissues tucked inside her bra just in case.

With the right players in place, a re-launch could be exactly what *Demon Dogs* needed to break past the barriers that kept them semi-successful, but mired in the local scene. New lead singer, maybe a few new songs and a feature article strategically placed on the best music blog. Potential for another viral musical success a la Mandy Hayworth.

"Would this plan include an exclusive with your favorite photographer?" Mandy pasted the flirtiest smile she owned on her lips and pushed her chest out which always helped when dealing with a dedicated boob man like Jay. "I can't wait to meet this mysterious guy who apparently owns a rocket."

Jay's gaze flicked to her chest for a long look before

he shook his head. "I'll see what I can do." He grinned, pointing at the closed door to the back of the club. "But you just met Lucien. The guy carrying the guitar."

The guy with the almost see-through white shirt, the jeans that left her drooling, and the mysterious tattoos that sang her name.

"Son of a..." Mandy growled.

She'd met the new lead singer of *Demon Dogs*.

And he told her not to take any pictures.

CHAPTER TWO

Damn, Lucien hated when Jay was right. The photographer had been waiting outside the club just like he warned, almost ruining his strategy for keeping his debut with *Demon Dogs* a secret. Create a little mystery and people will flock to uncover the puzzle. A marketing gimmick he planned to exploit.

Hiding in plain sight was a talent Lucien learned years ago. Act like a nobody and people saw you that way. Thankfully, it worked on the chick.

Lucien smiled to himself. He hadn't gotten a good look at her while trying to act like a roadie, but what he had seen was enough to make any guy's blood burn. Right now, his might as well be on fire.

Short, even in heeled boots, thin, but curved in all the right places. Rain plastered her coat tight against her form. The top of her chest glistened with water where the top snap had come undone. Damn the rest of her jacket for remaining closed. Or was that something she had done on purpose? He shook his head. Maybe he wasn't the only marketing genius around here.

Too bad Jay's warning hadn't come with the photographer's name or mention she was hot. Lucien might have rethought his strategy before stepping out of the van and into the lion's den.

"Hey, Lucien. Need help?" Carl called out, breaking into Lucien's errant thoughts.

"Hey, man, you working security here now?" Lucien

shook hands with the brawny bouncer who normally worked at his father's private club, Solvak's. He handed him the amp and one of the boxes. The guitar slung across his back, he didn't entrust to anyone.

Around anyone else, Lucien's six-foot-one height and broad shoulders made him stand out. Next to Carl, he felt like a stick figure. "Not enough hours for you at Solvak's?"

"Naw, I'm just filling in here at Gallery during the art re-hang." Carl shrugged. "Christophe wanted extra security. I just do what I'm told."

"Wise choice." Christophe's voice echoed from the back of the bar.

Lucien stiffened. "*Tata*, what are you doing here?"

A shrewd businessman, Christophe Solvak maintained a hands-on approach with all his investments. Including his only son, until recently. The chill seeping into his core he might attribute to the wet t-shirt and hoodie clinging to his skin, but Lucien knew better.

Clad in a three-piece suit, Christophe presented an air of formality. One that would exist even if he dressed in nothing but shorts and flip-flops. Not that his father would be caught dead in anything less than tailored pants, crisp shirt and tie. His father pressed his mouth into a thin line. Lucien, returning the gaze, forced himself not to shuffle his feet.

"I'm surprised you weren't the one here to receive the paintings." Christophe stated. "I thought you were working for Robert today."

Typical. His father never did like to answer his direct questions. Instead, he disguised his displeasure in Lucien's choices as casual remarks. Robert might be a silent partner in most of his father's companies, but Lucien's decision to work for Robert instead of Christophe still irked the man. And his father made sure to remind Lucien at every opportunity.

"Later." With no intention of accounting for his time

to his father, he also didn't feel like arguing right now. The rest of the band members were just outside and Lucien didn't want to air the family drama in front of strangers. "Staying for rehearsal?" He wasn't sure if he wanted his father to stay or go. Music had been one love they both shared, at least until his mother died.

"No." A pained expression pulled at the lines around his eyes. Christophe turned away. "I needed to collect some quarterly reports and check on the extra security," Christophe claimed. "Your *boss* insisted upon it. Luckily, Carl seems to have things covered."

The rejection stung like a slap to the face. "Whatever," he mumbled.

Where Shoalman paintings were concerned, Robert didn't believe there was ever enough security, and he'd never leave the task to Christophe or Carl. Clenching his teeth, Lucien refused to rise to his father's baiting. He and Robert delivered the art themselves before the sun rose. More likely, his father only wanted to make sure the band wasn't something Lucien made up as an excuse to avoid him.

"Make sure you lock up. The paintings are in the secure storage room." Christophe nodded to Carl, who hadn't moved, before exiting out the side door.

"Got it." Lucien exhaled sharply. He knew exactly where the paintings were stored because he'd put them there.

"That went well," Carl murmured.

The absurd comment drew a chuckle from both men and diffused the lingering tension. "Yeah, sorry about that." Lucien placed the sound equipment case next to the now unwrapped amp. Sliding his guitar case off his shoulder, he leaned it against the backstage wall. "Dad's almost as intimidating as Robert when he wants something."

"No one is that intimidating." Carl shook his head. "I don't know how you work for the guy."

"He's not that bad," Lucien stated. Thankfully, both

Robert and his father had allowed *Demon Dogs* to use Gallery for the next three weeks to rehearse during the day. Dismissing both men from his thoughts, Lucien refocused on rehearsal. Which brought him back to the sexy chick outside.

"Hey, Carl, have you been here all day?" Lucien asked.

Carl nodded. "Yeah, pretty much. What's up?"

"You wouldn't happen to know who the chick with the camera is outside would you?" Sure, Lucien knew she was a photographer and Jay mentioned she had a blog but man was he holding back on information where she was concerned.

"Ah, I see you met Mandy." Carl grinned. "She's kinda a fixture around town. My favorite fixture, if you know what I mean. She has connections inside of connections. If it involves music, she knows about it. Loves getting to know the artists, lives the music scene, and endorses local talent when she thinks they're worthy. But don't touch her camera. Like ever. She'll bite your fucking head off if you mess with her baby."

"Yeah, I noticed." No wonder she stabbed him with a look that felt like a dagger to the solar plexus. If he could control her photo-happy clicking, she could be worth getting to know. Her connections could be exactly what *Demon Dogs* needed to break out in the music scene. "Might just have to introduce myself. *Demon Dogs* could use a few endorsements."

"Hate to burst your bubble, little Lucien," Jay taunted. "But Mandy is so far out of your league, you might as well be playing a different game."

Carrying the rest of their equipment to the stage, Adam and Rusty, the other band members, snickered.

"At least we're both playing," Lucien dared. His little game of hide and seek with the photographer might have pissed her off but from what Jay told him about her, he hoped it sparked a mystery about him instead. "You scumbags wouldn't even rate a second look from her."

"Like you would?" Adam teased.

"A second look and more," Lucien countered.

"Do I sense a bet?" Jay's sly grin grew. "You wouldn't even score a date. And trust me when I tell you that you will never get *more* from the likes of Mandy. She doesn't do strings. Ever."

"We'll see about that." A handshake sealed the bet. Lucien feared Jay might be right, but at least if he were in pursuit the others would back off. Band Rule number one. You didn't go for a girl one of the others had marked. As sexist as it sounded, that particular band rule was unbreakable. Something about this chick prickled Lucien's protective tattoos. A warning he didn't dare ignore, even at the risk of sounding sexist.

"You think you have a shot?" Jay threw fifty bucks on the table. "Go for it. Can't wait to see the crash and burn."

To distract himself, and make the other guys think he wasn't as interested as he actually was, he checked all his equipment to make sure the rain hadn't damaged anything. He'd figure out some way to get Mandy to go out with him.

"Set up and do a sound check guys. I'll be right back. I need to change, shirt is soaked." He pulled the white t-shirt away from his skin to emphasize even though it had started to dry in the warm club.

"You're fine," Jay said, smiling. "Shit don't melt."

"You should know." Lucien headed for the back of the club, snickering at the taunts Jay received after that dig.

Stripping off the hoodie and t-shirt, Lucien checked to make sure the photographer chick hadn't gotten inside. Or maybe he was hoping she was right around the corner and would walk in on him bare-chested.

Earlier Mandy stared at his shirt like she saw straight through it and smiled at what she'd seen.

Still, half-naked in a green room wasn't exactly the marketing image Lucien was trying to create for the band. The former lead singer left the guys in a bad spot with every local venue owner when he entered rehab. For the tenth time. They had to cancel all their shows, leaving openings on lineups all over town. Lucky for Lucien, that same incident left *Demon Dogs* in need of a lead singer and a band in need of a relaunch, one he intended to take farther than the band ever managed before.

Making sure no one else was around, Lucien unlocked the partially hidden door that secreted an office Robert kept in Gallery. His reason for keeping his debut with *Demon Dogs* secret appeared to revolve around his master marketing plan, but in reality, music was Lucien's only chance to find purpose outside his hidden life. A life he could never expose.

Using his fingers, he combed his damp hair back into some semblance of order. He stared at the white tattoos crisscrossing his chest and forearms in the antique oval mirror hanging on the wall. Robert Shoalman kept secrets from the world. Secrets Lucien swore oaths upon his life to protect and keep. The marks upon his skin a testament to those promises. But what if he already failed in that duty?

Mandy had taken pictures of him.

She *couldn't* have seen anything unless Romani blood flowed through her veins. Even then, the significance of the white tattoos remained a secret except to a select few.

He twisted the shirt between his hands. A slow chill slithered down his spine. Why did knowing Mandy had pictures of him sit like a cold, dark pit within him?

CHAPTER THREE

Mandy was accustomed to using what passed for restrooms in bad nightclubs for many things. As a dressing room to change an outfit that went horribly wrong or as an escape from a drunk pawing admirer. Once, when a band insisted they wrote their best material in the can, she used a dirty bar bathroom as a backdrop for some photographs. The band wasn't lying. But for the first time ever, she found herself using the hand drier to dry her hair.

When the dryer proved no match for the mess of thick tangles, she gave up. She shoved her fingers through the dark chestnut strands, and twisted it into a sloppy bun. She let a few red-streaked pieces dangle from the rubber band to frame her face. Not her normal look, but desperate times called for less than stellar hairdos.

In the mirror, she patted her chilled cheeks dry and applied a clean layer of mascara before pressing her lips with her favorite lip-gloss. Lifting her cleavage into the right position, she popped open the next button of her blouse. No way would Lucien walk away from her again. Not until she got exactly what she wanted.

She'd only gotten a brief glimpse of the singer, but what she saw she thoroughly enjoyed. Every step he took towards her was borderline thrilling. Right up until she mistook him for a roadie and he forbade her from taking his picture.

But the pictures didn't show anything. Nothing. No hazes hovered around his form, no odd coloring emanated from his core. Nothing that hinted to Mandy who this guy was or was not.

Mandy exited the bathroom, adjusting her footsteps so the heels of her boots didn't echo down the short hallway. She stopped just short of the perfect location; at the end of the bar where she could see the entire stage, but no one would see her. And since the club didn't open for another six hours, no one would be vying for that spot.

Jay already sat behind his drum kit on stage. He adjusted his stool and tapped the cymbals on either side a few times. Rusty grabbed his bass and the lead guitar player, whose name she'd forgotten, joined him a moment later. Practice obviously hadn't started since only the soundboard operator seemed ready to go.

Snapping a few pictures, she tested the dimmed lighting without a flash. The images appeared clearer than she expected, so she sat back and awaited Lucien's arrival on stage.

Mandy strained to hear the mumbled voices, but it sounded like the usual pre-set conversation. Planning the song order and discussing a few shows lined up in the near future. Tapping her finger along the edge of the camera's lens, Mandy wanted to scream for them to get started already. She hadn't planned to be here all day. On the other side of town a band waited for her. A band who actually wanted her to take their pictures.

"You know, Angel," a dulcet voice sang behind her. "I don't recall sending press invites out for this rehearsal."

Mandy stilled. Hot breath warmed her neck. Every hair on her body stood straight up and a few curled. "And here I thought mine had just been lost in the mail." She turned, facing the solid mass of gorgeousness.

"I would hand deliver any invite I intended you to have." Lucien paused just inches from her and Mandy reminded herself that breathing was not only allowed, also a necessity for survival. Leaning against the edge of the bar, Lucien lifted his gaze to hers and smiled.

"Wow," she mouthed but couldn't be certain whether she said the words out loud or let them linger in her head. Mandy inhaled the scent of freshly shaven skin, soft and tempting. Restraining herself from reaching out to touch him, she settled for leaning in closer and letting his smell inhabit every one of her pores.

"Consider this an invite to stay." His hand lingered in the air between the bar top and Mandy's arm. Mandy didn't back away, watching his movement until he brushed a lock of hair off her shoulder, his finger lightly trailed across her skin. Most times the move would have the perpetrator on his knees in agony. This time Mandy's knees were the ones to shake.

"But absolutely no pictures," Lucien whispered. "Or I'll have Carl over there carry your fine ass right out that door."

Laughing, Mandy hesitated. First, no way would Carl touch her. She'd have his parole officer over here so fast he wouldn't see her ass. And Carl knew this.

Second, who did Lucien think he was? A rock star? He was barely a member of *Demon Dogs,* and at this rate he'd never take them to rock star status. Not without her laying the foundation of information for the local music scene to absorb.

Third, he had noticed her ass and this pleased her a whole lot more than it should.

Mandy hugged her camera tight to her chest. No one had ever forbid her from taking pictures.

"Fine, I'll just listen," Mandy said. He might not want her taking pictures with her camera, but that didn't stop her from raking her gaze over every inch of his body. The dark alley hadn't done his hotness justice.

She itched to see him through the lens of the camera. What would it reveal? Not that her imagination wasn't filling in its own blanks, but her imagination didn't reveal truths the way images did. But how could she convince someone to be photographed who didn't want to be?

She gave him an award-winning smile. "So go sing, handsome. But your voice better give my ears an orgasm or I will make sure *Demon Dogs* never gets any exposure."

Lucien chuckled. His laugh half-faded and his voice cracked when he tried to speak again. He cleared his throat. Mandy admired the nerves he tried to swallow. She was getting him to exactly where she needed him so he would finally relent on the whole no pictures situation.

"Your ears are sexy as hell and all." Lucien ran his tongue along his plump lips. Mandy squirmed. "But they're not the place I'd be worried about getting too worked up if I were you."

Lucien walked away before Mandy could respond, or consider the many ways she'd like to respond, none of which included any words. Except his walk swayed more like a saunter and his steps were far more relaxed than she'd be able to pull off considering how bothered she was watching him walk away. This assignment just took on a whole new level of difficult.

CHAPTER FOUR

Sexy ears?

He wrote song lyrics, composed music that people adored and all he came up with was sexy ears? But her look. Damn! One word and he would have been on her in a second. Screw practice.

Lucien forced himself to saunter away from Mandy despite the fact that he probably just blew any chance he had of winning his bet. Or a date with a gorgeous woman who was quite possibly completely out of his league.

"I see she nailed you with her fuck-me look." Jay rattled off a *ba-dun-chee* on his drums. "Probably should have warned you about that too. Oops."

"You know, you can be a real dick sometimes, Jay." Lucien just hoped the other guys hadn't noticed. The harmonic funeral march from the bass and lead guitarist echoed in the empty club. Lucien groaned. So much for secrets. "Very funny. Can we actually get a rehearsal in sometime today?"

"Waiting on you, lover boy." Jay dismissed the glare Lucien threw his way with another drum combination worthy of a solo.

"Start at the top of the list." Lucien grabbed his guitar and plugged into his amp. Turning around, he avoided making eye contact with Mandy, instead flicking brief glances over her form. Even that threatened to derail his thoughts. His concentration already teetered on the edge of a cliff and the chances of falling off multiplied exponentially if he spent another minute staring at her. "We'll work through everything once, repeat any you three bozos need to, and then fine tune the order later."

"Remember, no pictures, Angel." He flashed a smile, encouraged when she returned it, but he looked away quickly on account of the second fuck-me look she shot his direction. Maybe there was hope yet. Or a lot of trouble.

The opening chords of the guitars, followed quickly by the pounding of Jay's drums, pulled Lucien in and he lost himself in the music. Appropriate song, *Fascinate*. Mandy had definitely done that. His body vibrated. Mind clearing of anything else, he let the music fill him. Here he was free. No responsibilities weighing him down. No secrets to hide. On stage, he could let go, if only for a short while. A freedom that would end too soon.

Forty-five minutes later, the final chord echoed into the empty club. Lucien held his breath waiting for the other band member's reaction. They had loved his initial tryout, and he worked with each of them separately to learn the older songs, but this was the first time they played together as a group.

D-Day.

If any member had their doubts, this was their last chance to speak up before his contract became final.

"What the fucking hell was that?" Jay finally said. Lucien's gut twisted into a cold rock.

"I know I was a little slow on some of the entrances. I, um..."

Adam stalked towards him, while Rusty stood with arms crossed over his chest. Shit. He must have really blown it for them to be this upset with him. Lucien tried to swallow, his mouth now a dry desert.

"You'd think with a voice like his," Adam paused, the other two band members coming to stand directly in front of him. "He'd have his own record deal by now. Solo. Good thing we found him first." Adam smacked him on the shoulder.

"Welcome to *Demon Dogs*, Lucien." Jay stuck out his hand.

Lucien stared at the outstretched hand as though it was a snake ready to bite him. Rusty tousled his hair and Adam just laughed at him. Welcome? Lucien's brain reconnected.

"You bastards." He grabbed Jay's hand, shaking it. "Okay, you had me. Assholes." Lucien laughed, pushing off Rusty and brushing his hair back into place. "New Band Rule. No messing with the hair."

"Oh great, now he turns into a Prima Dona." Rusty made one last swipe but Lucien blocked him.

"All right kiddies." Jay waved them silent. "Enough screwing around. We have a lot to do and only three weeks before our debut. Stash your gear, Lucien, and meet us in the green room. We'll go over details for the show and get an update on this marketing plan of yours."

"I'll be right there." After slinging the guitar to his back, he unplugged and replaced his mic in its case. Lucien looked out from the stage. The club stood empty. Blank walls, paint drop cloths and ladders the only witness to his new status. Not even Carl was around.

More importantly, Mandy was gone. He shouldn't be surprised, but he had hoped she might stick around. He would have liked to return the favor for that sexy as hell undressing she gave him. She was definitely a woman who knew how to get what she wanted. If she looked at him like that again, he might just let her.

"Get a grip," Lucien muttered to himself. "It's not like you could sing your way into her bed." He couldn't even take her to his place. A stranger in his world wasn't only unwelcomed, but forbidden. One rule of Robert's he didn't want to test. Besides, he only needed to get a date with her to win his bet, not sleep with her. Still, apparently her opinion could either sink *Demon Dogs* or make them soar.

Walking into the green room, Lucien caught the water bottle thrown at him. The guys already loved pointing out that at eighteen he couldn't drink at any of the clubs they planned to play.

"Damn good year," he said, cracking open the top and downing half the bottle in one swig.

Moving past the dressing room area, Lucien decided against the sandwiches laid out on the kitchenette counter. He wasn't in the mood for real food yet, still too hyped from rehearsal. Adam and Rusty once again commandeered the comfy couch & flat screen TV. Sound effects from their first person shooter game and obsessive swearing filled the small room. Lucien shook his head and chuckled. And they called him a kid. Thankfully, someone painted the walls a vibrant red instead of the traditional green meant to soothe. Red he liked. Especially when attached to a sexy camera jockey.

"I see you have the publicity ads, flyers and social media blasts ready to go." Jay motioned him further into the room, a wad of papers clutched in one hand. Lucien's marketing plan. "I thought we could add an interview with one of the hottest music blogs in the area to introduce you to our fans," Jay stated flatly but Lucien's perfect pitch detected a hint of amusement in his tone.

"Sure. I'm game." Lucien's skin prickled, the air stagnant as though everyone held their breath at the same instant. Adam and Rusty became absorbed in their game, but the swearingfest had gone quiet. Something was up.

He took another drink. If Jay had managed to get in with *BehindTheImage*, it would mean huge local exposure. The blog hadn't responded to his email request about publicity and a possible interview, but he had used the name L.J. Slone, a nobody right now. He couldn't use Robert's connections. Too dangerous. Nor did he want to use his family name. He'd make it on his own or not at all.

Jay stood waiting, the corners of his mouth twitching to contain his smile. Lucien chuckled. Okay. He'd play Jay's game. "When did you want to set it up? I have to make sure I'm free."

"How about right now?" Jay sidestepped to reveal Mandy sitting on a tall bar stool at the intimate table already prepared for the occasion, camera in hand.

Ah, shit.

She had changed clothes. The wet jeans and t-shirt replaced with a short mini and bright red blouse that highlighted the red streaks in her hair. Did he say he liked red? He suddenly fell in love with the freaking color.

Black heeled calf boots displayed her crossed legs to their best advantage. One foot rolled in lazy circles. Each twist flexed toned thigh muscles, and the length of the skirt gave way too much exposure to for him not to notice. Lucien blinked to disrupt thoughts of what else those thighs could do. The button down blouse, top button barely hooked, showed off impressive cleavage rising and falling with each breath. Did he imagine it or did her breathing increase the longer he stared at her? She kicked out the other chair with her booted foot.

"Lucien, I'd like you to meet, Mandy from the blog *Behind the Image.*" Jay smirked.

Lucien's jaw slacked. Mandy, as in *Mandy's Musical Mondays?* As in photographer extraordinaire of the scene, local bands and the ability to capture every emotion the music stirred in a single shot? The image of playing with fire burned through him along with several inappropriate thoughts. He swallowed hard.

Managing to snag an article out of this situation would take a miracle, much less score a date. He straightened his shoulders. If he could deal with Robert and his demons, he could face a sexy, opinionated, and distracting as hell photographer. Flashing his best smile, the one that usually got him out of trouble—or sometimes into it—Lucien hoped he could keep it cool long enough to hide his nerves. And his love of the color red.

Marketing genius indeed. He just wasn't sure who owned that title right now.

CHAPTER FIVE

Mandy sat back in the tall leather stool, wishing it would recline so she could enjoy the show as Lucien walked towards the table. After listening to him sing two songs, eargasm had been an understatement. The timbre of his voice nearly melted her into the wall she'd been leaning on, until she was a puddle at her own feet. The anticipation of sitting across from Lucien, her camera in hand and questions that needed answers resting on her tongue strained the edges of her patience. Answers only Lucien could give. And he would give them. After all, she hadn't rushed home mid-way through the band's practice to change into dry clothes and fuck-me boots for nothing.

"Well, this is almost embarrassing," Mandy quipped. She shrugged, tilting her head back to swing her hair over her shoulder. Also to put her cleavage on center stage. "You see we've run into each other several times today and have yet to be formally introduced. I'm Mandy." She extended her hand.

"Uh, Lucien," he said grasping her tiny hand in his. Mandy nearly bit her tongue at the warmth.

Lucien positioned himself on the chair. He set his guitar case next to the table, leaning it against the chair she had offered him. "Sorry," he muttered when his foot tapped hers as he scooted the chair under the table.

"No problem." She hardly reacted, continuing to

twirl her foot. If she stopped, she worried the nerves that kept it circling would land on her face. Now was not the time to show her nervousness. Not when his ironclad facade finally started to chip away. "So you're the new singer of *Demon Dogs*." Her finger tapped the top of her camera, but not quite hard enough to depress the button.

"Yes and no." Lucien teased a smile. Mandy raised an eyebrow. "Yes, I am the group's new singer but we're considering a name change, something that will give us a clean slate."

"New name?" When rumors of a new singer began running rampant a couple weeks ago, it didn't include that little nugget. Mandy didn't like not being in the know. In fact, she hated it. Finding out first was what Mandy did best. She smiled, running a finger along her bottom lip. "I hadn't heard that."

"No one has heard about that." Lucien leaned back in the chair with his arms stretched out. The faint white lines covering his forearms shone in the light, a beacon for Mandy to lift the camera. As if he anticipated her move, he reminded her, "No photographs." Open palm covered her lens before his hands relaxed at his sides. His shoulders filled more space, creating a broad line she wanted to measure.

Mandy gritted her teeth. "I'm not just some random fan taking a picture for my wall." She sat up straighter, poised to make her point. "I'm the reason *Demon Dogs* remains an integral part of the local scene despite their obvious shortcomings." Mandy had single-handedly hyped the group until club owners were forced to listen. Once they did, and crowds filled the venues, *Demon Dogs* practically wrote their own tickets despite the baggage they carried.

"I'm sure that's true but now *Demon Dogs* may as well be synonymous with a rowdy crowd and fights that break out during every show." Lucien barely broke a smile. Thin lips drew tight. After a few awkward silent seconds, he took in a deep breath. "I'm looking to take it to a whole new level, one where the group is appreciated for our music."

Mandy remembered a time when Jay might have said the same thing. Their music contained power even he couldn't understand. Mandy had seen it. She'd photographed that power, the looming aura of their music, so many times she could fill a room full of the images. The practice session alone evoked a powerful influence strong enough to grab the audience by the balls and squeeze until they begged for more. She'd happily capture it with her camera and share it with the world, or anyone interested in seeing it. Except Lucien wouldn't let her.

"You talk like you have all this experience but you're new to the scene, at least locally."

"Let's just say I have some marketing experience." Lucien lifted his eyebrows, widening a stark blue gaze that captured hers and refused to relent.

"Let's just say," Mandy held the stare unapologetically. "I can't write an article if the band doesn't have a name."

"Good." Lucien tapped the top of the table. "I don't want you to write any articles, post any photos, don't even mention the band. Not yet."

"You're kidding right? You have a show in, what, three weeks?" Exactly three weeks. When Jay called to beg her to be there for the new singer's debut, she circled the date on her calendar and assumed it meant some promotion on her blog. "And you don't want to create any traction now? Not a smart marketing move, in my opinion."

"I have a plan for the perfect buildup beginning six days out and leading right up to the date of the show. Right now, I want them wondering, curious. Hungry for more information with no way to get it." Lucien paused. Mandy couldn't quite read the hesitation without taking a picture but she had to admit his plan was working. She wanted more.

"Look, you're new to the local scene, and around here, people need the info to stew on until all the juices are simmered and ready." Mandy had worked several promos for local bands. She'd won awards for her photographs, scored a feature in *The Scene* music and art magazine before anyone knew there was a local music scene. And because of her uncanny knack for picking the next rising stars in the area, she'd managed several main feature articles since, always maintaining a love for the neighborhood bands. With her help, *Demon Dogs* would be the next. "Do you know what my help can do for you?"

"Oh, I'm aware of who you are," Lucien stated. His hand flinched when Mandy adjusted her camera on her lap.

"So who do you *think* I am?" Mandy shifted slightly in her seat, unwilling to be pegged as nothing more than her father's daughter.

"You're the author of the most visited blog highlighting area bands. Every venue in town has you on a permanent VIP status. Need I go on?"

Mandy nodded, enjoying the sound of Lucien's voice as much as she enjoyed how well he'd done his homework. "What else?"

"Well," Lucien drawled. Leaning forward on the table, he cut the distance between them in half. "You're a local music photographer. Or should I say, *the* local music photographer. Your images tread a line between haunting and fascinating. And you have connections any band would jump at making."

Leaning forward herself, she closed the distance between them. An inch more and she could kiss him. "Except you." Mandy pointed out. "You are not jumping." Except for maybe his heart rate. She smiled when the pulse in his neck increased with each breath he took.

He swallowed hard, but held their close proximity.

"Have dinner with me," he whispered. "And I'll tell you all about it. Discuss a feature. Create a stir around the mystery enough to make your readers drool."

"Wow." Mandy laughed. She settled back into her chair. "Do you use blackmail to get all your dates? That's classy." Mandy aimed her camera to the corner of the room where Jay talked into his phone. She snapped another photo, more interested in the darkened shadow behind Jay then capturing another picture of him.

"Do you even see the world around you without looking through that camera lens?"

"How do you expect me to do a feature without any photographs?" Mandy ran her hand across the metal body of her camera, the most reliable thing in her life and her only source of truth.

"Dinner and we'll talk about it." Lucien tempted.

"Fine." Mandy pushed away from the tall table. Her boots hit the cement floor below and she pivoted so she faced the door. Lucien scrambled to follow, almost tripping over his precious guitar.

She walked away, feeling his gaze on the swing of her ass, the click of her heels down the back hallway the only sound besides his rapid breath. She wanted answers, none of which she'd gotten yet and his control of the information was tighter than the CIA. He wanted to play games? She'd play. Only she was changing the rules.

One hand on the outside door, she paused, taking a deep breath. She looked over her shoulder. "Meet me at Casa D' Angelos."

Pushing the door open wide, she hurried through before she changed her mind. She'd relent to a date with tall, dark and mysterious. She just wasn't sure when.

But then, he didn't know when either.

CHAPTER SIX

"And you said she was out of my league." Lucien leaned against the doorframe of the green room unable to contain his smug grin. Somehow, the red walls paled in comparison to the shade Mandy wore. Not only had he managed to win the bet, he shifted the interview to a location where the guys wouldn't be hovering over his shoulder.

"You got a date?" Adam pumped his fist. "Yes! Pay up, Jay."

"Not so fast. Where's this date happening? Burger joints and coffee shops don't count."

"Italian restaurant, Casa D' Angelos," Lucien said. Why did Jay flinch?

"Nice place," Jay mumbled. Swiping his beer off the table with a jerk, he downed the rest without taking another breath. Stalking over to the metal trashcan, he slammed the empty bottle into it hard. Lucien jumped as the glass shattered on impact. Jay was pissed and Lucien couldn't quite figure out the attitude flip-flop.

The bet had been Jay's idea. It's not like money was something he hadn't coughed up before. On the night Lucien auditioned, Jay bet him it was going to be a waste of his time. Yet, he didn't hesitate to hand over the fifty bucks when he not only didn't choke, but gave Jay a hard-on with his voice.

"So when does the event take place?" Jay pointed a

finger at Lucien. "It better not interfere with rehearsals."

Lucien's grin faded, reality a gut punch to his ego. She hadn't given him a date or a time.

The mimicked sound of an explosion came from Rusty. "Crash and buuurn. Ouch!"

"Nice try, Lucien." Jay grabbed another beer from the fridge. "Don't worry. I know how to get a hold of her."

"I'm not giving up that easy. And I certainly don't need your help." Lucien grabbed his hoodie and raced for the backstage door. The alley was empty. Running to one end he scanned the street left and right. Nothing. He sprinted to the other end, almost careening into a pedestrian in his haste.

"Watch it, buddy." The suit pulled his phone away from his ear long enough to give him a cold stare.

"Sorry." Holding his hands up in front of him and kicking on his charm seemed to mollify the man. Damn it. She couldn't have gotten that far. At least the rain had stopped.

His racing heart had nothing to do with his running. She threw down a challenge and he accepted without really understanding what he was getting into. Fine. He'd play the game her way. Except he intended to win.

Lucien tried to walk the four blocks to Casa D' Angelos, telling himself she wouldn't be waiting, that would be too easy. Half a block away he conceded to a light jog. The outside looked like something from the Italian Riviera. Directly on the water, the restaurant touted an outside balcony upstairs and a glass wall with a breathtaking view of the Patapsco River on the first floor. Inside, the atmosphere reeked of class and sophistication. Lucien wasn't dressed for this place and almost hoped Mandy wasn't here. Almost.

"Welcome to Casa D' Angelos." The host eyed Lucien's jeans and sweatshirt. "Just one, sir?" he asked in a curt tone. "I have a coat and tie you may borrow if necessary."

Lucien dismissed the haughty look, scanning the few patrons in the restaurant. No red caught his eye. "Look, uh..." Lucien waited pointedly for the maître d' to give him his name, which he ignored in favor of giving his hoodie a dour look. "Um, Marco—" Lucien guessed. The temperature dropped about ten degrees to sub-pissed.

"Anthony. Anthony D' Angelo."

"Of course." Not just a waiter, but the restaurant owner himself. Could he do anything else wrong today? Lucien kind of doubted it right now. "Anthony, if an angel comes walking in here I need you to call me at this number immediately." Lucien pulled out a business card and a wad of cash. Reading the card, Anthony's eyes widened, the cold demeanor replaced immediately with contrition.

"Mr. Solvak, forgive me. I did not recognize you."

Lucien pursed his lips. He couldn't get away from his family name even if he wanted to. The notoriety had its advantages sometimes, but he wanted to use his own abilities to get Mandy to recognize the band's—and his—talents. At least he hadn't given them the antiquities card for Robert's business. That would have ratcheted the sucking up tenfold. "My *father* is Mr. Solvak. My name is Lucien. Just Lucien."

"Of course, sir." A slow nod assured Lucien his identity would remain confidential. The tip made sure his request would be fulfilled. "How may I assist you today, Lucien?"

"There's a girl, I mean, a woman about this tall." Lucien hovered his hand level with his shoulders. He hadn't really been paying attention to her height when she left. Not when her ass was a much more interesting focal point. "Well, maybe taller. I don't know. She was wearing heels and sitting down most of the time. Anyways, she has darker hair with red streaks, full lips and looks like an angel."

Lucien smiled at the image in his head. As exciting as traveling the world was, the constant moving made it hard for him to meet people, make friends. Hard to create lasting relationships when you might have to disappear into the night without notice.

It's just a fucking date. You're not asking her to marry you. Lucien shook his head. A soft throat clearing caught him off guard.

"An angel, sir?" Anthony smiled. "How will I know she's an angel?"

"Her name is Mandy and she'll be the one with wings." Wings he hoped would help him soar, not crash and burn. Now he had to wait. A text message pinged his phone.

WHERE ARE YOU? TRUCK IS HERE. YOU ARE NOT ~ CARMEN.

"Shit, sorry. I have to go. Please call me the minute she shows. I don't care when or what time of day. Understand?" Anthony nodded.

Lucien raced out of the restaurant and headed back to the club. Mandy distracted him so much, he forgot all about loading the artwork for Robert's German tour. Responsibilities crashed down hard.

One more screw up today and if Robert found out he wasn't doing his job, he wouldn't need Mandy to sink his music career. Robert would rescind their tenuous agreement before Lucien even got to play his first gig, denying his dream as surely as Robert's immortality denied him rest.

CHAPTER SEVEN

"He went straight to Casa D' Angelos." Camera in hand, Mandy smiled standing at the window of her apartment. The window faced the street and lent the perfect spot to see Lucien leave the restaurant.

As soon as she mandated a location for dinner, she sent the cab waiting to take her across town for a show tonight away empty. Once the decision started swirling in the air, she couldn't force herself to stand in another crowded bar listening to another mediocre band. Not after the sounds Lucien had treated her to earlier that made her want so much more.

If she'd thought before she spurted out the name of a restaurant, she might not have named one across the street from her apartment. Except it was her favorite restaurant and the first one that came to mind. And if it hadn't been that restaurant, she wouldn't have been treated to the sight of Lucien scrambling after her.

"Excuse me?" Kyrissa asked. Mandy hadn't heard her roommate enter the apartment. Mandy turned just in time to see Kyrissa plop a box of paint supplies onto the coffee table that made the wooden piece of furniture sag a bit in the middle. "Who went to Casa D' Angelos?"

"Just a guy," Mandy said, her camera still pointed in Lucien's direction. Depressing the button a few more times, she closed the window covering to examine the images. Though his form outside the window appeared clear as day, the blurry image of the picture showed nothing, highlighting the rain more than it showed off Lucien's hotness. She could barely tell it was even him. "Damn it, too far away."

"Just a guy that you happen to be stalking right now?" Kyrissa peeked out the drapes.

"Stop looking out," Mandy said, swatting at Kyrissa's hand. "He might see you." She nudged Kyrissa away from the window without peeking herself, despite how tightly her fingers clung to the drapes. Any movement of the fabric could flash like a signal to draw Lucien's attention from the street. The last thing she needed was more of his attention. Wanted? Maybe. But she didn't need it.

"It's not like you to stalk a guy." Kyrissa laughed, shaking her head. "I have to say I'm not sure I've ever seen you this," she waved her hand at Mandy, "whatever you are, over a guy before."

"I'm nothing over this guy. He's just some nobody and so what if he happens to be the new lead singer of *Demon Dogs*?" Mandy gave away more information than she'd planned.

"Ah, a singer." Kyrissa hummed. "I bet he plays guitar too."

"Just. A. Guy," Mandy insisted without confirming or denying Kyrissa's correctness.

"I bet he is also incredibly good looking." Kyrissa tried to pull back the drape again. Mandy swatted her hand away.

"Whether he is hot or not doesn't matter."

"So he's not good looking, but he is hot." Kyrissa crossed her arms over a black, paint-splattered sweatshirt with frayed edges. Mandy thought she had hid the atrocious article of clothing well enough that Kyrissa could never wear it again. She hated being wrong almost as much as she hated that damn sweatshirt. Almost.

"That's not what I said," Mandy scoffed. She also

hadn't denied the accusation because Lucien was not only hot, but also lead singer, guitar playing hot and Kyrissa knew, admittedly, that was Mandy's favorite kind of hot.

"Then let me be the judge." Kyrissa extended a hand toward Mandy's camera.

Under normal circumstances, Mandy showed Kyrissa every image she captured. She'd shown her more pictures of up and coming bands than her friend cared to see. This was not a normal circumstance.

"I don't have any pictures to show you," she admitted walking towards the door to their apartment building to answer the security system's ding. The last person she expected to see in the screen was waving at the camera. She buzzed him in and waited for him on the landing outside the apartment.

"Why don't you have any pictures of this guy?" Kyrissa asked when Mandy walked back inside with Jay following.

"Because Lucien doesn't want her to take any," Jay stated, a crooked grin showing his amusement at her predicament. Mandy glared at his relaxed stance against the frame.

"Just a guy who's rock star hot and is going to make you work to get a picture of him?" Kyrissa laughed, turning towards her bedroom. "He sounds perfect for you, Mandy."

Mandy stuck her tongue out at her best friend's back. The one thing she refused to acknowledge—Lucien was exactly her type, a guitar playing lead singer that plucked strings in her body she didn't know existed. Mandy didn't date musicians anymore and the reason for that rule stood at her front door.

"I'm no longer speaking to you," Mandy called into the abyss of their apartment.

"Like you could ignore me." Kyrissa flipped around to call over her shoulder, "Oh, I forgot to tell you. Your dad stopped by. Said something about being in the neighborhood and wanted to make sure you were still on for dinner."

"Of course we're still on for dinner." Mandy squirmed. She hated talking about her father with anyone else in the room. Kyrissa knew all the sordid details of her life that Jay wasn't privileged to. "But the next time my father stops by uninvited, be sure to tell him to stop stalking my best friend for information."

"Then answer your phone," Kyrissa called out from her room.

"There is a reason I'm ignoring his phone calls," Mandy said softly. And her father knew them all.

Jay might be the reason Mandy no longer dated musicians, but her father was the reason she no longer trusted her heart. He'd broken it into tiny pieces so long ago; there were no strings strong enough to put it back together.

CHAPTER EIGHT

Drenched from the rain once more, Lucien snuck in the loading dock of the warehouse through the metal security door. The wet chill was worth it if he avoided Robert's wrath. Too bad his sister was on him the moment he began to open the door to go inside.

"About time you got here. First truck's about loaded. They are doing the final check now." Carmen slapped the clipboard against his chest with a wet smack that echoed even among the grunts of loaders. "Why are you drenched? What did you do, run from rehearsal?" She poked her head out the loading dock and spied the fire-engine red of his truck, eyes narrowing at him.

"Heavy rain." Lucien shrugged out of the wet hoodie to avoid more questions and his sister's scrutiny. He'd have to live with the wet t-shirt for now. For the second time in one day, Mandy managed to get him soaked and partially undressed. Too bad she wasn't around either time to see it. He fought the smile that threatened to sneak out.

Focus, damn it.

Flipping through the inventory lists, he compared his counts with the driver's manifest. Signing final approval, he darted looks around the warehouse. "Where is he?"

"I shooed Robert to the office to sign contracts." Carmen waved towards the business office at the front of the building. "You know how he gets when people are handling his artwork. Especially, when we—" She emphasized the pronoun and Lucien cringed. "Aren't around to coordinate."

"I'm sorry, okay? Rehearsal ran over and it slipped my mind." Lucien had said too much, or too little, it was hard to tell with Carmen. Either way, the lawyer in his sister perked up as if she had a case to crack. Mandy was a definite puzzle, one he looked forward to figuring out, but not one he wanted to share with his sister. "Don't start, Carmen."

"Start what, little brother?" She pulled down and locked the loading dock door with a loud bang as the first truck rumbled away. With a single raised eyebrow and sly smile, Carmen took slow measured steps in his direction.

Lucien backed up. Here comes the interrogation. Redirect. That's what lawyers did. "Does he know I was late?"

"I do now." Robert's baritone voice was quiet in the warehouse, but the flat intonation shouted his irritation like the squeal of microphone against an amp. Lucien grimaced. He couldn't see Robert, but Carmen's pale face and stiffened pose told him everything he needed to know. Robert was pissed.

Swallowing, Lucien turned.

"Robert, let me explain—"

"Save it. We have another shipment to load and we are already behind schedule."

"Actually." Lucien checked his watch and the checklist of items loaded onto the second truck. "We are five minutes ahead of schedule. I built in extra…" Robert's gaze bore into him. The black of his eyes a portal to the hidden pain Robert always carried with him. Painting was his lifeblood. Literally. And no one else was protected from the extreme emotions painted into the art besides Lucien, a fact Robert hounded him with constantly, as if Lucien didn't understand the risks.

"It won't happen again." Lucien would never forgive himself if someone else got hurt because of his lack of planning.

"Finish loading." Robert stated. "We will discuss this later."

"I made a mistake—"

"Mistakes get people killed in *my* world," Robert snapped. Tight fists loosened as he took a deep breath. Robert curbed his volume as the remaining loaders looked over but the fury remained. "A demon hunts me. We have returned to the last place he almost found me because of your Grandmother's vision. Dangerous under normal circumstances." Robert exhaled. "Your music hobby makes it more so. It draws greater attention to us." A sharp jab caught Lucien in the chest. Robert pressed forward, forcing Lucien to step back until he hit a stack of crates. "A mistake could cost everybody their lives. Including yours."

"I know what's at stake." Lucien's heart raced. He would never put his family or Robert in danger, but after he finally convinced Robert to let him audition, the thought he might have to leave his music behind tore him in two. "I'm being careful." Robert scoffed but released the pressure on his chest. "The interview will only contain pictures of the band and I'll be using a stage name. Slone, not Solvak."

"Interview?" Robert's dark gaze bore into him. "No. Too much exposure."

"I know what I'm doing." At least Lucien hoped he did. He hadn't exactly told Robert he planned to hit the local music scene with *Demon Dogs*. Lucien shook his head. That name *had* to go. He would expose the band slowly. Keep the mystery about him as the lead singer under wraps as long as possible. Once on stage, L. J. Slone would make his debut, not Lucien Solvak.

He designed all his plans to minimize the chances of anyone discovering his secret life—Guardian to an immortal who had been outrunning a demon for over five hundred years. Lucien would not be the reason the demon caught Robert now.

"You promised you'd give me a chance." Lucien kept his voice steady, hiding the twisting acrobatics his gut currently performed. It had taken almost two months to get Robert to even agree to this arrangement. Only after years of subjecting his family to private concerts and becoming an often-requested fixture at an open mic concert venue in the last city they hid, had Lucien even worked up the nerve to announce his interest in the audition.

"Yes, I did. No more mistakes or our agreement is revoked. Understood?" Robert waited until Lucien nodded. "I need to go paint." Robert rubbed at the back of his neck, a wave of pain cresting over his features. A pain Lucien didn't yet understand, but felt like it was his own. Pausing at the bottom of the stairs leading to the upper apartments, Robert warned Lucien one last time. "You have three weeks to prove this hobby of yours is worth the risk."

Lucien uncurled his fingers from the clipboard. The term hobby hurt, especially coming from Robert. He thought if anyone understood what creating music would mean to him, it would be another artist. Obviously, he was wrong.

"Who's the girl?" Carmen shot out.

"What?" Lucien's voice cracked. "Girl? What are you talking about?" Most of the time his sister was practically a surrogate mother to him. But sometimes, she was a royal pain in the ass. His gaze shot around to make sure Robert hadn't overheard the real reason he was late. If his efforts at the restaurant panned out, it would be worth keeping the secret, if only he could hide it from his nosy sister.

"She's nobody," he lied. Carmen stared at him. He sighed, "Fine, she's just the hottest photographer in the music scene." He flung the clipboard against a stack of boxes, the crack not quite loud enough to dissipate his frustration.

"A hobby." Lucien glared at the staircase. "That's all he thinks this is to me. Fucking immortal bastard." Lucien managed to keep the epithet mostly quiet. The hand on his arm told him it hadn't been quiet enough. Lucien slumped down on the crate.

"So tell him it's more."

"You really think he'd let me pursue a music career? No way." Lucien stalked over to where he could watch as they loaded the last paintings. "These guys are already counting on me to catapult them into rock stardom, while Robert thinks this is only a one-time gig. How am I going to make this a career if he treats it like a fuckin' hobby?" He slumped against the crate. "Maybe he's right. I should just give up on this whole idea of a band before I get any more invested."

"Don't you dare," Carmen smacked his arm.

"Ow."

"That was to remind you what it's like to feel. Your music does that. Makes you feel alive. And I don't even want to mention what your music does to anyone else who hears it."

Lucien stared at her. "Who are you, and what have you done with my sister?" He flinched away when she half threatened to smack him again. "You're not normally this supportive."

"Your music is as much a part of your life as painting is a part of his." Carmen touched the Romani guitar tattooed on his upper arm. The one he got in their mother's memory and as a reminder to strive for his own music dream. "Just like it was Mother's. Don't give up."

"I can't keep things from him, Carmen. My oath…" Lucien shrugged off the rest of that thought. How could he explain what it was like to be a Guardian to the one Solvak who wasn't one? He couldn't. He barely understood it himself.

"I know," Carmen whispered. Lucien almost

believed she did understand. Except she couldn't possibly.

Picking up the clipboard, he rifled through the pages. Each piece listed was a masterpiece. "He shares these with the world and the world benefits. Is it wrong that I want to do the same with my music?"

"No. But it's not just your music you want to share is it?" Carmen teased. So much for redirection. "Thought so." She grinned. "Who is she?"

Lucien stiffened. "I really need to make sure all these paintings are accounted for, before—"

"For a person who hates secrets," Carmen snatched the clipboard out of his hands, "you are trying to keep this one. Spill. Or do I need to go get Mama T to worm it out of you? So, you said she's hot."

"That's not what I meant. And don't you dare bring our grandmother into this." He wouldn't stand a chance against Mama T's matchmaking.

"So she's completely hideous and you can't get her out of your head." Carmen couldn't stop being a lawyer for two minutes. She continued to grill him. "Or are you having trouble getting her into the sack?"

"Stop that," Lucien warned. Visions of that short skirt riding up farther on those fantastic thighs... Lucien shook his head. "You're putting words into my head. I mean my mouth. Ugh." Times like these, Lucien wanted to strangle his sister. Constantly on the move, never staying in the same place for long, intimate relationships weren't something Lucien had ever had a chance to pursue and his sister knew it.

Carmen laughed. "Wow, she must be something special to have you wound this tight. How long has this been going on?"

He shouldn't tell her, but she'd get it out of him somehow. At twenty-three, the youngest lawyer ever at her firm, Carmen earned her reputation as a tenacious attorney. If she wormed the details out in front of Robert, or worse, Mama T, Lucien would never hear the end of it.

"Four hours." Lucien shrugged. "I just met her. Today. At rehearsal." Each addition made it sound more and more unreal. A hot chick, whose smile captured a piece of him like a photo. An image he would keep forever.

"Seriously?"

"I know it's stupid. And that damn camera of hers adds a whole new level of dangerous but—" Lucien swiped the front lock of mostly dry hair out of his face. Everything Mandy represented should make him stay away. He had a secret to protect. But everything she offered taunted him—a life outside all the secrets.

"But?" Carmen prompted.

"There's something about her. I can't figure it out." But man, did he want to. It started out as a bet, now he wanted more than just a date. He wanted to get to know Mandy and not just for the band. Lucien shook his head. "I don't think she's interested in me as much as what the band's re-launch can do for her blog," he mumbled. The guys were probably right. She might be out of his league. Hell, he wasn't sure they were even playing the same game.

He dared to look at Carmen. His body tensed as though expecting a blow, ready for her teasing, only to see her smiling at him. "What?"

"You want the dream, the music...the girl." Now a bit of a smirk appeared. "What's stopping you?"

"You heard Robert."

"I heard Robert give you a challenge to prove him wrong in three weeks." Carmen's eyes flashed with mischief.

"I can't tell Robert what I'm really doing, can I?" Lucien asked. He already knew the answer.

"You have to make a choice. How important is your music?" Carmen closed and locked the last loading dock door and started heading upstairs to her apartment. From the first landing she called down,

"How important is the girl?" Jogging up the remaining steps, she left Lucien alone.

A quiet stilled over the warehouse, but the music in Lucien's head sang loud and clear. New lyrics formed, the melody wrapping around the image of a dark haired angel with streaks of red. Mandy. With the first guitar strum and the first notes he sung that morning, he made his choice. Now he had three weeks to prove he made the correct one.

CHAPTER NINE

"Evening Love," Jay tried to sound more British than he actually was which only came off as him sounding like a bigger douchebag than he actually was. On stage, his image so pure and captivating, it had enchanted Mandy. It wasn't until she saw him off stage that she learned the pureness ended the moment he stepped out from behind his drum kit.

"I'm not your love." Mandy opened the door to her apartment wider, handing him the same towel she'd used when she got home. Jay dragged his drenched ass inside, running the fabric over his long brown hair. "What are you doing here, Jay?"

"Wanted to touch base about the article." Jay smiled. His boyish grin had a whole lot less effect on her than it had at one time. "Lucien ran out after your little interview. I didn't get a chance to discuss it with him."

"There won't be an article." Mandy clenched her teeth. If Lucien wanted to play hardball, she'd throw the ball out of the freaking court.

"Look, I know the new guy is being a little difficu—," Jay said before cutting himself short. "He's different. I know." His lips curled in one corner as though trapping an apology inside his crooked smile. "But if you don't run the news of our newest band member, get the buzz out, *Demon Dogs* is finished before we even get started."

"Not my problem." Mandy crossed her arms over her chest. She leaned back on the granite island, the one major compromise her father gave into during the hundred-year-old building restorations. Mandy insisted on an open layout with an island in the center that could seat six. She loved to cook and wanted an audience when she did it. "Besides, according to Lucien, *Demon Dogs* may not exist. Says there's a name change in the works."

"Hmmpf." Jay cleared his throat. "He's tossed a few suggestions around, but nothing's sticking yet."

"Well, when something sticks you let me know," Mandy said. She couldn't figure out if Jay agreed the band needed a name change or was annoyed by the mere mention of it. "I'll be sure to not care."

"Look, Mandy. I'm desperate, all right? I'm getting too old for this trying to cut into the music business shit." Jay took two steps towards her. He swept his finger across her cheek. Too bad it no longer carried any influence over her.

"You're twenty-five," Mandy huffed, sidestepping when Jay tried to press his body closer to hers. "And you've managed just fine so far. If it doesn't work out with Lucien, you'll land on your feet, find another band. You always do."

"Lucien is different," Jay said. Mandy couldn't agree more, though she wouldn't admit it to Jay. "There is something powerful behind his voice, commanding the stage; I know he'll be able to embrace the crowd. Damn. At the risk of you thinking I have a hard on for the boy, his voice makes love to my fucking ears."

"Eargasm," she whispered. Jay nodded. How she wished she could deny she had experienced it too. "Still, doesn't matter if Mr. Uptight and Mysterious doesn't want my assistance. If he won't let me take any pictures of him, that means no promos, no on-stage presence to blog about, well, I got nothing to share. That simple."

"When did Mandy Hayworth ever need permission from a guy to do, well," Jay hesitated, "anything? You took some pictures before he politely asked you to stop, so use them."

"Politely asked?" Mandy mocked.

"Fine, demanded. Whatever."

"None of those images are useable." Mandy hadn't erased them, but she might as well since she didn't plan to share them with anyone. "Unless you want a close up of his teeth and a glimpse at the tattoos under his shirt." In all honesty, Mandy was fine with that image. She also had an image mostly of his hair that she considered stroking and one that only showed him from so far away it's hard to determine if the image was of Lucien or a homeless guy.

"Wow," Jay mouthed. "He's gotten under your skin, hasn't he? You can't get a good picture of him. He's making demands of you. And you're listening. Just thinking about this guy is eating you alive."

Mandy scoffed.

"You told him you'd go out with him, so go out with him. There's no guy in his right mind that can turn down a chance to—" Jay cleared his throat, shaking his head. "Pose for you. No guy."

Jay posed for her only once and the images she captured proved he wasn't the guy she thought. Dark and twisted, mist filled the air behind him like some sentient fog from a B-movie horror flick. She broke things off the next day.

"If I wanted to go out with him I would have given him my number. Not named some random restaurant for him to meet me at."

"Since when is Casa D' Angelos random?" Jay asked.

Though surprised he remembered her favorite restaurant, she doubted he recalled why it meant something to her.

"But I didn't set up an actual date," Mandy stated.

"For a reason." A reason she still wasn't sure. She meant to tell him tomorrow night at eight, but she got too flustered and ran off before the heat she felt seeping up her neck flamed her cheeks.

"Don't make me beg," Jay said. He dropped to his knees. "Because I am not above groveling at these legs." He slid a hand up the back of her calf, behind her knee, stopping just short of the hem of her dress. She glared down at him.

"Get up you moron." She kicked his hand away. His gentleness, his mischief, provided a peek into the past Jay, before she saw his real image. She'd never be with Jay again, but maybe she could do this one favor for him.

"I'll see what I can do. No promises," she added quickly when Jay's face lit up like a little kid in a toy store. "I don't know where you found this guy, but Lucien is pretty guarded and I'm not sure I want to unlock whatever secrets he's hiding."

"Like you could stop yourself," Jay laughed. "I've never known you to turn down a challenge. And Lucien Solvak is a challenge with a capital C."

Solvak. The name sat on the edge of familiarity that Mandy couldn't quite place.

She hated how much Jay knew her. How she hated secrets because of the power they had to destroy lives, the way her father's secrets had nearly destroyed hers. Maybe Lucien's secrets were better off where Mandy couldn't find them. Then he couldn't disappoint her too. Too bad Jay gave her a piece to a puzzle she had to put together now.

CHAPTER TEN

"You're here bloody early," Jay exclaimed, dropping his bag next to Lucien in the greenroom. "Not interrupting anything am I?"

"Mandy's not here." Lucien slammed his mouth closed before the next words snuck out—*like I hoped.*

"Mandy?" Jay chuckled. Lucien squirmed. "I didn't mention her."

"I wanted to go over the press releases and…stuff." He sounded desperate even to himself. "I have limited time and I want to make sure I get this right." That and he had no idea how to find Mandy other than the email he'd already tried through her blog.

"Uh huh." Jay snaked the chair around and sat on it backwards. "Don't worry about Mandy. She'll be around. I saw her last night and smoothed a few things out."

"You saw her?" A surge of jealousy that had no right to be there, flared hot enough to reach his neck. Digging his fingers into his thigh, Lucien managed to keep it from showing on his face. He hoped.

"After you ran out, I went to see her." Jay's smug smile turned Lucien's stomach. "Mandy and I go way back. You're right about screwing the pooch on that interview, but I got her to reconsider. She's willing to give you another shot."

"You?" Lucien forced a smile. Anything to keep the pictures of Mandy and Jay together out of his head.

"How much did you have to pay her, 'cause you and I both know your charm ain't worth shit."

"Damn boy." Jay grabbed his chest, pulling out an imaginary dagger. "Wound a guy's ego while you're at it."

"You have more than enough to spare, Jay," Adam called out. "Hey, Lucien." The two bumped fists as Adam passed. Truthfully, Lucien felt like part of a group for the first time in his life. "So what's on the schedule for today's practice?" Adam asked.

"I had a couple of ideas I wanted to float by you guys for the stage show. See what you thought." He shuffled through some papers of hand drawn images filled with lighting and staging cues. A few he had taken extra time to use color.

A sharp whistle filled the room when Rusty moved to pick up one of the drawings. "You do these?"

"Well, kinda. They're based off some paintings by an artist I know." Lucien held his breath, hoping the guys didn't press him too much. They knew he worked for an art collector, but that was about the extent of their knowledge. He needed to keep it that way.

"Dark. Powerful." Rusty grinned. "I like. Goes good with some of the new songs."

Lucien relaxed his tight shoulders. Adam loved the haunting new harmonies Lucien had created between the bass and lead guitars. Rusty had been the hard sell to the new sound.

The stage show was the next step in his rebranding of the band. Killing the old image and resurrecting it with a newer, fresher one. One that would invigorate the sound and immortalize the band. An idea teased at Lucien. A name. Jay squawked, destroying the thought before Lucien could grasp it.

"Keep this up and we're going to lose everything about the band image," Jay grumbled. Dropping the illustrations back to the table, he moved over to the fridge and popped a beer.

"I thought that's what you wanted." Lucien spun in his chair. Jay had sought him out after his audition and invited him to join the band on the spot. Pushed him to come up with a fresh sound for the *Demon Dogs* focused on his unique vocal talents. Take them to the top. It was a dream they shared. Or so Lucien thought.

"I wanted to clean the act up, find a way to finally break into the bigger scene." He sloshed the beer toward the three of them. "Not lose the entire bloody identity."

Lucien looked at Adam and Rusty. Adam shrugged. Rusty frowned. He knew Jay the longest. Catching his eye, Lucien opened his hands palm up, asking silently.

Rusty flicked his gaze to Jay before he shook his head at Lucien. Moving closer to return the drawings, he whispered, "Another time."

Seemed Lucien wasn't the only one with secrets.

"Let's get this rehearsal started." Jay grabbed his sticks and headed for the stage. "You." He pointed his sticks at Lucien. "Make sure you give Mandy the damn interview. Charm her pants off. Not literally." Jay took a long swig of his beer, a shadow of pain lingered for a split-second. Brief enough, Lucien wondered if he'd imagined it. "She can make or break this band. I personally am tired of obscurity. That girl and her camera can get us where we want to be."

"I don't know how to contact her."

"She said she'd contact you. Said you'd know where to get her message." Jay's sly smile crept out. "Don't make me have to break Band Rules to get this interview. I'd be more than happy to rekindle that old flame." He started to say more, but closed his mouth, his jaw settling into a hard line.

This time Lucien saw the shadow. He had been around Robert too long not to recognize deep-rooted pain. Something was going on between Mandy and Jay. Had Lucien crossed a line he didn't know about? If Mandy and Jay had been together—the thought sent another flush of jealousy rushing through him—Jay should have said something.

"Jay, I didn't know," Lucien started.

"Know what?" Jay scoffed. "Mandy and I are old news." He threw his arm around Lucien's shoulders. Jay's voice carried only to him, "Just make the goddamn date before I make it new news." The threat, and Lucien took it as such, was very real. "Now get your pretty-boy ass on stage. We have a new sound and show to practice." Jay released him and shoved past Adam and Rusty.

"Was that an endorsement?" Lucien asked.

Adam chuckled. "About the closest you're gonna get from him. You get used to his mood swings. I should have given you a whiplash brace to welcome you to the band. Worse than any woman I've ever met on PMS."

"Truth," Rusty agreed.

Said you'd know where to get her message. The restaurant. He checked his watch as Rusty and Adam left the room. Casa D' Angelos was only four blocks away. He could slip out and be back before the others noticed.

Music and Mandy. The two collided at every turn. He wouldn't have met Mandy without his music. He eyed the backstage door.

"Lucien, get your ass out here!"

He shook his head. And both demanded he play by their rules. Lucien turned towards the stage. That would be the first thing to change.

CHAPTER ELEVEN

With Jay on her side, Mandy technically had a lot more access to the band. He texted her the rehearsal schedule, shared a list of new songs the guys had been working on and promised she'd be the first to know if, or when, the band changed its name. He even sent her the first of the media teasers Lucien drafted.

She had to admit, she was impressed by what she'd gotten her hands on so far. Lucien had created an enticing mystery around both the band and himself. The one thing Jay couldn't give her was a backstage pass to Lucien. To gain access to that show, she could only rely on herself, starting at Casa D' Angelos.

"Ah, Mi Amanda," Anthony cooed as Mandy entered the restaurant. Holding her one free hand, he kissed both cheeks. "It has been too long since you come to visit. Let me get your favorite table ready."

"I'm sorry, Anthony." Mandy pulled away from the older man. "I'm not here to eat. I need to ask you for a favor."

She'd known him since she was a little girl and had been dining at Casa D' Angelos once a week for most of her childhood. Her mother adored the restaurant, cared for the people inside, even considered Anthony family. Mandy's visits now were more sporadic, even though her apartment window faced the restaurant's front door. Perhaps it was her love for this very restaurant that had driven her to choose the neighboring apartment building when her father wanted to restore one for her and Kyrissa to live.

"For you, mia bella, anything." Anthony smiled the way he had always smiled, calling her the same thing he'd always called her mother, *my lovely*.

Mandy returned the warm greeting. The past lingered here, both good and bad. The latter being the most recent. Maybe the time had come to make new memories, new beginnings. She tightened her grip on her camera. Lucien might be a good image to start.

"There's this guy," she began. "He's going to come in looking for me and I want you to give him a message."

"Is this gentleman your boyfriend?" Anthony raised an eyebrow.

"No," Mandy said, shaking her head. They were barely acquaintances; certainly not her boyfriend. "Absolutely not."

"Ah, that too bad." Anthony grinned. "He *molto bello*, no?"

"Molto bello?" Mandy asked, unfamiliar with the Italian term. Mandy loved to listen to her mother converse with Anthony whenever they dined together. But it had been years and the phrases less familiar to her now than they once were. Her mother had been fluent in Italian. Also German and spoke another language she'd never admitted she knew but Mandy suspected was Romanian given the closeness to a few Latin phrases Mandy recognized.

"Handsome," Anthony said. "This young man is handsome, no?"

"Sure, I guess." Mandy squirmed. Talking about a guy with Anthony felt almost as awkward as talking to her father. Almost. "I hadn't really thought of him as handsome." Because she had been too busy thinking of him as completely to die for rock star hot.

"Well, beautiful woman." Anthony gestured to her and Mandy fought the heat rising to her face. "Handsome young man. What could be the problem?"

Mandy chuckled. She considered Anthony many things, maître d extraordinaire, restaurant owner, not to mention a classically trained chef. Matchmaker had never been on that list. "There isn't a problem. We just met. That's why I need your help."

"Ah, I see. Tell me how I can be of assistance." Anthony offered his arm and escorted her towards a tall table in the corner.

Mandy held a folded piece of paper out to Anthony. "Could you just give him this note? I'm not entirely sure how to get in touch with him," Mandy lied. If she really wanted to see Lucien, she knew exactly where his band was practicing at this very moment. "He's supposed to come in here looking for me so I wanted to leave him a message, in case I'm not here." She did not intend to be here when Lucien arrived. If he wanted to play hard to get with the interview, she would play harder.

"Of course, I can do for you." Anthony took the piece of paper from Mandy's hand. "But let's seal it." He lifted the candle burning in the center of the table. Letting the melted wax drip on the paper where the two ends touched in the middle. "Wouldn't want your privacy invaded. Now, let me see that necklace of yours, to mark in the wax."

Anthony gave a mischievous grin. Mandy suspected he was up to something. She rubbed a thumb over the Angel pendant she'd worn ever since her mother gave it to her when she turned twelve. The intricate design, carved in white gold, had been her grandmother's and her grandmother before her. Each woman passed it onto their daughters on their twelfth birthday. Only her mother died two days later and Mandy never took the necklace off.

"Ah, mia bella." Anthony's warm brown eyes softened. He understood the significance of the pendant and what it meant to Mandy. "No harm will come to the necklace."

Slipping the chain over her head, Mandy only hesitated a second before letting Anthony's fingers take hold of the jewelry. He pressed the carved pendant into the heated wax. When he lifted it, it left a perfect indention of her pendant.

"That's incredible," she whispered, slipping the chain back around her neck. She lifted her camera and snapped images of the sealed envelope from several angles. When she looked into her lens, the lighting on one of the images lifted the angel right off the page. Or maybe it only looked like that to her, on her camera screen. She could never be certain what anyone else saw in the images she captured.

"Ah, so I will be sure to give this Lucien of yours this message." Anthony nodded.

"He's not *my* anything," Mandy stated.

Anthony smiled, eyes gleaming with mirth. "No young man in his right mind could tell mia bella no."

"Unless he's not in his right mind." Mandy smiled back. She lowered herself off the tall stool, making her way out the front door. *Demon Dog's* practice should be over any minute and Casa D' Angelos was the last place she wanted to be when Lucien came looking for her. If he came looking at all.

Not until Mandy reached the marble steps of her apartment building did it strike her. She steadied herself against the front door, her heart racing as though she sprinted the four blocks from the club where the band rehearsed.

Anthony used Lucien's name.

She never told him who would be looking for her. He already knew.

CHAPTER TWELVE

"What is with you man?" Rusty demanded. "I said take your shirt off."

"What?" Lucien snapped his head back to the conversation. Nearly tripping on a chair in his haste to step backwards, he tried retracing the half-heard conversation to the point where Rusty demanded he strip.

After rehearsal he planned on racing over to Casa D' Angelos but the guys wanted to discuss the new songs and how everything would come together. Then Jay and Rusty got talking about tattoos and dragged Lucien into the argument. That promptly turned into a pissing match with them stripping off their shirts to compare tats.

Rusty chuckled, "You're more nervous than a teenager waiting on the results of a pregnancy test." All the guys howled except Lucien.

"It helps if you sleep with the girl first though," Adam added. "Unless she's the Virgin Mary and that I know isn't the case."

"Shut up," Lucien snapped. Nobody talked about Mandy like that. Not while he was around.

"Whoa. Touchy." Adam nudged Jay. "I think *someone* has got it bad for our little photographer." He held up his hands in front of him, still laughing, when Lucien stood up to come after him.

"Easy, Lucien." Jay interposed himself between the

two. His colorful Calaveras tattoo on the center of his chest distracted Lucien from doing something stupid. "We're just givin' ya shit. Don't mean nothing. If I thought they were disrespecting Mandy for real, I'd help you beat their asses."

"Sorry." Lucien ran his hands through his hair, cracking a smile when he recognized the move as one of Robert's nervous habits. "She's just—"

"Gotten in your head," Jay finished.

Stalking to the fridge, Lucien grabbed a water. The guys wouldn't care if he grabbed a beer, they'd never rat him out, but Lucien couldn't risk being even a little tipsy. Mandy had him rattled enough. Wanting to use some of *The Shoalman Collection* images in the stage show, he'd need every ounce of control and all his wits to convince Robert in their meeting later.

Lucien played with the cap of the water bottle before cracking it open with a rough twist. "She's got me chasing my own tail," he finally admitted.

"Yeah, she's good at that," Rusty said. "Toss me a beer to make it up to me." Lucien thought about shaking it up for the pregnancy test comment, but a single finger twitching back and forth from the red-headed bassist told him the payback outweighed the mischief. This time.

"No worries man." Adam walked over and smacked Lucien on the shoulder. The easy-going manner and the infamous panty-dropping smile of the blond Irishman drained away the last of Lucien's agitation. "We've watched Mandy work before."

"Speaking of Mandy," Jay interrupted. "Did you know what she meant about where to get her message?"

"Yeah." Lucien nodded. He was used to teasing by his sister and family, but the guys played at a whole different level. "She does like her little games, doesn't she?" Mandy added a spin to the entire thing that kept him in a perpetual whirlwind.

"Oh hell yeah." Rusty chuckled. "That minx could set up a politician to admit his own crimes and make it his idea to do it on national TV."

The sudden splash of water as his hand squeezed the plastic bottle reminded Lucien to pull it together. Mandy was going to take some serious handling if he planned on coming out of this date unscathed and with the secret of Robert's immortality intact.

"Don't worry. She likes you, so you're probably safe." Adam grinned. "Probably."

"So?" Jay coaxed

"Huh? Oh. The message." Lucien shook his head. Damn. She really did have him spinning. "She'll leave it at the restaurant." Lucien checked his watch again. Adam laughed, followed quickly by the other guys.

"So go already," Jay exclaimed, rolling his eyes.

Lucien didn't stick around to hear how the rest of the Mandy conversation ended. Better if he didn't know. He raced for his truck. The drive took less than two minutes, but he wasn't sure he had taken a single breath along the way. What if she didn't mean the restaurant? What if he had this all wrong?

"Signore, Lucien. What a pleasure to see you again." Anthony gestured for him to approach the reservation desk. "Michelle, give us a moment *per favore*."

Lucien did a double take. Heat crept up his neck at the sultry look the hostess washed over him. Being ogled at still made him squirm. At least on stage he could lose himself in the music and not be so aware. He flashed a quick smile before dropping his gaze. Lucien focused on a chip in one of floor tiles until she retreated down the hallway towards the kitchen, leaving the two men alone.

Anthony smiled at the exchange. "Forgive her, she has good taste. As does Mi Amanda."

"Amanda? Oh, so she was here?" His stomach tensed. "Did she, um, leave me anything? A note maybe."

"Si, Signore. An angel indeed." He handed the folded paper to Lucien, his eyes shining.

In his haste, Lucien almost missed the impression in the wax. "I've seen this symbol before." Lucien traced a finger over the delicate imprint of an angel. Sculpted like a lithe dancer, the arms wrapped in a protective embrace around where the heart lay, her wings arched upwards to meet over the figure's head.

"It is a family heirloom, I believe," Anthony said.

At the mention of family, the image connected. Mama T. "My grandmother has a Guardian Angel almost exactly like this one," Lucien whispered.

"It seems your angel has arrived."

"One I don't intend to lose." Digging into his pocket, Lucien grabbed his knife to cut the wax, preserving the image on the paper. Scanning the tight, elegant script, his brow raised at Mandy's demands. "Exclusive, huh? Well two can play this game. Anthony, she said you knew how to contact—" The black receiver hovered in the air in front of him. Lucien laughed. It was already ringing.

"Hello?" Mandy's voice sounded excited in his ear.

"So you want an exclusive with me?" Lucien heard the hitch in her voice before she caught herself. "I mean, we just met. I'm not sure I should commit myself like that so soon." He couldn't help himself. Anthony coughed and turned away, but couldn't hide his smile.

"If you want the exposure I can give you," Mandy countered, a hint of amusement coloring her tone. "Then you need to bare it to me and only me."

Now there was one hell of a thought. Lucien cleared his throat. Gesturing to Anthony, he mimed writing. Scribbling a quick note on the pad the maître d handed him, he continued his banter with Mandy.

"Well, if I am going to bare it all, then I think I get to dictate the terms of our encounter. I mean, certain protection needs to be in place before I allow poking around in secret places." Lucien knew he was pushing his luck, but this time, he was going to enjoy the puzzle that was Mandy. Anthony caught his attention and pushed back the pad with a time noted.

"True." Her voice turned soft and sultry. "One should always protect oneself, but that doesn't mean it won't be fun."

A heated thrill shot straight to Lucien's core. Oh hell, the woman was going to be the death of him. He took a steadying breath before replying to that challenge. "Tomorrow night. Eight o'clock at Casa D' Angelos. Dinner first and no shop talk."

"Fine," Mandy muttered.

"Bring your wings."

"My wings? Oh."

The blush was almost audible over the phone line, right along with her increased breathing. Damn what he wouldn't give to see her flushed. Preferably beneath him. Or atop. So not picky. He pulled the mouthpiece away so she wouldn't catch his breathy response. This girl was freaking fire to him.

"One last condition."

"And that is?" Her voice drew out the question and each second burned, like flames licking at his ears.

"I need you bare too. No camera. After dinner, we'll discuss continued…exposure." The silence was deafening. Lucien held his breath.

"Fine. No camera. But you better put out, or we'll have a real problem."

Lucien barely held onto the phone. "Agreed." The single word all he managed to get past the tightness constricting his throat.

His body burned as he stared at the receiver. His chest ached and it took a moment for Lucien to realize it wasn't Mandy's comment that caused the sensation. Tingling seeped over his forearms. His white-ink tattoos glowed in the dim light of the restaurant for all the world to see in a rare call for help, just as his phone pinged with the sound of an incoming text message.

"I have to go. I'll see you tomorrow night." He dropped the phone on the cradle and raced out the front door. Lucien didn't need to read the text from his sister. He knew. Robert was in trouble.

CHAPTER THIRTEEN

"What the hell just happened?" Mandy held the phone away from her ear. The line had gone dead. Why couldn't he text her like a normal person?

"From the looks of it, you just got hung up on." Kyrissa snickered. "Can we get started now?"

For days Mandy promised Kyrissa that she would photograph her new paintings before she turned them in to her professor. The creepy older man offered Kyrissa commissioned artwork and no matter how many times Mandy asked Kyrissa to stop working with the guy, Kyrissa couldn't walk away from the money.

"Who did you say bought these?" Mandy asked. It wasn't that Mandy didn't think Kyrissa's paintings were amazing, she did. Mandy would feel a little more at ease if she could figure out where Kyrissa's course advisor found patrons for the artwork of an art student when there were professional artists showing their work all over town. Not to mention, some of those artists asked for far less compensation than offered to Kyrissa.

"You know I don't get their names, just their money." Kyrissa smiled, more than happy to be living off her art. If Mandy hadn't suggested it after Kyrissa's mother died, there's no telling whether Kyrissa would have ever applied to art school.

"I'd burn any money that passed through Professor

Creeptastic's spindly fingers." Mandy grinned back. Her father bought the building they lived in so they didn't have to pay rent. He provided most of the furnishings in their apartment, minus the few pieces Kyrissa's mother had made.

"You know I can't do that." Kyrissa rolled her eyes. "I like paying my share." Her smile teased, taking any sting out of her words.

Mandy had a clothing allowance, travel budget and access to any number of credit cards, all of which she loved sharing with her best friend. Yet Kyrissa insisted on paying the utilities herself, putting them in her name before Mandy knew her plan. And like clockwork, every Friday Kyrissa filled the refrigerator with food even though Mandy couldn't figure out when she did so since the two were together more than they were apart.

"Fine." Mandy didn't need to hear once again how much Kyrissa thought of her professor. Kyrissa usually took most of her warnings into consideration. Her professor being the lone exception. Nothing about the older man screamed safe in Mandy's opinion, but her friend refused to listen. She'd rather not hear about the walking skeleton at all. "Let's get started."

Mandy had already set up her tripod in the corner of the spacious room where she had hung black drapes as a backdrop. No matter how many times Mandy attempted to use white behind Kyrissa's dark thoughts, the paintings always required a dark background. This time was no exception.

Kyrissa set the first canvas on the easel in front of the backdrop. "I think this one is my favorite so far," she said.

"Not mine." Mandy disagreed. The grey and blue colored skies made the field of flowers pop right off the canvas. Only on closer inspection did Mandy see that the stems and leaves of each flower displayed a corpse. Somewhat disturbing, borderline demonic. But then

Mandy didn't appreciate any of the commissioned work Kyrissa painted for her professor. It seemed whatever clients he lined up to buy Kyrissa's paintings were patrons of the dark arts more so than anything else.

"So you going to tell me about mystery guy that hung up on you or what?" Kyrissa changed the subject.

"You know as much as I do." Mandy bit her tongue.

"And that is driving you nuts." Kyrissa smirked.

"Yes it is." Mandy admitted. She took the images of the next three paintings in silence. But by the time she had finished she was seething.

"Who does he think he is?" Mandy asked. Bad enough he ramped her up so hot with almost phone sex that she thought her phone would melt. Then he just dropped the line, leaving her dangling from the cord.

"I have no idea." Kyrissa shook her head.

"I'll tell you who he is. He's a freaking nobody and he will remain a nobody unless he lets someone get close enough to figure out who he is." Lucien was rock star material all the way. But rock stars have their pictures taken. A lot. She just needed to be the one who took the first ones. Challenge replaced irritation. "That somebody might as well be me, right? I mean who is better at launching local talent than me? Who, I ask?"

"Definitely it should be you." Kyrissa snorted.

"You think this is funny, don't you?" Mandy accused. "Finally a hot guy that I want to plaster all over my bedroom walls, who's not begging me to take his picture. Instead he wants me to go out on a date with him, without my camera no less, and you are laughing at me."

"It is kind of comical." Kyrissa nodded.

"Not funny at all." Mandy glared but she couldn't force venom to go along with the look.

"So that's what this is about. That he isn't falling down at your feet begging you to take his picture?"

"It's not just that," Mandy said. She fidgeted with her camera strap, trying to compose her thoughts so that Kyrissa didn't think she was truly as insane as she felt right now. "When he sings," Mandy paused. She had only heard him sing once, and for a very short time at that, but she couldn't erase his voice from her mind. She'd tried already and failed miserably. "The world stops spinning. Every worry I had leading up to the moment he opened his mouth disappeared the instant the words came out."

"So, he's a good singer?" Kyrissa asked. "You know hundreds of good singers."

"Not like this." Mandy shook her head. "He is so much more than just a good singer. His voice is, I don't know, eargasmic," she finally stated. "And it's not just me. Jay mentioned it too."

"Wow, you need to get laid. I've never seen you worked up like this."

"First, you of all people are not allowed to tell me I need to get laid." Mandy might have taken a break from guys for the past six months; Kyrissa had given up on them years ago. "Second, now that I've heard him sing, I feel like not sharing this guy's voice with the world would be a crime against humanity. And not doing everything in my power to make that happen would make me a criminal."

"Then do whatever is in your power." Kyrissa folded her arms over her chest.

"I would," Mandy said. "But Lucien doesn't want my help. Or if he does, he's hiding it really freaking well." And Mandy wasn't sure exactly where to look.

"Well, then I'd suggest you start with your own advice. Let him get close enough to figure out who you are. Then he's sure to trust you with his image."

"Since when did I ever take my own advice?" Mandy scoffed. Unfortunately, Kyrissa's suggestion made sense. She just wasn't sure she could follow through. Letting Lucien get close wouldn't be so hard, except she could still feel the embers smoldering from her last burning. And Lucien threatened to ignite another fire all his own.

CHAPTER FOURTEEN

Lucien paced the balcony at Casa D' Angelos and checked his watch yet again. Straightening the collar of the grey shirt tucked into his dark jeans, he tugged at the sleeves of his borrowed jacket. Adam told him it was his lady killer. Lucien didn't want to kill Mandy, just charm her. Casual, confident. He scrubbed at his face. Yeah right. He checked the time again. Five until eight. He didn't have time to go change.

"Calm the fuck down," he muttered. Great, now he was talking to an empty room. He re-seated himself at the only table left on the balcony. He requested a quiet table up here. Anthony removed all the other tables.

Well at least there wouldn't be anyone to see his complete screw up of a date. If his date even showed.

A boat whistle sounded across the water. Calm, the midnight blue reflected the bright moonlight like a giant mirror. If not for the cool, late summer breeze causing tiny ripples, he might mistake the vast expanse for land. However the serene water view soothed Lucien. With a slow exhale and a final wipe of sweaty palms on his jeans, control reappeared.

"I can do this. I've performed in front of hundreds of people in different clubs all around the world. She's just one person." Okay maybe just the hottest freaking woman he'd met in ages. Or ever.

Groaning, he dropped his head into his hands. He was so screwed. The French doors clicked open. Lucien bolted to his feet.

Holy shit. Angel had been an understatement.

Dressed in a vibrant blue dress, short enough to show off her magnificent lean legs, with her hair up in some intricate, twirled hair style, moonlight bathed Mandy in its glow. The orb as captured by her beauty as him. Did he say hot? At this point, the sun would be jealous of the fire she sparked in him. Lucien stared at the vision in front of him. She stared back, smiling.

Forcing his brain to engage, Lucien walked over to greet Mandy. Anthony assisted her in removing her light wrap before lightly kissing her hand. The beading on the back of the dress caught the soft lights and wings appeared in the design.

"Wings," Lucien whispered, his smile growing larger yet.

"Pardon me?" Mandy turned towards him. "Oh the dress."

"*E bello*, no?" Anthony prompted.

"Very beautiful." Lucien interpreted Anthony's compliment.

Mandy's blush stole every thought from his head and set every part of his body on fire in an instant. So much for control.

Anthony cleared his throat.

"Sorry." Lucien was not sorry for staring. If allowed, he'd drink in the vision before him for eternity. *Show you manners.* His grandmother's broken English echoed in his head. *Treat her like angel, and all go well.* Lucien smiled. That he knew how to do well. Clamping down on his raging hormones, he fell into the formal manners drilled into him by Mama T since he was very young.

"Thank you, Anthony. I think I can take it from here." Holding open his hand, Lucien waited as Anthony placed her fingers gently on his palm. Her touch set every nerve tingling. The tight coil in his core strained for release. His gaze never left hers. "Shall we sit?"

With Mandy's hand tucked securely into the crook of his arm, he escorted her to the table. He held her chair as she sat. Her surprise turned into a smoldering look that about dropped him to his knees in front of her. Mama T was right. Manners opened amazing doors. Lucien knew what he wanted before he took his seat. Her. He wanted Mandy and would do whatever it took to get her. Even pose for a few pictures.

"Thank you," she whispered. Mandy looked around, frowning slightly. "Aren't there normally more tables out here?"

"Um, I don't know, maybe?" Lucien stammered, almost missing his seat. Anthony's knowledge about Mandy's full name took on a much deeper meaning than a detail-oriented restaurant owner knowing his customer. He held up his open hands in front of him. "Honest, it wasn't my idea."

Did he imagine it or was she disappointed that he hadn't set it up? The puzzle that was Mandy grew. One minute she blows him off, the next she demands an exclusive. Now she looked disappointed after getting exactly what she wanted. It was like trying to sing underwater—every time he opened his mouth, he started to drown.

"Anthony." Mandy chuckled.

"Yeah, Anthony." Lucien smoothed the napkin on his lap as the silence grew.

The waiter came by just then with a bottle of wine. "Compliments of the house," he stated.

"He's going all out tonight." Mandy shook her head.

"Actually," Lucien corrected her, "I picked that out."

"You?"

"Yeah." He smiled, happy he surprised her once more. "It comes from a vineyard I visited in Italy when I was younger. That vintage is one of their best years."

"Wow. I'm impressed." Mandy reached for her side, her smile fading as she came up empty. She covered the instinctive grab by shoving her hands in her lap.

Lucien reached over and picked up her hand. She stiffened at first but relaxed as he rubbed his thumb over her knuckles. "Isn't this a much better way to get to know me than through the lens of a camera?"

She glared at him. The spark flashing beneath long lashes made him glad for the napkin covering his lap. If his demand to come sans camera got this kind of reaction, Lucien decided he liked her just a little bit irked at him. Her dark eyes smoldered and the rapid rising and falling of her chest accentuated her curves. It was hotter than hell. The trick—not getting burned while playing with fire.

CHAPTER FIFTEEN

Mandy wanted to tell Lucien he was wrong. The only way she ever knew who someone truly was lie in the images she took. Without her camera, she might as well be naked, leading to an entirely different way of getting to know someone, a way she'd consider with Lucien if she hadn't sworn off band guys. Or guys in general.

"We'll see about that," she smirked. Restricting the dinner to non-band talk proved far more difficult to adhere to than she anticipated, she eased into a conversation that hadn't quite started yet and she wasn't quite sure how to begin. With him sitting this close, Mandy wanted to know more about his singing, how he managed to make every syllable sound as if it were alive, about to take flight. She stopped herself from asking how long he'd been performing and if he knew what affect it had on the people who heard his voice.

"Ma'am?" the waiter questioned, holding the bottle of wine.

"Yes, please," she replied taking a deep breath. *And keep it coming,* she wanted to tell him. He poured her a glass, setting it beside Mandy.

"No wine?" Mandy asked Lucien when he covered his glass. She enjoyed the slight shift he made in his seat.

"I'm only eighteen." He shrugged. "I'll be nineteen in

a couple weeks," he added quickly.

"Wow." She took a swig from the glass to compose her thoughts. Eighteen. Four years younger than her. How had she not seen that coming? "And yet you've picked the best wine I've ever tasted," she said, considering downing the entire glass to calm the frayed nerves she couldn't control.

Glad the waiter left the bottle.

"My, um, friend is something of a wine connoisseur. He taught me. Drinking age in Italy was sixteen when I visited. Think they've raised it to eighteen since, but I could be wrong." Lucien shifted in his seat again before lifting a glass of water to his lips, licking them when he finished.

If he hadn't brought her attention to his lips, perhaps she could focus more, but now the fullness of them all she could see, wet and glistening in the candlelight. Her finger itched to capture a picture of the curve, a slight sheen of moisture highlighting the fullness. Her mouth itched to do something else entirely.

Mandy shifted in her seat. Why had she picked this dress? Yes, it matched the deep blue highlights she added to her dark hair this afternoon. And yes, her cleavage had never looked better. But every time she moved, the beads woven into the back of the dress reminded her that she practically wore wings and she didn't have one angelic thought right now.

A few moments into an awkward silence, Anthony appeared and placed a plate of hor d'oeuvres between them. Mandy went for the caprese, without hesitating, to settle her stomach.

"So, uh, you must come here often," Lucien said. "Wait. That sounds like a bad pick up line. I meant, Anthony knows your tastes pretty well so you've obviously been here before. And for him to call you *mia bella*, my beautiful, although it fits." Lucien wiped his mouth with a napkin, replacing it on his lap. "Is it getting warm in here?"

Mandy chuckled. Did he realize how adorable his rambling made him?

"I find the temperature perfect actually." Containing the smile from widening on her face fared impossible. "And yes, I do come here often enough for Anthony to know my tastes. Perhaps too well." If seating them in the balcony area, the candlelight and clearing the dining area of any other tables any indication, Anthony thought Lucien was exactly her taste. So far, she couldn't argue, but only her camera could confirm or deny that. "And he's called me *mia bella* since, well, as long as I can remember. Can't say the name is fitting."

"I disagree." Adjusting his tie as though the offending item constricted his breathing, Lucien cleared his throat. Again. "I take it you live close by."

"Correct." Mandy did not intend to disclose more than that. "How about yourself? You obviously travel, but where do you live?"

"Not far from here, just the other side of town." Lucien didn't seem willing to share either.

For a moment, Mandy considered the dinner a stalemate, at least the conversation portion. While the tension in the room rose with each silent moment that passed, both were anteing up for some sort of control.

Anthony brought another course. Neither of them questioned his selection of the chef's choice tonight. Mandy couldn't question it since, conveniently or not, he brought her favorite meal, eggplant parmesan. She had yet to find another chef to prepare it as light as the chef at Casa D' Angelos did and Anthony always portioned the plate especially for her.

"I brought my portfolio." Mandy turned the conversation to business as soon as the dinner plates were cleared. "Perhaps I might be able to persuade you into letting me take pictures of you if you saw my work." She lifted a small book onto the table.

"And dinner is over." Lucien laughed.

"My plate's been cleared." She shrugged, ignoring Anthony headed their direction with dessert plates.

Shaking his head, Lucien flipped through the first couple of pages of her portfolio. Mandy held her breath, awaiting his approval. Or his disdain for her work. She could handle either.

"Your work is," Lucien began, and then he swallowed hard. "Powerful," he finally said.

"Thank you." Mandy poked at the desert placed in front of her. She normally devoured the tiramisu, but tonight, not having her camera began to weigh on her mind. "That is only a small sampling; I have a lot more at home."

"Have you ever thought of putting these into a digital library? I could help you catalog all your images and make it searchable by subject, date, whatever you think would be best." Lucien's eyes gleamed brighter with each new image. His fingers stopped to trace certain photos. "You then load your portfolio into a tablet and can carry more images."

Mandy stared blankly.

"Sorry," Lucien said, grinning like a kid with a new toy. "Got carried away. I really like the technical aspect of creativity."

"No, it's fine," she said. "I've never had time to catalog my photos properly much less create a digital library." One day she posted a few pictures of bands online, within a month she ran a full on music blog with more visitors and images than she knew how to handle. Now she had no idea how to construct a filing system for the countless images.

Mandy dreamed about someday displaying her work gallery style, she just hadn't been organized enough to approach any of the area galleries with her ideas. And she definitely didn't want to use her last name to get her own show. Maybe she needed Lucien as much as Lucien needed her. "Personally I think seeing them larger gives a better impact, but you know they can only be so big for today's viewing on small screens."

"I would love to see the larger images." Lucien pushed the sleeves of his jacket up, a hint of the white tattoo underneath peaked out. "I mean, if that's an invitation." He swallowed.

Of course she wanted to invite him to come home with her. But seeing more images ranked far below exposing more of his arms, and maybe his chest, to see all the white lines he had hidden beneath those clothes. Also touching his lips. With her mouth.

"Sure," Mandy squeaked. Maybe it was the wine speaking. "That would be great."

"It would?" Lucien asked as surprised as her when she accepted his offer.

"Uh, yes, it would," she repeated.

"Maybe for the right incentive I could help you create a database and you could conduct your interview."

"Right incentive?" Mandy was willing to go pretty far to get what she wanted, and she wanted Lucien any way she could get him, but she didn't give her endorsement away for free.

"Yes. You have the platform and connections that would take me months, if not years to form. Influential blog and you're on a first name basis with several music reps. I have the exclusive you want and the know-how to make you a kick ass digital library." He flashed that damn smile of his, the one that made her squirm. "Win-win if you ask me."

"So you'd allow me to use my connections for you? How generous." Mandy tapped her foot. "I want unlimited access to the band and get to take all the photos," she demanded.

"Access is yours and only yours, but I control the pictures."

"You drive a hard bargain, Lucien, but you can't really dictate my picture taking in my own apartment."

Lucien paused and licked his lips, as if he knew they drove her to distraction. Leaning on his arms, he cut the distance between them. Blue eyes reflected the candlelight, but his smile flashed brighter still. "So I'm supposed to let you take unlimited pictures of me just because I'll be in your apartment?"

Mandy smiled. She didn't need unlimited pictures, she just needed the right photo to capture the essence of Lucien Solvak. "How about if I even the stakes and agree to take only one photograph of you a day until the re-launch?"

"One photograph?" Lucien raised an eyebrow. "Some might call that bribery."

"Some might call it compromise to get what both sides want. What harm would one photo do?" Mandy sat back in her chair. "Unless you have something to hide."

All color blanched from Lucien. "No, one image a day is fine." Lucien leaned back in his chair, arms crossed over his chest. His expression had grown more thoughtful, guarded. "You better make it good though."

Mandy closed her portfolio. She stood up, tucking her book under her arm. Lucien scrambled to stand beside her.

"Oh, Lucien Solvak," she said, straightening the lapel of his jacket. Fisting the edge of the garment, she gently pulled him close enough for her to gaze into his eyes, nearly getting lost in the blue abyss. She lifted her hand to his face, patting his cheek lightly. "Sooner or later you will learn. Everything I do is good."

Releasing her grasp, Mandy turned and walked away.

CHAPTER SIXTEEN

The heat of her body pressed close to his had been hot enough to stir his arousal to a blazing-freaking-nova in two seconds flat. All he had to do was lean forward, claim that pert mouth with his. Drink her down like a fine wine. But no. Like a gentleman, he let her leave.

Watching Mandy walk away was always a treat and this time was no exception except for the raging hard-on she left behind. Lucien shifted uncomfortably. Grabbing the glass of ice water, he held it against his cheek where her touch still burned before downing the entire glass. It wasn't until the waiter came in to clear their dessert plates that two things struck him.

Mandy knew his name, his real name, not the stage name of Slone. She'd also agreed to have him come see her photographs, but hadn't yet come back to the table so they could leave for her apartment.

Damn it, she suckered him again.

Hell no. Not this time.

Lucien rushed through the French doors and into the lower dining room, dodging waiters and a few patrons. The other diners gawked at him but he didn't care. If she left the restaurant before he caught her, he'd be at the mercy of Anthony, who, he had a feeling, would follow whatever orders Mandy left before he'd even consider a request from Lucien. The flash of blue caught his eye at the front desk. Relief flooded his system until he saw her reach into her purse and pull out something small and square.

"There is no way I am letting you pay for anything—" He stopped and Mandy blushed a deep crimson. In her hand wasn't a credit card or cash. She currently crushed a camera strap in one hand, a coat check card for the item in the other. The hostess froze in mid grasp of the claim ticket.

"Seriously?"

"I followed your rules," Mandy stated. Her voice pitched a bit higher than from a moment ago on the balcony. There, the sound had been sultry and provocative. "No camera for dinner. We're done with dinner, so I'm reclaiming my camera." She thrust her chin up at him, daring him to argue while shielding the object under discussion safely behind her.

"True." He took a step closer to her. She stood her ground. Damn she was hot when she got riled. He had to curb thoughts of that feistiness playing out in other places. "Are you trying to back out of our agreement?" He hated to admit it, but Lucien needed her more than she needed him.

"I was waiting for you," she countered.

"And were you going to inform me you would be waiting down here, or just let me linger on the balcony thinking I'd been ditched again?" Fingertips slid over her bare shoulder, following the line of her arm until he reached the hand holding the camera strap. Her skin dimpled and he didn't miss the slight shiver either. He lifted her hand, camera and all. "If you want help with this," he teased, not specifying whether he referred to the camera or the goosebumps, "you have to hold up your end of the bargain."

"My connections for an exclusive?"

"I told you I'd give it to you." Lucien managed to suppress his chuckle, but his grin couldn't be contained.

"Are you going to be this much of a tease all the

time?" Mandy tried not to smile, but the corners of her mouth twitched.

"Depends."

"On what?"

"Whether it turns you on or not." Lucien held his breath, not sure where that comment came from. Maybe it was payback for how she left him. Probably more his dick running away with his mouth. So much for manners.

He let go of her and shoved his hands in the back pockets of his jeans. Licking his lips he forced himself to continue. "So what's it going to be?"

Mandy grabbed one of the restaurant business cards and flipped it over. Accepting a pen from the hostess that Lucien had totally forgotten was there, Mandy scribbled out an address. She presented the card to him, but didn't release it right away.

"My truck is right outside," he said.

"Not sure that will work." Mandy chuckled, finally releasing the card. "You might want to look at the address."

Lucien groaned. "No wonder they know you so well here. You live across the damn street." God he was a fool. "I notice there's still no last name on here. You know mine." He wasn't quite sure how she got that, but he had an inkling Jay had something to do with it. "I think it's only fair if I know yours."

"Eventually." Mandy smiled, but her gaze turned his blood to molten lava. Lucien shook his head in surrender. If he had an address, he could *find* her last name. Public records were an effective marketing tool and dating tool as well it seemed.

"Well then, we best be going." Holding out his arm, she raised one brow before tucking her arm around his. The moonlit night would have been perfect—a beautiful woman next to him, an invitation back to her apartment—if only his music career wasn't riding on the outcome.

"This is a magnificent building," he said, admiring the architecture of the restored four-story brownstone. Robert would love this place.

"My dad is in the process of restoring it. It's kinda his hobby. Kept as much of the original structure and fixtures as possible, except insisted on a top of the line security system." Her fingers tightened slightly on his arm. "Only the best for his daughter," she grumbled under her breath.

Attuned to the tiny nuances of tone from singing, he caught the layers of sarcasm in the last part of her statement. Mandy obviously came from money if her father did this as a hobby, but her comment and reaction had him wondering about her relationship with her dad. Lucien could relate to troublesome father issues.

"If he's that protective, he'd probably hate that you're bringing home some band guy you barely know," he teased.

She tensed and Lucien feared he pushed his luck too far. "Look, if you'd rather—"

"Don't worry. I can handle myself." She touched the camera at her side.

"I'm sure you can." The buzz of the door lock coincided with the unique ring tone on his phone. Lucien frowned. That was Robert's ring tone. "Excuse me a moment." Disengaging her hand from his arm shouldn't be that hard, but his fingers lingered on hers until a second insistent buzz from his phone sounded.

"Everything okay?"

His face must have shown his agitation at the text. He needed to leave, but couldn't explain the real reason why. *The person hunting my boss almost killed someone trying to get to his paintings.* "Yeah. I, um, have a security issue at my job I need to deal with."

"You have another job other than singing?" Mandy sidled up closer to him and he blanked the screen.

"Yes. Sorry. Can the interview wait? I really need to

take care of this."

"Of course." Her hand smoothed across his chest. "How about we pick up right here, well, inside, tomorrow morning." She grinned and Lucien's temperature shot up at least ten degrees.

"Tomorrow works for me."

"Nine in the morning?"

Nine o'clock gave him three hours before he had to meet the guys for rehearsal. Plenty of time to setup the initial framework for a database. He could even use the template he created for archiving Robert's massive art collection.

"Perfect." Great, his brain was stuck on single word answers. She was so close, her breath a warm temptation gliding over his lips. This time he wouldn't back down. A hand against his chest brought him up abruptly as he leaned forward.

"Business arrangement." She stepped back holding out her hand in front of her. "Nothing personal." The hitch in her voice betrayed the contradiction in that statement.

"Of course." He grasped her hand. But instead of shaking it, he raised her fingers to his mouth, eyes locked on her face. With the lightest touches, Lucien bushed his lips against the softness of her skin. Mandy's mouth parted slightly, breath catching, never breaking his gaze. In this modern day, the old world mannerisms, traditional in his culture, always made an impression. It was a move that worked every time.

"Until tomorrow."

Jogging down the entrance stairs, Lucien heard his name one last time. Turning, the click of a camera echoed. He should have seen that coming, irked that she once again got the better of him. "Only one," he reminded her.

"Until tomorrow," she whispered back. "Then I get another."

He hadn't been kidding when he described her

photographs earlier as powerful. What he hadn't mentioned was the layers of truth exposed behind every single one. Lucien had no idea what truths would show behind an image of him, nor how to keep secrets from someone with her kind of ability. He also wished he didn't have to.

CHAPTER SEVENTEEN

Mandy wasn't sure she'd ever had a dinner date end so abruptly before, not that dinner with Lucien had technically been a date. She also wasn't sure the last time she'd had more fun. Before she could wrap her head around his absence Kyrissa texted asking for a ride home from her studio.

"I'm glad you texted," Mandy said bouncing into Kyrissa's campus studio.

"Amanda," the sinister voice rung out into the dismal space. "I thought you graduated from our fine institution already."

"Kyrissa needed a ride." She turned to the figure gliding out of the shadowy corner. Stooped, thinning white hair and she swore, he wore the same white shirt, brown jacket and pants every time she met him. Professor C evoked the same image from Mandy, one she refused to confirm with a picture, of a walking bag of bones. Every hair on the back of Mandy's neck stung her like a thousand tiny needles pricking her skin. "Where is she?"

"The ladies room," the professor stated so calmly Mandy detected zero emotion in his words while her heart began to race away along with her paranoia. "I'm afraid I may have pushed her boundaries to get her to see the potential of her talents with this series. Though I am still convinced she can tap into the gifts she's been given and produce these paintings before my buyer begins to look elsewhere for his art needs."

"And who might this patron be that he desires...this?" Mandy pointed toward a mess of swirls and darkness gathered on the canvas on Kyrissa's easel.

"I am sorry. But he has requested his identity remain hidden as he does not wish for every art student in the vicinity to make contact looking for work." The professor edged his way across the studio space and stood in the open door. "Tell Miss Spears that I stand by what we discussed and look forward to seeing the completed pieces."

"Hmm," Mandy hummed. "And what *exactly* did you discuss?" She wouldn't tell Kyrissa anything except to stop working for the man in front of her.

"A pleasure as always, Miss Hayworth." Professor C offered her a fake smile, ignoring her question. "It is quite charming that after Kyrissa lost her mother, she somehow found more family in you than should be possible."

"Just remember I protect my family, Professor, from whatever dangers that may lurk." Mandy had never heard such guttural force leave her mouth. "Kyrissa is more than just family to me."

"I will keep that in mind." The Professor nodded. Mandy stood in the doorway until he disappeared down the hall and Kyrissa exited the bathroom in the center of the building.

"You got here quick. Didn't mean to keep you waiting." Kyrissa wiped the corner of her eye. "Where'd Professor C go?"

"He's gone." *And good riddance.* "Unfortunately, I don't think his absence is permanent."

"Stop," Kyrissa warned. Other than Mandy, her art advisor was the only person who had known Kyrissa's mother. He'd even taught her mother more than twenty-five years prior, before either Mandy and Kyrissa were born. Somehow he'd managed to wedge himself into Kyrissa's life in a way that no matter how hard she tried, Mandy couldn't extricate him.

"Fine. Tell me what you've been working on when you're not at the apartment."

"I'm supposed to be painting this new series for another patron of Professor C's, but haven't quite found the inspiration I need yet." She placed a paint brush still filled with a blue gray wetness into plastic wrap. "I might keep playing with this image or scratch it altogether and start over in the morning. I don't know."

"It's interesting." Mandy held her camera close to the wet canvas to capture a tiny spot where the color seemed to bleed. In her lens the blue relaxed and put her slightly at ease, if not for the layer of gray underneath that made her eyes burn and water after a few seconds of staring.

"You can hate it. I do." Kyrissa grabbed her bag. "Let's go home. Maybe tonight I'll actually see my pillow before midnight."

The problem for Mandy wasn't so much that she hated the painting as much as she couldn't decide how she felt about it. With one moment, the chaotic swirls of paint zapped her emotions right out of the air she breathed leaving her struggling for another breath. In the next, a glimmer of something else, hope maybe, infused that same stagnant air with a fresh breeze.

"Sounds good to me." Mandy glanced over her shoulder and snapped another picture before shutting the studio door behind her.

CHAPTER EIGHTEEN

The whine of the ambulance sirens assaulted Lucien's ears upon exiting his truck. The blue and red flashing lights hypnotizing him in place. Someone got hurt. Who? And why? Rushing towards Gallery's back entrance, the young beat cop hauled him up short when he attempted to cross under the yellow police tape.

"Behind the line," he commanded.

"I work here. My father owns the place," Lucien said impatiently. God, what if it was Christophe. He didn't want their last fight to be the final words they had together. His chest seized. *Robert!* His Guardian marks tingled, making the hair on his arms rise, but didn't glow. Robert was near, but not in trouble. Yet.

"ID please—"

"Lucien!" Carmen ran towards him. "It's okay, officer, this is my brother. We've been waiting for him." She dragged him forward as the cop lifted the tape. "You need to get in there before the two of them kill each other."

"The two of whom? Carmen, what the fuck is going on? Who was in the ambulance?"

He hunched his tall frame behind the slew of bodies, thankful the press had been kept at a discreet distance. Not being a Guardian, Carmen chose to go to law school while Robert dragged Lucien all over Europe. Now she worked in one of the biggest law firms in Baltimore, was short listed to make the youngest partner in the firm's history, and knew half the cops in the city. At least a handful owed her favors. One particular detective that had shown more than feigning interest in his sister would do whatever she asked for free.

"Short version." Carmen rushed him through the crowd of cops swarming the area. "Someone broke in, blindsided Carl with a bottle to the back of his head, broke his arm and attempted to get to the artwork. Silent alarm triggered and Carl managed to trip the audible alarm."

To keep the media backed off tonight, Lucien gladly supported Carmen calling in a few favors in to hide this situation. Both Robert and his father held a bit of local influence and the last thing they needed was bad publicity. He didn't want *any* where Robert was concerned. Too dangerous. *The Shoalman Collection* was legendary but people only had a name and no real face attached to the art. Something Lucien worked hard to accomplish.

"Okay, that answers two questions, but who the hell is fighting with all these cops around." Loud voices emanating from the back office answered the question for Carmen. "That explains this." Lucien rubbed at the marks on his forearms, the hairs still standing tall.

He sprinted down the back hallway. Placing Robert Shoalman and Christophe Solvak in the same room for any length of time was like adding potassium to water. A dynamite explosion would be quieter and less destructive.

"And where in hell have you been?" Robert snarled. Lucien hadn't even cleared the doorway before the full force of Robert's aggression descended. Robert's gaze impaled him, his hair rifled and disorderly, body tense to the point of shaking. *Out of control.* Warning bells screamed in Lucien's head.

"Well maybe if you had let him work for me, instead

of stealing him away, he might have been here to prevent this, Robert."

"Do not start this again." Robert pointed his finger, moving toward Christophe, his other hand balled into a fist. Lucien jumped to interpose himself between the two men.

"Enough! Both of you just stop." Tension pulsed and beat at Lucien from every side until it settled into a pounding headache. An off-tune instrument screeching in the background would have been more welcomed. The silence raged until Christophe finally stalked to the other side of the office with a loud huff. Lucien sighed, turning to question Robert. "Tell me what happened."

"I told you the security here was inadequate." Robert paced, rubbing at the back of his neck, his other hand clenching and unclenching. "I never should have let you talk me into this display."

"Security wouldn't have been an issue if you and Lucien had let me help, or hell, bothered to keep me apprised," Christophe accused. "But no, things always have to be on Robert Shoalman's terms. Lord forbid someone else—"

"Sometimes things happen for a reason." Robert spun to face Christophe, eyes almost solid black with anger. And pain. "The choice must be acceptable to both Guardian and charge. Why do you think your son is my Guardian and not you? You made your choice, just as I made mine." Robert staggered. Catching himself on the back of a chair, he squeezed his eyes shut. "If the paintings had fallen into the wrong hands..."

Who was supposed to be Robert's Guardian? Him or his father? A sense of inadequacy filled him. Was that why he had so much trouble learning how to heal Robert or prevent the attacks of his curse? Lucien twisted to confront his father. Christophe wouldn't look him in the eye. Fine. There were more important issues right now anyways. Lucien took a deep centering breath, burying his own pain.

"*Tata*, how's Carl? Did someone go to the hospital with him?"

"No, I...I don't know," the sudden change of subject throwing Christophe off balance.

"Have you spoken to the police? Filed a report? Is anything missing in the bar? Is there any damage?" Lucien scrambled to cover all the issues that needed to be taken care of. He had his debut and the band re-launch coming up, not to mention the implications of an attempted theft. Lucien couldn't help but wonder if there was more to this than an art thief looking to make a quick score. Had Robert's demon found them?

"I'll see to Carl and the police report." Christophe stared at him, jaw set in a hard line. He flicked his gaze towards Robert, the anger still evident yet tempered by something else.

"Thank you." Lucien sucked in a breath of air, dealing with his father a battle he rarely won. "When I'm done here, I'll check for damage to the bar and see if the security system needs any upgrades." Christophe opened his mouth but Lucien held up his hand to stop him. "I'll call you with anything I find."

"I'll hire two additional security guards while I'm at it," Christophe said.

"Two?"

"After this." Christophe scoffed, gesturing to the cops still milling about the outer area collecting evidence, his gaze settling on Carmen's tense form. "Don't you think it might be a good idea not to leave *anyone* here alone?"

Lucien bit his tongue. It was a dirty trick bringing Carmen's safety into question, but arguing money or business with his father was a pointless endeavor.

"Do whatever you want." He would anyways. Lucien grunted. The pain running through his marks pulsed and grew. "Now leave and let me do my job."

Without a further word, Christophe turned in stiff military fashion and exited the room. Lucien tilted his head at Christophe's retreating back and Carmen nodded. She closed the door behind her when she left.

Lucien inhaled sharply when painful muscle spasm traversed his forearms and across his chest. With his father's overpowering presence gone, the pain radiating from Robert magnified. A crash had Lucien spinning. Previously neat and organized files now spilled across the floor and desk. The slick sheen of sweat covered his brow. Pale, eyes wide and unfocused, his breathing short and ragged, Robert shook his head repeatedly. Muttered words too garbled to understand rolled continuously from someone who rarely spoke more than a few sentences at a time.

Panic brings pain—and the curse. Mama T's training echoed in his head. If he didn't get Robert calmed down quick, he'd succumb to his curse in front of an audience who would never understand. Maybe he wasn't Robert's first choice, but he was his Guardian now.

"Breathe, Robert. The paintings are safe."

"I need to see them." Robert paced the room like a caged animal. Hands ran through his hair one minute, then picked up and dropped random items the next. "I need...I need..."

Lucien scanned the room. Moving to the wet bar and pouring a double shot of scotch, he shoved the glass into Robert's hand. "Here. Drink this."

"I hate scotch," Robert complained, but downed the drink in one quick motion. Some of the wildness left his eyes, his color returning. Gripping the glass in a death grip, Robert fought to slow his breathing. Lucien matched him breath for breath, laying a hand on his shoulder to help ground him. "At least I buy good scotch."

Lucien cracked a grin. "Sit. Do you want another one?"

"No."

"Mind if I grab one?"

Robert nodded. Lucien poured more of the amber colored liquid into the tumbler and tossed it back. Fire burned a line down his throat and ignited in his stomach. Bent over the bar coughing, he blinked to clear the tears from his eyes. "If that's good scotch, remind me never to drink the bad stuff. Damn. How does Jay drink this?"

"He has good taste."

Lucien turned. Robert stared at him. The intensity used to bother him, still did at times. But not today. Violence lingered beneath the surface, chained up, contained, but still there. Stories told in whispers the last remnants of a violent past reflected in the scars covering Robert's arms and torso. With five centuries of practice, Robert learned to channel the impulses. Only in paintings did those repressed tendencies come out, the agony of his curse freeing them to wreak havoc. Deep rooted pain lingered in Robert's eyes, but their color had returned to their normal dark brown instead of the anger filled blackness.

"I owe you an explanation."

"No. You don't." Lucien didn't want to delve into that hurt just yet. "Let's just figure out who was here and why. The rest can wait." For eternity as far as he was concerned. Making sure Robert was steady on his feet and under control once more, he crossed the bar to the glass enclosed art gallery. A familiar tall cop stood checking the unbroken glass. No wonder so many cops were here. Carmen's on-again, off-again boyfriend must have rattled some cages.

"Dante?" Lucien held out his hand, the detective offering a firm handshake. "I mean Detective Reese. I forgot you worked burglary."

"Except nothing seems to have been taken and the thief seemed to know exactly where the cameras were stationed, so we didn't catch much on the surveillance recordings." The detective nodded to Robert behind him. "Any thoughts on who might try for your paintings?"

Lucien butted in. "*The Shoalman Collection* is well known in the art community. We haven't made a secret of it being shown here this month. We did take extra precautions though."

"Good thing." Detective Reese ran his hand down the unbroken glass. Waiting.

"I'd let you in." Robert stiffened behind him. "But until I reset the security system it's in lockdown mode and I can't do that until everyone is done poking about. Safety precaution." He shrugged. "You understand."

"Of course." He might accept Lucien's explanation, but he wasn't buying it. "I'll keep you apprised of the investigation, but for now, we're treating it as a simple B&E into the club." Dante handed Lucien his card. "If you find anything more on the video footage, let me know."

"Thanks. I will." Dante and the rest of the officers collected their gear and filed out of the club. Carmen must have gotten his father to leave for the hospital. He heaved a sigh of relief for that small blessing. Locking the doors and setting the alarm, he returned to Robert who stared through the glass panes at his paintings.

"Do you smell it? The stench?"

Lucien inhaled. Sweetness and the lingering odor of decay teased at his nose, turning his stomach sour. An invisible film formed on the roof of his mouth, leaving him wanting to scrape his tongue against his teeth to remove it. "What the hell is that?"

"The scent of death denied."

"He's found us?" No. Not now. Not when things were finally settling down. Lucien growled. The band. Mandy. His heart clenched. None of it mattered.

Mama T's Second Sight about the curse always

centered on Robert needing to be here to find answers. She couldn't or wouldn't say more. Having the support of his sister while he learned his role, especially in light of his father's apparent potential as a Guardian, gave him a sense of stability he never had before now. He suspected his grandmother's vision had just as much to do with Carmen being in Baltimore than anything else.

His oaths were the strongest hold on his life. "I vowed to protect you. If we need to leave—"

"Not yet," Robert stated. Lucien detected an odd confidence in his tone. "You have a music performance to put on and I have to find out why your Grandmother's vision brought us here."

The constriction around Lucien's heart relented but didn't go away. He'd have to cancel with Mandy tomorrow. Instead of spending time sneaking sly glances as her sexy legs while he worked, he'd be assessing and fixing the damage to the bar. But it was the secret he kept from Robert that weighed heaviest on his shoulders. One day, he'd have to choose between his Guardian vows and his love of music. It just wasn't today.

CHAPTER NINETEEN

"I thought you were going to cancel on me. Again." Mandy tensed with Lucien standing on the other side of the doorway. In the three days since their date, she'd nearly forgotten how much he electrified the air around him. "Come on in."

"If I recall, you canceled on me yesterday." Lucien flashed a half-crooked grin. The boy could melt an iceberg with his smile. As he walked inside her apartment, Mandy soaked in the view. Dark jeans, loose, but fitted in the places that counted most. Her cheeks heated just glancing at the exposed forearm holding his laptop bag. She'd never seen white tattoos like the ones that wrapped around his wrists and scrolled over his skin.

"And you canceled on me the day before that." Mandy shut the door a little harder than she intended. She hadn't asked for explanations when Lucien called to tell her something came up and nine wasn't going to work for him. He offered to come by at three that afternoon, but Mandy had other plans. Finally, their schedules matched.

"Yes, I did," he said, nodding. He didn't offer another word on the subject. Mandy hated not knowing. "Where do you want to do this, Angel?"

"Uh." Mandy's eyes widened, not a single angelic thought swirled in her mind. She imagined Lucien lounging on her couch, sprawled on her bed, preferably shirtless. Hell, she pictured him on... "The table is fine," she managed to say. Her laptop wasn't the only thing in the room charged and waiting.

Did her voice quiver? Mandy worried when Lucien turned to stare at her. He cleared his throat, licking his lips, slow, as if deliberate to drive her insane. It was working. Never had her tongue fumbled as much as it did staring at Lucien.

"Yeah, sure." He shook his head. "The table will work." He set his laptop next to Mandy's on one end. At the other end of the table, Mandy opened a large leather portfolio; stacks of larger images piled beside it.

"You want something to drink?" She'd almost offered him a beer. Eighteen. Not twenty-one, or even twenty. Eighteen, she reminded herself. "Water? Mint tea maybe?" *Me?*

"Water is fine." Lucien sat at her laptop. "Are all your photographs on your main screen?" Lucien faltered when she set the water bottle beside him, their fingers touching for maybe longer than necessary. He stared. Blue eyes so pure, so seemingly innocent, yet the heat of his look, anything but. She wanted to know what thoughts could possibly be running through that head of his. She hoped every one of them contained her. Things he'd like to do to her. That he'd let her do to him. Different positions they could try.

"Just the ones I'm currently working on," she said, forcing herself to pull her hand away, break the gaze. Kyrissa's paintings were her current project, one she continued to drag her feet on. She had promised her she'd transfer them to a flash drive but hadn't done so yet because Mandy hated giving Kyrissa a reason to go see her professor.

"Uh, where do you put the pictures you're not working on?"

"I put them in that folder." Mandy pointed to the

sole folder in the center of her laptop screen.

"You put them all in one folder?" He asked. His mouth hung agape.

"Yes." Mandy sat at the table beside Lucien. She clicked open the folder. Thumbnail images covered the new window. She scrolled through the long list. Lucien gasped. "I kept intending to go back a arrange them, but when I started the blog, it sort of blew up so fast I didn't have time and then the problem grew and I honestly had no idea how to fix it. Sorry. I should have warned you how much of a mess my filing system is, or lack thereof."

"They're all in the same folder," he whispered, eyes widening the further down the never-ending list of titles he got. "Wow. That's a lot of pictures."

"Not all of them. The raw images are over here." Mandy clicked another folder open. "I don't touch up the images or anything, just resize them. I never add anything that isn't already in the frame," she clarified, though not sure why she needed to.

"Two folders." Lucien stood up. His hand covered his mouth, scratched at the scruff along the edge of his chin. If he had an itch there, Mandy could certainly offer to scratch it. With her tongue. "You keep thousands of images in two folders." He wove his hand over his head, staring at the floor.

"On that hard drive, yes. I have a few externals as well. They're a little better organized, but not much." Mandy shrugged. She ached to grab her camera and capture the moment, strong hands intertwined with the rich black hair. But she could take only one picture of him today. One. And this wasn't the one she needed.

"Let me guess, the externals only have two folders, too?"

"That's a problem isn't it?" Mandy asked without confirming or denying anything. "Luckily, I'm not including the binders of negatives I have from when I first learned how to develop film myself in this database you're creating."

"Not feeling too lucky with all these images right now."

"Seriously, there aren't that many images. I don't need like a hundred folders or anything. I wouldn't know where to find which image I was looking for."

"You're kidding right? There's zero organization of what might very well be a million images." Lucien shook his head, a worried look on his face. "I don't even know where to begin." Lucien paced from one end of the room and back. "I'm not sure I can do this."

"I thought that's why you were here." Mandy flipped her hand in the air. How hard could this be?

"Okaay," Lucien drawled out. "But this is going to take longer than I thought. A lot longer. Probably a couple of weeks." He laughed.

"As long as you give me the exclusive for the band, I don't care how long it takes."

"I already said I'm yours," Lucien gleamed. "Exclusively."

"Huh. I might like the sound of that," Mandy pulled her hair up off her neck and into a loose knot at the back of her head. The ice-cold bottle of water sitting on the table looked refreshing, if she could hold it up to her neck. And her cheeks. Lucien didn't hold all the cards on overheating this time. This fire belonged to her. "Perhaps too much."

"Or not enough." Lucien winked.

Clearing her throat, Mandy clutched her camera. "If this task is going to take so much work, we better get started. I pulled some pictures for you, but also a thumbnail of all of the images I'd want included in the digital library." Mandy set out a few proof sheets from some of her favorite photo shoots. Along with her portfolio, these were still only a small sample of her entire body of work. "Maybe seeing the originals would help categorize them." Mandy shrugged. She really was so far out of her comfort zone that she couldn't feel the boundaries anymore.

"These are good," Lucien said. He laid some out, scattering a few and matching others to the corresponding proof sheet like a master puzzle maker. "Are the titles on this proof accurate?"

Mandy nodded. All the images lined up created something she hadn't noticed before. Pieces to a puzzle she hadn't know existed.

"Okay, good. This gives me something to work off of."

I'll give you something to work off.

Around Lucien, Mandy found herself refraining from saying everything that popped into her head. Definitely not something she was used to.

Lucien went silent while he worked, killing Mandy with the lack of conversation. Every few minutes she clutched her camera, readying for the moment when she would take her one picture. She just couldn't make up her mind whether to photograph his concentration, the way his brows inched together every time his fingers sped across the keyboard of the laptop. The movement of his long, lean fingers had her thinking about all kinds of things, none of them concerned her article.

After several near clicks, Mandy settled the frame of her camera on Lucien's face. So deep in concentration, he didn't notice her hesitation as she adjusted the lens, zooming in close to capture his eyes then back out again to see the whole picture. Highlights hit his jaw line whenever he looked at the proof sheet and back to the screen. Short stubble against smooth skin. She could think of at least three things she wanted to do to that jaw rather than take a picture of it.

In the end, it didn't matter. Her finger pressed the button just as Lucien looked up and the shot she captured was neither the one she intended nor one she regretted. Focused tight in on his face, a smoldering gaze aimed in her direction, his crystal clear blue eyes framed by thick lashes with a strand of dark black hair curling along his cheek. Perfect.

At least the image of Lucien would be perfect if it showed anything deeper. It didn't. No colors highlighted his face. No shadows cast across his eyes. And no deep dark secrets revealed themselves in the photo. Almost as if something protected him from her sight.

Holding up a finger, Lucien gestured her one photo had been taken.

Mandy unstrapped the camera, laying it on the table in front of her. "I only need one," she said. Needing one and wanting a thousand images of this guy were two very different things.

"You barely even looked to see if that one is any good," Lucien smirked. Mandy considered taking another because of the super sexy arch of his raised eyebrow. She cleared her throat, not remembering the last time she decided not to break rules.

"I trust my instincts to take the exact picture I need." Or needed. But who really knew the difference? Even though her faith in her ability wouldn't waver just because Lucien Solvak was trying to hide something from her, she did wonder what the picture didn't show. Would it be shrouded in dark and mysterious shadows like Jay? Or would his coloring bleach white more like Kyrissa? Or would all pictures of Lucien come up empty?

"I think I have the framework for this database mapped out at least," Lucien said. "But I have to go. Rehearsal. If it's okay with you, I could take a thumb drive to come up with most the categories myself, but I'll still have to come back tomorrow night and finish before the images can be relabeled to fit the categories."

"A thumb drive is fine as long as you swear on your life not to misuse any pictures and I get a free pass for a second photo to be taken at any time of my choosing." Mandy flashed a smile she was certain he couldn't refuse. He grimaced but agreed to the terms. "But tomorrow night doesn't work for me."

"You already have plans." Lucien took a deep breath. All the color had blanched from his face; pale, as if someone just revealed that Santa wasn't real. Mandy wouldn't be the one to burst that bubble.

"There's a band playing at Metro."

"I just assumed our exclusivity clause went both ways." He stood up, snapping his laptop shut. "Guess I was wrong."

"You're barely giving me anything to be exclusive with." Mandy crossed her arms over her chest. Exclusivity? On her part? Not a chance. "How about we meet up again on Thursday night?"

"I have to work." Lucien frowned. "Friday?"

"Another band photo shoot and interview," Mandy said.

"And I'm out of town this weekend," Lucien added. "Unless you want to wait until next week."

"Looks like tomorrow's our only option." No way Mandy wanted to wait a week to see Lucien again. Three days had been torture. She leaned back against the table, letting her legs stretch out as far as she could until they were just a few feet from Lucien. His gaze followed their every move. "If I make myself available tomorrow night, are you going to make it worth me changing my plans?"

"Absolutely," Lucien said. Placing his hand beside her, he leaned down, close to her ear. "How about two pictures and an interview? Exclusive, of course."

"I might be starting to enjoy this exclusivity thing after all," she mumbled, never lifting her eyes from his.

"Me too." He leaned closer, the need for her to take a drink increased. His gaze followed her tongue but just when Mandy thought he was close enough to kiss her, he took a deep breath and straightened back up. "I have to go," he said.

"You what?" Mandy asked, clearing her throat.

"Rehearsal. The, uh, band." Already at the front door, his hand rested on the doorknob. "Be back tomorrow."

Mandy couldn't decide which emotion to embrace in the moment the door closed behind Lucien. Pissed, because he had managed to get her to agree to change her plans, got her all worked up, then walked away. Or relieved that he saved her from making a huge mistake. The last thing Mandy needed was strings to some music hungry adolescent. But dammit, she wanted to tie a few strings around Lucien Solvak.

CHAPTER TWENTY

"Make sure you tuck him in early, Carmen," Jay called out from the back door. "We have a long day of practice tomorrow and he needs all the beauty sleep he can get."

"Screw you, Jay." Lucien laughed. One of these days, he'd wipe that smirk off Jay's face. Sitting at the bar, he waited for Carmen to finish inventorying the liquor. "You know I could have done that after I was done."

"I don't mind. Makes me feel useful."

Lucien narrowed his eyes. "What's that supposed to mean?"

"Nothing." She smiled at him. "Sing me a song while I finish up."

"You mean you're not sick of *Demon Dogs* music?"

"I want a real song." She laughed when he scoffed. "Serenade me with the song mother used to sing to us when we were little."

The smile faded from his face. "I'm not supposed to play that."

After his mother's death, he retreated to music for solace, playing the many songs she taught him. Only one gave him any peace—*The Long Walk*. It was the last song she taught him. Had she known she was going to die when she taught it to him? One night, after crawling into a bottle, his father caught him playing it. It was the one time Christophe ever hit

Lucien in anger. The command forbidding him to ever play or sing the song again backed up with the threat of destroying his guitar if he disobeyed. Lucien promised never to play it in the house again. And he hadn't.

"Please." She laid a hand on his arm. "For me?"

Lucien crossed to the stage and picked up his guitar, unplugging it from the amp. Settling on the edge the wooden platform, he wiped the sweat from his hands onto his jeans. Heart racing, he closed his eyes. His mother's face hovered behind closed lids. Smiling. His mother had always smiled when they played music together. She would have liked Mandy.

Thoughts of Mandy comforted him and he began to pluck out the beginning chords of the melody, the lines cutting into his skin where he pressed against the fret board. Cold beneath his fingertips, the vibrations of the gut strings glided over light calluses, each note a separate thread pulling at his heart. Plucking rhythmically, music surrounded him, weaving its sound around his soul. The skin on the back of his hands warmed like his mother covered them again. Just as she had when teaching him the song. He could almost smell the light herbal scent from the hand cream she always used.

There is a walk all must take, but be not afraid young one. The journey is your own, but always by your side will I be.

Lucien let the Romani lyrics flow, his voice shaky at first, gaining strength as memories flooded through him. It had been so long. Music. From his earliest memories, it had been a part of his life. No matter where they traveled, he always had the songs of his people and family, their stories embedded in the notes of every melody. The one constant he could always count on.

Stronger and stronger, Lucien's voice filled the bar. The tempo rising and falling along with the emotion of each stanza. Life. Death. The road between them varied for everyone and the journey itself was what shaped each person. His mother's journey had been short, but she filled each day, each moment with joy. Sharing her love of music with him, encouraging him to take risks and embrace the gift given to him. Yes, she would have loved Mandy. She too made him embrace the possibilities offered to him, both with the band...and her.

His hand stilled, the last note and chord fading into the silence. Fingers brushed moisture from his cheek and he opened his eyes to see Carmen sat next to him, her face streaked with tears. His throat tightened. The song lifted a weight he hadn't realized he carried all these years, freeing him from the chains of fear holding him back. Gasping ragged breaths, he fought against the emotions crashing over him. Loss, but also joy. The last being the true gift his mother gave him.

"This is why you can't ever give up on your music," Carmen whispered. She crossed her hands over her heart, the Romani gesture of giving of one's self. "You put more emotion into a single note. And share that joy, leaving a person with more than they ever expected."

Lucien pulled his sister into his arms and hugged her. "I miss her."

"You shouldn't." Carmen pulled away from him, her smiled warm and bright. She wiped her face with her sleeve. "Every time you sing, you cherish her memory and bring her back into our world."

"Let's go home. I have a sudden need to be around my family." Sliding his guitar to his back, he pulled his sister to her feet. "And if you ever tell Jay about this, I'll make sure *you* never get another night of beauty sleep as long as I live."

CHAPTER TWENTY-ONE

Mandy had to admit that lately Kyrissa spent more time in her campus studio, out of Mandy's watchful eye, as she did at home. And Kyrissa's safety was always a concern for Mandy. But since finishing art school, Mandy didn't find herself on campus nearly enough to know exactly how safe campus was for her best friend at any particular moment, at least not without taking some precautions. Precautions that glared right at her from behind the security desk of the Naylor Building.

"Uh, Mikhail is it?" Mandy asked staring at the security guard's name tag. He was young, and cute with dark complexion and darker eyes and thick black hair that reached his shoulders. But he was almost too pretty to gawk at. Exactly the type Mandy could convince into doing whatever she needed and make him think it was his idea. At least she hoped.

"Yes. And you are..." His smile, warm and sincere, oozed enough charm to make her pause, but couldn't throw Mandy off her game.

"I'm Mandy," she said sliding onto the top of the desk. She almost felt bad the way her lashes fluttered and she licked her lips. Mikhail squirmed just a little bit in his chair. "Just Mandy."

"How may I be of service to you, just Mandy?" One brow raised, his grinned curled around a dimple and Mandy almost lost her train of thought. If Lucien had worn that look, she likely would have melted into a puddle in his lap. But he wasn't Lucien and she needed this guy's help.

"I was wondering if you could tell me..." Mandy swung her legs around to his side of the desk. "I'm sort of looking for someone. A former professor of mine and I was hoping you could tell me his course schedule. The catalogue didn't seem to list faculty names so..." Mandy twirled a lock of hair around her finger.

"I would be happy to help." Mikhail stood, leaning down on the desk. He towered Mandy, easily over six foot. "As soon as you get your ass off my desk."

"Fine," Mandy snapped, placing her feet back on the floor. She moved back to the other side of the desk, exaggerating her steps so he could see what he was missing.

"Now," Mikhail crossed his arms over his chest. "Why don't you tell what you're really looking for because every professor in this building, and every building on campus, posts their current semester class and advisor hours outside their doors. It's school policy so that those of us concerned about campus safety can do our jobs and not be bothered by trivial questions we're not required to answer."

Huh. Mandy huffed. "I see we're gonna have to do this another way." She pulled a twenty dollar bill from her purse. Always prepared, she had many more in reserve since she had no idea how much this information would cost.

"And this is for?" Mikhail shoved the money into his back pocket before Mandy answered. He sat back onto the chair behind him.

"My roommate goes here. She has a studio on the top floor and I'm worried about her staying too late. Are you, or someone equally serious about their job, on duty all night?"

"Yes. Since the building is open twenty-four hours, and believe me these artist types often take advantage of those wee-morning creative hours, someone is stationed here every hour."

"Good to know." Mandy used to be able to convince Kyrissa to walk home with her well before midnight. Not so much anymore. "What about faculty? Do any of them keep hours other than those posted? Does, maybe, Professor Calaul ever stay all night, perhaps he sleeps in his office occasionally?"

"Sorry. That's gonna cost ya another bill." Mikhail smirked.

Mandy cursed under her breath, pulling a second twenty from her bag. "So?" she taunted.

"Yes." He slipped the bill into his uniform pants.

"How often?" Mandy handed over more money before Mikhail asked for it. She'd played this game before, more than once, and she was definitely a pro.

"Hmm," Mikhail drew out a breath, leaning back into his chair. "Two, three times a week. But I'm guessing you already suspected as much. Your roommate wouldn't happen to be the cute blond in the corner studio on the third floor would she?"

"Why? Do Professor C's overnight visits coincide with her late nights?"

Mikhail hesitated. His eyes lightened, glare relaxed. Mandy offered twenty more dollars.

"I'll give you this one for free." Mikhail winked, pushing Mandy's hand back. "Yes. They do happen on the same nights, most times. But I don't think there's anything skeevy going on, if that's what you're worried about. Professor sometimes goes to the studio space, but he's never in there more than ten, fifteen minutes, max."

"And how would you know that?" Mandy worried whether Mikhail could be more stalker material than security guard extraordinaire.

"Hot chick like her and Mr. Creep-me-the-fuck out. I was curious." Mikhail shrugged. "Checked the video footage of the hallways a couple of times. On the nights your roommate is here late, Professor goes up and checks on her, usually only once. He pops into her studio, knocking on the door first, and always waits to be invited in. And then he comes back to his office a few minutes later. Passes by here like nothing happened, so I'm pretty sure nothing does."

"You ever go up and verify that?" Mandy opened her purse again.

"Of course. I make rounds every half hour or so and your roommate is always in there painting away. Some powerful stuff, too, if you ask me."

"Well, Mikhail. This might be your lucky day." Mandy slid a handful of twenties across the desk. "I'm willing to pay to make sure my roommate is safe if you're willing to make sure that is true as long as she is in this building."

"Just to make sure the Cooky Professor keeps his distance from the blond?" Mikhail swiped the cash into his grasp. "Consider it done, for now."

Mandy took a marker from the pen holder on the security desk. "And should that space be breached, you'll call me." She wrote her number on Mikhail's arm. In sharpie.

"Besides a few bucks, which I assure you I don't need, what's in this arrangement for me?"

"Let's just say I am one of the most connected people you've ever met in this city. And I use those connections to help my friends out. All they have to do is ask."

"Well, I don't mind keeping an eye out for friends. But for the right friends, I don't need to be paid for those services." He rifled the stack of money, adding the two bills from his pocket, before handing the entire stack back to her. "Besides I'm switching to the day shift after tonight. Going into the family business."

"I hope that's not some weird reference to the mafia or something." Mandy tried to laugh it off but couldn't help and wonder what kind of family business he meant.

"I wish." Mikhail chuckled. "The mob's gotta be a lot less complicated than my family." His physique was solid, muscles that were barely contained in the security uniform, and an ease surrounded him that said he could take control of any situation. Whatever business needed those traits, Mandy almost wanted to become a part of his family.

"Don't I know it." Mandy smiled at Mikhail, certain she'd see him again. Soon. And often.

"Listen. Part of my duties in the morning will consist of running the tapes back from the night before. Since I have a strong tech background in the security field, I might be able to make sure you have access to a live feed, if that would make you feel better?"

"You have no idea how much better." Mandy narrowed her eyes. "Why would you do this and how many other people have you done it for?"

Mikhail chuckled, "Suspicious sort. I like that. I'm only doing it for you because anyone who has drawn extra attention from that crazy old Professor needs someone looking out for her."

Mandy vibrated with the truth of his words. "Maybe you're not the complete ass I originally took you for. Thanks."

"I'll get it set up and send you the link provided you give me an email." He handed her a piece of paper. "Preferably not on my arm this time." He tucked the paper into his shirt pocket after she complied.

"Fantastic. Looks like today was actually my lucky day." Mandy grinned, holding out her hand. "It was a pleasure to meet you Mikhail...." She waited but he didn't offer a last name, only a slight smirk.

"Likewise, Mandy, girl with no last name." Mikhail squeezed her hand, smiling.

Mandy walked away feeling just a little bit better now that she had a pair of eyes on Kyrissa, even when she wasn't within sight.

CHAPTER TWENTY-TWO

"Hungry for Romani?" Lucien asked when Mandy opened her apartment door. Her eyes flashed wide for a second, her skin flushing color into her cheeks. Damn she was hot when she blushed.

"Takeout?" Mandy tried peeking into the bag.

Lucien pulled the bag away. "Eat in," he teased and was rewarded with Mandy licking her full luscious lips. The act caused him to swallow hard. He was supposed to be the one ramping her up, not the other way around. "Provided you let me in," he said.

"Oh, right." Mandy pulled the door open the rest of the way

"I figured I'd treat you to dinner since I requested you cancel your plans tonight." The thought of Mandy being with another guy—Lucien refused to let his brain finish that line of thinking, or the images it conjured up. She's part of the marketing plan, he reminded himself. Yeah right. He always cooked for publicity agents. And imagined them in his bed. Or being between their legs.

Lucien shook his head. Averting his gaze from Mandy's form he restrained his thoughts—and his wayward body—refocusing on the job at hand. Dropping his laptop by their worktable, his arms full of groceries and a pot tucked into a bag on his back, Lucien headed for her kitchen.

Dressed in shorts that showed off long legs and a

formfitting t-shirt that read *Take a picture. It will last longer*, Mandy scooted onto a tall barstool. Lucien chuckled, especially since her camera sat next to her on the countertop. Waiting as always.

"Typhoon Bordeaux?" Lucien pointed to the countertop. Robert had the exact same color granite in his apartment.

"Yes," Mandy said. She ran her hands over the smooth top. Hands Lucien tried hard not to imagine elsewhere, on other places, preferably him. "I'm impressed. No one else ever knew this color. But I figured if daddy was remodeling, he might as well put in the best."

"And you only keep the best," Lucien teased. Flashing his most brilliant smile, he winked, determined to make sure Mandy thought he was good enough to keep around. Reaching into his backpack, he pulled out a battered pot. Mama T's favorite.

"You can cook?" She asked.

"Yes, I can cook."

"Spicy and hot I hope?" Mandy tilted her head to the side. Arching a single brow, her dark, wavy hair cascaded over one shoulder exposing the long curve of her neck. Lucien walked into the kitchen counter. Damn it. He cleared his throat, managing to cover the stumble by pushing the grocery bag further onto the counter, blocking the view his body wanted to devour raw.

"If it's not hot and spicy," he quipped back, "It's not true Romani."

"Mmmmm. A man who cooks and sings. Now that's hot."

"Do you always say whatever pops into your head?" Lucien was glad for the tall counter between them. He wouldn't have to say a word for her to know what thoughts were running through *his* head. He focused on pulling the supplies out of the bag.

"Oh, I'm holding back a few choice thoughts," Mandy said. His perfect pitch caught the waiver in her voice and Lucien looked up in time to see Mandy squirm.

Grabbing the large stew pot, he turned towards the gas stove behind him.

"So, um, what's ready to eat?"

The cast iron pot dropped to the stove with a loud clank. Lucien licked his lips trying to moisten his dry mouth. "Cabbage rolls," he managed to get out. "Well, they're not ready yet, but it won't take long to heat them up."

"Sounds good actually." Mandy walked over, her proximity sent shivers all through his body. "Can I help?"

Lucien stared. God she was so gorgeous. With curves in all the right places and dark wavy hair Lucien longed to run his fingers through, his concentration sunk lower in his core. How had he lost control of the situation so fast? How had he ever thought it was possible to have any control where Mandy was concerned?

Lucien spread out single pieces of cabbage on the countertop "We need to stuff these with rice and seasoned meat." He nodded to the two containers of the pre-cooked items. "I'll get the rice. Grab the hedgehog meat, will you?"

"Hedgehog meat?" Mandy faltered, her hands rubbing against the top of her shorts. "Seriously?"

Lucien held the snort in as long as he could. The look of sheer panic on Mandy's face pushed him over the edge.

"Why you…"

He ducked the blue kitchen towel she threw at him, but couldn't stop laughing. When Mandy picked up the wooden spoon, he grabbed her wrists pulling her against him. Laughter faded as he gazed down at her. Deep brown eyes stared into his. The hint of her scent tickled at his nose. Light and somewhat fruity. Not overpowering like so many of the Romani women. He licked his lips again. It would be so easy to lean down and just...

Lucien took a half step back, pulling the wooden spoon from her now lax grip. "Thanks. We'll, um, need this to mix the rice and meat." He chuckled. "Promise. It's just ground beef seasoned with peppers, although Mama T told me she has cooked hedgehog before."

"Who's Mama T?" Mandy peeked at the container of meat before bringing it over to Lucien.

"My Grandmother. Her name is Tila, but we all call her Mama T. Well, except for Robert. He's known her as Tila for too long to call her anything else." Snapping his mouth closed, Lucien turned away from Mandy.

"You okay?" Mandy laid a hand on his shoulder. Lucien started mixing the ingredients together to hide the taut strain in his muscles.

"Yeah, fine. Just need to get these cooking if we plan to get any work done tonight." Heat from her skin thru his shirt set his heart pounding into overdrive almost as much as the mistake he almost made. Mandy was an outsider. Robert would kill him if he ever disclosed his immortal secret. Unless the demon hunting them did it before Robert got the chance. As much as he hated secrets, Mandy couldn't know anything else. Stick to music and cooking. "Here, let me show you how to make these."

Standing behind her, Lucien grabbed a handful of the sticky mixture and placed it on a cabbage leaf. He used his hands to guide hers, showing her how to wrap the stuffing into the leaf so it wouldn't fall out during cooking. "You just tuck the end under that seam to seal it closed."

"Like this?" Mandy folded the edge, pinching the leaf to make it stay.

"Exactly like that." His fingers lingered on hers a moment longer, taking the round ball from her. "You sure you haven't done this before? How did you know to pinch the leaf?"

Mandy shrugged. "You have your secrets. I have mine." He wanted to kiss the smug smile right off her face.

"That trick is only known to Romani cooks." It was as though she belonged in his world. He couldn't explain the feeling of rightness around her. Of being safe. Nothing in his life was safe, not with all the secrets he had to hide. Lucien shook his head, dismissing the sensation. Mandy was definitely not safe. She was like playing with freaking fire and all he wanted to do was fan the flames.

Arms on either side of her, he trapped her against the counter. Her increased breath gave him a very nice view. "Help me make the rest of these and it will be our little secret."

"Deal." She pressed closer to him. Neither moved for several heartbeats. "You'll have to step back if you want me to help with the food," Mandy whispered. "Unless you had another recipe you wanted to try."

The hairs on his arms stood up where their skin touched, the rest of his body stirred. Food was not on Lucien's mind. At least not the kind he was supposed to be making for her. They just met. He barely knew anything about her, although had finally uncovered her full name—Amanda Hayworth.

"Right." Dragging his feet backwards, Lucien forced himself to put some distance between them. Was that a frown?

Mandy exhaled sharply before a slow grin crept out. "Bet I can make more then you."

Lucien laughed, the action releasing some of the pent up tension. "Go!" he called but started before he spoke the words.

"Oh it's going to be like that, is it?" Mandy reached across and pulled the bowl of meat closer to her.

"Cheater," Lucien cried out when her hip bumped

into his, not that he moved any further away.

"All's fair in love and...non-hedgehog meat," Mandy quipped.

Her hands covered in meat and rice, her laughter loud and boisterous, Lucien didn't think he'd ever seen anything so sexy before.

"I still won," Lucien chuckled. "Even with your meat stealing, hip checking, cheating ways." He managed to turn his attention to the food, placing all the cabbage balls in the pot. Lucien covered them with sauce, seasoned them with fresh ground pepper and added a dash of salt.

"Trust me." Mandy placed her freshly washed palm flat against his cheek, transferring an energy he didn't recognize and didn't want to lose. "If I had wanted to win, I would have won."

"I'm sure you would."

He could stay like this forever. Her touch on his skin. The spicy tang of the meat still clung to her fingers, mingling with her own intoxicating scent. Lucien inhaled. Capturing her hand, he turned and placed a kiss in the center of her palm.

Energy crackled between them. Alive. Tempting. Dangerous.

He had to stop. Now, before it was too late. Lucien pulled away, releasing her hand. Turning away, he fiddled with the stove controls. Anything to keep from seeing the disappointment on her face. And keep her from seeing his.

"Now what?" Mandy asked. The tone was casual, but Lucien caught the edginess to it.

"They cook for about three hours. A slow simmer is the best way to heat them up." Lucien grinned. "Food, like life, best enjoyed slowly." Mama T's favorite saying had no meaning before he'd met Mandy.

"So that's how you work." Mandy's breathy voice, very different from her carefree laughter of a few minutes ago, captured his attention.

Lucien turned at the sound just as the click of the camera went off. He frowned. "That's one. You only get one more tonight. I hope it was what you wanted."

Mandy smiled, her gaze raking him from head to toe. "Yeah, I got the one I wanted."

She sauntered into the living room towards their makeshift worktable, her hips swaying with each step, as if her ass didn't already claim his full attention. Life might be best enjoyed slow, but Mandy was going to burn him up from the inside out at this rate.

"There's water in the fridge."

"What?" Lucien asked.

"You're sweating." A sly smile teased him from the living room. "Kitchen must be...hot. Thought you might need a drink or something."

Or something. Water wasn't going to cool the burning inside him with that kind of look. He licked his lips and grabbed two waters from the fridge. Heading into the living room, he held the ice-cold bottles against the white tattoos crisscrossing his forearms. Cooking with fire took on a completely new meaning when applied to Mandy Hayworth.

CHAPTER TWENTY-THREE

"This is actually good," Mandy said, plating another stuffed cabbage in front of her. Authentic Romani meals had been a staple of her childhood. Now she could count on one hand the last times she enjoyed such cuisine. Four years ago, when she went to Romania to get a tattoo. The time before that was at her mother's funeral.

"Your faith in my cooking skills was clearly underrated because these are the best stuffed cabbage you will ever taste, notwithstanding my grandmother's." Lucien sucked the juices off his fingers slowly, moaning with each one. Mandy had to look away.

"Did you make this corn bread yourself or should I be thanking your grandmother?"

"With my own two hands." Lucien cleared his plate, replacing it with a platter filled with some sort of dessert, warm honey dripping over one side of the plate.

"Just wait until you taste these sticky dough balls," Lucien whispered in Mandy's ear. He placed a clean plate in front of her. "You will never question my skills again."

Mandy wanted to question how he made every hair on her entire body stand up when he breathed that close to her neck. Or how he knew that stuffed cabbage was her favorite Romani meal. It seemed inappropriate to tell him that as a child, her mother made the meal once a week, sometimes twice if Mandy was having a particularly rough day. And Mandy had eaten her fair share of traditional dough balls smothered in honey.

"I don't know." Mandy leaned back in her chair. "You know what they say about a guy with sticky fingers." She took a bite out of the dough ball.

"Uh, no. I actually don't know what they say." Lucien glanced up at her, eyes narrowed. She tried not to melt at his gaze, but when he wore innocence the way Mandy wore flirtation, like a second skin, melting always occurred.

"He'll need help cleaning his fingers," Mandy said sucking honey off each of her fingers while Lucien looked on, mouth open wide. "You're right. These gogosi are delicious. Maybe the best I've ever had. I won't ever question your skills again."

"You know about gogosi?" Lucien asked.

"Of course," Mandy said.

"And how exactly do you know about them?" Lucien asked. The brightness in his eyes tempted her to use her last picture for the day.

"It's a secret. Besides, I thought I owned this interview," Mandy teased. Mystery worked both ways and disclosing that her mother had Romani ancestry needed to remain a mystery for now. At least to Lucien. "Now are we going to get back to work or what? I believe I have one more picture to take and at least a thousand questions to ask."

"I did not agree to answer a thousand questions." Lucien pushed his plate away from him, leaving one unfinished dough ball glistening in the light.

"I don't recall agreeing to have dinner with you either, but here we are." After cleaning her hands, Mandy reached for her camera. It may have sat within an arm's length but nothing comforted her more than wrapping her fingers around the metal case.

"At least you enjoyed dinner," Lucien grumbled. The way he glanced at her camera, as though it might bite him, Mandy barely managed to contain her chuckle.

"I'm sure you'll find my interview techniques enjoyable." Mandy let her cardigan slide off her shoulders, exposing a tight fitting, black tank top. "And, you can always choose not to answer any question you don't want to answer."

Lucien cleared his throat. "Ask whatever you like."

"What's your middle name?" Mandy asked.

"Jaren," Lucien replied. "But if that ever leaks, I'll know the source."

"So you're planning to use a stage name?" Mandy's finger tapped the tiny button on her camera. Patience had never been her strongest skill, but the longer she hung out with Lucien, the more self-restraint she seemed to hold in reserve.

"L.J. Slone." Lucien never lifted his eyes from his laptop screen.

"Hmm," Mandy hummed. "Very rock and roll sounding."

"I thought so." Lucien continued pouring through a barrage of images that swept across the screen. Some were so old Mandy hardly recognized them until the subtle emotion shone through. He didn't blink twice at the lighting her images seemed to capture or the shadows that sometimes lurked behind her subjects. In fact, he made no comment at all about the photographs, she wondered if he saw them the way she did.

"Any chance L.J. Slone emailed me about exposure for his as of yet untitled band?" Mandy vaguely recognized the name from amongst the clogged email box of wanna-be bands looking to hit it big. She sent the request straight to junk mail when she couldn't locate any more information on the name.

"I may have sent an email or two that went unanswered."

"Sorry about that. I get plenty of requests from bands I wouldn't even categorize in the mediocre folder and I don't endorse mediocre." Mandy considered eating another gogosi just to watch Lucien stare as she licked the honey off her fingers.

"Apology accepted." He smiled and her insides melted. She debated using her newly won picture concession, but held back. Barely.

"Where did you learn to play guitar?" If nothing else, she could use the moment to pry whatever info from him she could since she couldn't use her camera to do the job.

"Taught myself mostly. I listened to music non-stop for years then figured out how to make the same sounds." He shrugged. "Started playing and singing for family. By the time I turned ten, the audiences had grown. Started writing my own lyrics, singing along. Next thing I knew, there were more strangers in the audiences than family. Moved onto bigger stages, mostly local clubs, festivals, stuff like that. Music, singing, art. I can't imagine my world without them surrounding me."

Mandy understood that sentiment. Her world had been a lie up until her twelfth birthday. That's when she turned to her camera for truths everyone around her had hidden, starting with her parents. Learning they were her biological parents after spending the first twelve years being adopted left Mandy struggling with an identity crisis of proportions so big, they swallowed her entire world. Mandy shrugged off her thoughts.

"What kind of art?"

Lucien squirmed. Why would a simple question, one he brought up, make him all of a sudden break out into a sweat?

"Well," Lucien puckered his mouth. "Recently, paintings, but really, I like all kinds of media art." He grabbed his water bottle, draining the liquid in several long pulls. Holding the empty plastic to his chest, almost like a shield between them, Lucien gestured to several photos open on his laptop screen. "Right now I am rather enjoying photography. Do you have any of these enlarged?" He pointed to a few shots that Mandy liked most and kept close.

"Of course. There's a couple..." Mandy froze. She'd been particular about the art that hung on their apartment walls, insisting that Kyrissa's paintings decorate much of the shared rooms. Enlargements of the images Lucien pointed to were kept somewhere more private. "In my bedroom," she admitted.

"Is that an invitation?" Lucien's smile widened, more of the blue showed in his eyes. Mandy wondered when this particular shade became her favorite color. "I accept," he said, nodding. "You're right; I do like your interview techniques."

"Just to see a photograph," Mandy snarked. Inhaling his scent, like her favorite worn leather jacket, her chest relaxed, letting out all the air she'd been holding in. "Follow me."

She led him to the far end of the apartment. She never invited men into her room. If she spent a night with someone, she never shared her domain with him, too worried about not being able to hide in the one place she could be herself.

"Wow," Lucien whispered behind her.

"I know, the bed is totally over the top, but it's so comfortable." Mandy apologized for the oversized four-poster, king-sized behemoth in the center of the room. Dark, hand carved wood. An intricate diamond pattern repeated across the back. "It sort of came with the apartment."

Her father found it in the room when he purchased the building and insisted on saving the history of the bed. Mandy hadn't expected to see it as the centerpiece of her bedroom when she moved in, but now she couldn't imagine the room without it.

"The bed," Lucien paused. "Right. Completely over the top." He nodded, a mischievous grin coming over his face. "But I was referring to that photograph." He pointed to the one photograph Mandy kept closer than any other. The large image flanked one side of her bed making it the first image Mandy saw every morning. "I will take your word on the bed's comfort, unless you extend an invitation to discover it on my own," he said adding a wink.

"As if—" Mandy rolled her eyes so hard, he definitely couldn't follow them. *As if* she hadn't already thought to extend the invite. Repeatedly.

"It's the first photograph I ever took," Mandy whispered. "It's a bit grainy because I had no idea what I was doing at the time. And there's a definite learning curve trying to work in the pitch black of a dark room." All excuses she'd long forgotten. "That's when I learned to develop my own film."

Even in the graininess of the amateur photograph, the image shone crystal clear, every detail bold and crisp, except for the tiny haze that lifted from the figure's shoulders. The woman's pure white energy always calmed Mandy. A connection long denied and taken away before fully revealed. The image wrapped Mandy in a cocoon of peaceful serenity, not so alone, as though the woman still watched over her. Her fingers sought the angel pendant, rubbing the stone, warm from her skin between her fingertips.

"Amazing." Lucien lifted his hand as though he wanted to touch the photo. She'd wanted to do the same thing, many times, but never dared for fear of losing the power that emanated from it. Now, glass prevented fingers from actually touching the image, preserving the connection of the utmost importance.

"It's my mom."

"She's an angel." Lucien hadn't looked away.

"She was," Mandy agreed.

"Sorry," Lucien said reaching for Mandy's hand. "I

didn't know.

Mandy shrugged, letting his fingers touch hers. She didn't pull away or move closer.

She thought of the woman as her adoptive mother, until she took this picture and the truth revealed itself, at least part of it. The same dark brown eyes, bordering on black. Waves of brown hair so familiar to Mandy, they could have been her own. The white haze surrounding her mother was the key that opened the lock to the truth. Every photo Mandy had managed to take of herself, through mirrors or using the timer on her camera, even the accidental selfie with her phone, the exact same haze was never far away.

This picture never lied, even though her parents had for so long.

Her father still hadn't explained why they did it and Mandy quit asking. Instead, she built up a wall separating her father's silence and herself. Every time he tried to break through, she added another layer. After ten years, only the truth could knock it down now.

"You look just like her." Lucien squeezed her hand gently. "You're both beautiful."

Standing here in her bedroom, her hand warm within his embrace, the compassion flowing from him a comforting cocoon surrounded her hidden pain. She almost felt content. Almost.

CHAPTER TWENTY-FOUR

Lucien rubbed his fingers along Mandy's knuckles. He knew the empty pit that sunk into your soul at the loss of a mother, yet her image contradicted that impression. Lucien stared at the white halo effect around her mother's image, narrowing his eyes. She could have altered the image. But had she? Doubt, something he couldn't quite name, gnawed at Lucien.

"The other images are over here," Mandy stammered. She moved in front of a series of three framed prints positioned in a cascading angle down the wall. Arms hugged tight across her chest, the self-confident, arrogant photographer Lucien had come to know disappeared, leaving behind a wall of cold stone.

He should be looking at Mandy's work, but instead a tattoo peeked out from under the right shoulder of the black tank top Mandy wore. The white ink lines set Lucien's heart racing. Without thinking, Lucien traced the lines of the half-hidden design. A Guardian Angel.

For a brief moment, Mandy leaned into his hand. The heat rushed through the white lines into his palm the way a fire rushed dry grass. His arms, where his own white ink resided, tingled and warmed, not in warning but in recognition—as if the same artist created both markings.

"What are you doing?" Mandy asked. A shiver rippled beneath his hand. Had she felt the same fire that burned between them? She moved away, but slowly, as though reluctant to break the moment, fighting for distance she didn't really want and he didn't want to give.

"I'm sorry." Lucien shoved his hands into the back pockets of his jeans. "But your tattoo. It's beautiful. I never saw it before."

"Most people don't seem to notice it." She frowned at him. "But you see it clearly?"

Lucien couldn't explain how he saw the ink without exposing his own. It shouldn't be possible. Only the Romani knew how to capture the power of the white inks and they restricted them to those of Guardian bloodlines. The photo in the center of the trio caught his eye.

"Wait, this is it isn't it? Your tattoo?" As if rendered in 3-D, the image seemed trapped under the glass as though opening it would release the tiny angel into the world.

"No." Mandy moved protectively in front of the photo. "That was my mother's tattoo."

"Your mother had one like this, with the white ink?" Living with a cursed painter who happened to be immortal, mystical images took on different meanings with Lucien. White ink tattoos were definitely not common. He only knew of one practitioner in Romania who did these Guardian tattoos. For both Mandy and her mother to have them suggested connections Lucien never before suspected. The possibilities sparked hope he couldn't ignore.

"Where did you get it?" Lucien tried to sound nonchalant but his body vibrated. "Maybe I'll look the guy up and add to my collection." He flexed his forearms and biceps making the existing normal tats dance between the white lines. True white tattoos didn't show up except to those with the sight.

"Well, unless you have travel plans to Europe, you're out of luck." Mandy's eyes smoldered. "I'd be happy to let you explore mine a bit for the price of a picture...or two."

Like a light switch, the old Mandy was back. Fingers traced up Lucien's forearms, setting his skin aflame once more. He could barely keep up with the emotional whiplash, but he didn't care. Stepping closer, until her body pressed against his, he wondered how long he could keep this charade up. Two steps backwards and they'd be at her bed. In her bed.

Lucien swallowed.

"You only have *one* picture left for today." How had his voice not cracked? Maybe it did crack but he couldn't hear it over the sound of Mandy breathing so close to his ear.

"Chicken," she whispered.

If she only knew. Taking a step back, Mandy leaned against a carved column at the foot of her four-poster bed. Her hands followed the spiral cut wood up and down. His body imagined them...

"Maybe we should get back to the photographs." His fingers drummed out a staccato rhythm on the side of his leg. "You know, the ones in the living room." If he didn't get out of the room fast, Mandy's interviewing skills would learn and see a whole lot more about him than he planned.

Mandy snorted. "If you insist." Her hand trailed across the front of his t-shirt as she walked past, the light touch tensing his abs even tighter.

Holy hell, the girl was going to kill him, a death he'd enjoy every minute of. Following her back towards the kitchen, the sway of her ass teased. Lucien blew out a slow breath. At least he'd die smiling.

"Still, I think tracing each other's white tattoos would be more fun than working on that database."

"What did you say?" Lucien froze, eyes wide, his heart skipping a beat before pounding double time. She couldn't possibly see his the way he saw hers, crisp and clear as if they were on display for all the world to see.

"Tracing the white ink tattoos." Mandy gestured toward his forearms, now taut with tension. "The intricacies of the ones you have are sexy as hell."

She could see his Guardian markings, marks that bound him to oaths she couldn't know about and she should be blinded from seeing.

"I have to go." Lucien scrambled to grab the cooking supplies, shoving the still dirty pots into plastic grocery bags. He had to get out. Now. "I forgot. Band rehearsal. I'll..I'll call you." The click of a camera stopped him in his tracks.

Mandy stared at the photo, her face a mask of confusion and hurt. "What did I say wrong?"

"Nothing." Lucien lied. "I just lost track of time." He opened his mouth to explain but nothing came out. His two worlds must never meet and they were currently on a collision course. "Later."

Lucien ducked his head to avoid making eye contact and sprinted out of the apartment. He didn't stop until he was out the front door and in his vehicle. His body continued to shake no matter how hard he squeezed the steering wheel.

What the fuck do I do now?

Breathe.

Uncoiling his hands, he flexed them to restore the circulation. The truck rumbled to life. Gunning the engine, Lucien raced away from Mandy as fast as he could, even as his body clamored for him to go back. On autopilot, the drive to the warehouse passed in a blur. He screwed up, said too much. Wished too hard for something he couldn't have. But nothing explained how Mandy could see his tattoos. Unless her photos did exactly what he feared and exposed his secret. No, not his. Robert's.

CHAPTER TWENTY-FIVE

Mandy needed to forget about Lucien, the object of her body's traitorous obsession. Forget about how he bolted at her touch, and most of all about how much he drove her absolutely insane. She needed to get back to a favorite pastime. At least for one night.

Find new music.

She craved new talent to highlight on her site. Any talent. She ached to hear songs echoing through her mind all night and well into the morning hours. She even missed waking up smelling like stale beer and cigarettes. Tonight she would remember. Even if it killed her in the process.

Mandy stood in front of the gilded, full-length mirror in the corner of her room. Pulling her hair up off her shoulders, she twirled once to make sure the silver and black wrapped heels were sturdy enough for a night out, possibly a long one. A bright pink sweater clung to her body and her black ruffled skirt was exactly the way she liked it, super short.

"Should I bother to wait up?" Kyrissa leaned against the door to Mandy's room.

"Probably not." Mandy winked. Grabbing her camera, she slung the strap over head and let the camera rest against her side. "There's a band playing at Metro I need to check out. They're from New York and Jay says they're pretty good."

"Jay?" Kyrissa asked. "Please tell me you are not

dressed like that for Jay Cooley."

"Definitely not," Mandy assured her best friend. When it came to the opposite sex, or anything else for that matter, Mandy confided in one person. Naturally, she'd told Kyrissa what a mistake it had been when she slept with Jay. Mandy didn't do strings and she thought Jay understood that. She'd been wrong. "Jay and I are just friends and that is all we will ever be. Besides, when have I ever needed to dress for a guy?" She winked.

Kyrissa didn't answer. She simply laughed, moving out of Mandy's way when she passed through the door.

"Hey," Kyrissa called out to her. "Will you please call your dad? He stopped by again and I'm getting tired of being your buffer."

"We wouldn't need a buffer if he'd tell me the truth." Mandy adjusted her shoe. *Or let me take his picture.* Seems the two men she needed the truth from most had both denied her from taking pictures. What exactly were they trying to hide?

Within minutes of entering Metro, Mandy had lost the nostalgia she waxed an hour ago. Along with the music and stench, she had also forgotten about the rowdy crowd bumping into her from every side. Already she wanted to forget the scantily clad chicks who kept giving her the stink eye because their boyfriends couldn't draw their gawking away from Mandy pushing her way to the front of the stage. She couldn't be blamed for having the attention of nearly every guy in the room. Too bad the one guy she considered wanting attention from wasn't interested.

The music played loud and hard enough to let her forget. Almost. She still compared every lyric to the new songs she'd caught *Demon Dogs* practicing. The drummer on stage wasn't as entertaining as Jay and the bassist hardly made any expressions while he played, unlike Rusty who displayed a complete range of facial expressions whenever he held his bass. And the front man might as well be lip-syncing. He smiled down at her. Mandy could hardly contain herself from laughing. No comparison. Lucien Solvak owned the stage. This guy didn't belong on it.

"Drink?" A cold beer touched her arm.

"Thanks," she said taking the bottle. "Figured I'd see you here."

"I told you these guys are pretty good." Jay smiled. Mandy didn't like the way his gaze dropped. "I'm always keeping tabs on the competition."

"These guys are no competition." Mandy lifted the beer to her lips. Maybe if she drank a few more, she'd finally be able to forget Lucien existed, at least for tonight.

"Glad to hear you say that." Jay glanced back on stage, shaking his head. The lead singer had picked up a guitar and the first few notes screeched over the microphone. "Guess there will be no Mandy Hayworth endorsement."

"May have to," Mandy said. "I haven't added any new music in almost two weeks and at this rate, if I don't post something this week my blog will be obsolete before I get the pictures I need of Lucien."

"Whoa." Jay turned towards Mandy. His hand gripped her upper arm a little tighter than made her comfortable. "You've spent plenty of time with that boy. If you haven't been taking pictures, what the fuck have you been doing?"

"First, let go of my arm if you intend to keep that hand." Mandy pulled away from the too tight grip. Jay unwrapped his fingers, taking a step back. She turned towards the stage. "Second, what I do or do not do with Lucien is none of your business."

Mandy lifted her camera to frame the lead singer. She clicked a few times, each time she regretted the moment her finger pressed the button. Dark forest green colors surrounded his form on stage. The captured images confirmed the guy's bloated ego that he no doubt used to cover his low self-esteem. Mandy could overlook many things while endorsing a band, bloat wasn't one of them.

"Sorry," Jay said. "I just...I mean I'm really hoping this kid is the key to *Demon Dogs* breaking through. Find a label. Finally land a decent record deal. Ya know?"

"I know." Mandy smiled up at him. No matter what color his character turned, Mandy would always have a soft spot for Jay. She lifted her hand to his cheek. "I really am trying to help you. I just need Mr. Evasive to loosen up a little bit."

Beside her, Jay downed his beer and helped himself to hers. She didn't mind, she hadn't really been in the mood for the drink to begin with. She hardly noticed when he walked away.

Shaking her head, she turned her attention back to the band. Once again, the lead singer smiled down at her, making every hair on the back of her neck stand up, but not in the good way. The intense stares actually creeped her out. She leaned back to contain more of the stage within her lens and snapped. The only problem, when she took the camera away from her eye, the guy standing in front of her was Lucien. Too bad, she just wasted a picture of him she hadn't intended to take. And he'd never looked more delicious.

CHAPTER TWENTY-SIX

"That doesn't count," Mandy yelled above the noise of the band. "I didn't even know you were here." She fidgeted with her camera. "And you ruined my shot."

"Consider it a freebie." Lucien barely contained his exasperation. He showed up tonight to hear this band and finalize his marketing plan, not play games with Mandy. Seeing her at the front of the stage fired off every brain synapses at once. The lead singer's continued lurid looks and thoughts of Pretty Boy Peters with his hands roaming over Mandy had finally been too much. Marketing became the last thing on his mind.

"Maybe if you weren't so busy looking through that damn camera, you might have seen me approaching," Lucien chided.

"Lucien?" Jay returned carrying two more beers. "Hey man, what cha' doing here?"

Great. When Jay walked away from Mandy earlier, Lucien thought he left for the night. Yet, here he was hovering next to Mandy like he owned her. Fingers curled tight enough to turn his knuckles white, Lucien tried to remember if there was a Band Rule against punching out another member. Lucien crossed his arms over his chest to keep from finding out.

"Well, it's not letting me take his picture that's for sure," Mandy sniped. "Remember that picture doesn't count."

"You got a picture of Lucien and you're not going to use it?" Jay flicked back and forth between Mandy and Lucien. "Why the hell not?"

"We have an agreement." Lucien tried to pull Mandy away from the leering gaze of the lead singer. She shrugged off his grasp, pointing her camera back at the band and clicking several pictures in a row. The singer's smile grew. "At least I thought we did," Lucien growled, stepping between Mandy and the stage. All her camera could possibly see now was Lucien, not that she bothered to look through the anger she stabbed his direction.

"Get out of my way." Mandy gritted. "I'm trying to take a picture here."

"Take one," he taunted.

"This isn't the one I want."

"What the fuck man?" Jay yanked Lucien sideways. "Are you trying to ruin the band before we even get started? Stop pissing off the ticket you're being handed and make nice with Mandy before she rescinds her offer to endorse us."

"I know what I'm doing." Lucien yanked his arm out of Jay's hold, shoving him back a step.

"Could have fooled the shit outta me."

"You think you can do a better job?" Lucien challenged, head lowered, squaring his shoulders towards Jay. "Have at it. You seem to know exactly how to work your magic on her."

"Hey." Mandy spun on him. The finger pointed but thankfully didn't stab. "No one works their magic on me. No one." She pushed between the two of them.

"He had one job to do. Give you an interview, let you take his photo and get your fucking endorsement." Jay puffed out his chest. "Don't know what else he's gotten in his head to do, but the band better fucking come first."

"You're one to talk." Lucien reached past Mandy, pushing Jay further from where her hand still lay against his chest.

"That's it." Mandy shoved harder on his chest. She pointed at Jay. "You. Go get another drink and cool off. Lucien, outside. Let's go. Now." A quick nod towards the approaching bouncers stifled anything he might say.

His connections had gotten him into the club, but at eighteen, the bouncers weren't going to take kindly to him starting a fight with a paying customer. Mandy continued to push at him and he gave way. Spinning, he shoved through the crowd to the exit, acutely aware of Mandy's hands hanging onto his waist.

"What the hell was that all about?" Mandy demanded. "I have a reputation to uphold, not to mention a blog to maintain and I'm always trying to find a larger audience for my photographs. All of which are in jeopardy because of you right now. Just because you're protective of your image doesn't mean everyone else is. I have requests from dozens of bands that want me to photograph them, write articles about them. But not you." She threw her hands up in the air.

"I'm sorry. I didn't mean to ruin your shots." He didn't either; he just wanted to get her attention out from behind her camera. He blew out a hard breath. *Fuck.* Pacing in a tight circle, he moved to release the tension from the near fight with Jay. He had to fix this. "I just wanted you to really look at who you were photographing, and to listen to the music. Not be blinded by a camera lens."

"You don't get it." Mandy held up her camera. "This tells me everything I need to know. I hear the music in every photo I take. They say a photo is worth a thousand words. Well, then, my photos sing a thousand songs."

Lucien had seen the proof in the myriad of images from her portfolio. Powerful. Revealing. But he worried what she'd hear in the images of him. Songs of an immortal cursed to paint death and linked to him through sacred white tattoos. Would the white ink she could already see reveal more than he intended to share in one shot? In the wrong hands those pictures could ruin more than just his music dreams. They could force Robert into hiding, taking Lucien with him.

"I'm sorry, okay." God Mandy drove him to distraction. Scrubbing at the light stubble along his jaw, he checked his phone. What if he gave her other photos to post, ones that helped both of them. "Let me make it up to you."

"I'm listening." Mandy crossed her arms over her chest. Lucien focused on her face instead of the view he'd rather take in framed within those arms.

"I can get you an exclusive on some other kinds of art."

He had toyed with the idea of using Robert's pictures to highlight the band's stage show. Brief glimpses, but with the power they held, the images would be the punch he needed to go along with the lyrics he'd already written. But so far, every attempt to capture that impact had failed. But if Mandy took the photos...

"Why are you looking at me like that?" Mandy asked.

Her vision, the ability to capture the emotional impact that lay beneath each layer of paint, combined with his words and the band's sound, would catapult them to the top of the scene. It would mystify people and linger with them for an eternity. Lucien smiled as the final piece of the marketing plan, fell into place. The band's name.

Eternity.

"How does exclusive access to some paintings that are about to tour the world sound?" Lucien cocked his head at her, pouring every ounce of his charm into his smile.

Mandy uncrossed her arms and fiddled with her camera. "Interesting."

Lucien chuckled. The icy walls melted a bit more. She could hardly resist an exclusive.

"I want to use pictures of some oil paintings for the stage show." He reached for her hand, encouraged when she didn't pull away. "I want you to take the photographs, as many as you want. And you can use them to start releasing info about the band on your blog. Teasers of what the audience can expect from us. But no names yet, for me or the band."

Ever so slowly, he brought her hand up to his lips. Her fingers tightened a fraction as he placed the feather-light kiss across her knuckles.

"Would that help with content for your blog until you have an article ready? And you'll get the credit line for those photos used in the marketing for the tour. I'm talking international magazines, global audiences, the works."

Mandy softened her stance further, looking up at him through her long lashes. Dark eyes smoldering, she captivated him with her gaze.

Heat rolled through him like a runaway train. His body hummed when she was near. He didn't want her mad at him. Just the opposite. A slight pout on her lips tugged at Lucien's control. God he wanted to kiss her right now. He licked his lips. She did the same. Focus. He needed to focus. Lucien took a step closer until he could lean his forehead against hers.

"Please?" He begged, his lips inched closer. Looking down at her was heaven and hell wrapped up in one sinfully hot angel. "I really am sorry about ruining your shots and I promise the pictures will be worth it."

"They better be." After a few muted pauses, Mandy backed away first. Lucien silently thanked her because another moment and he wouldn't have been able to stop his mouth from claiming hers.

"Is that a yes?"

"Alone with you and permission to take all the photos I want?" Mandy smoothed her hands up and down his chest. "How could a girl resist. Let's go."

In two hours, Robert would return. If he caught them in the warehouse... Lucien shook his head not wanting to contemplate those consequences, even though spending the next few hours with Mandy would be worth every single one.

CHAPTER TWENTY-SEVEN

"You don't have to do that, you know." Mandy nodded towards the door Lucien held open for her. He rushed ahead of her at the club before she could touch the outside handle. She'd never waited on someone else to do anything for her, starting now seemed counterproductive. "I can open my own door."

"I like to do these things, especially for you." Lucien shrugged. "Blame my grandmother for teaching me to respect women if you must." As old fashioned as the sentiment, Mandy had to admit that Lucien's gestures gave the moment a sense of sweetness she hadn't expected. And having him waiting for her at their destination with his arm extended was freaking sexier than she cared to admit.

"Fine," Mandy said stepping out of his truck. She glanced around the empty garage. "Where exactly are we?"

They'd only gone a few miles from Metro, but Mandy stopped paying attention to the lefts and rights the moment Lucien flashed his baby blue eyes her direction. Why was she such a sucker for dark hair and blue eyes? She barely noticed the darkened alleyway that ended at a loading dock until Lucien pulled through the open door.

"This is where I work." Lucien flicked on a few lights. "And live," he admitted. Mandy hoped he wasn't referring to the garage itself.

Lucien unlocked a metal, paint-peeling door and led her down a long hallway. A spiral staircase ascended to her right.

"Am I really here to take some photos or are you just trying to get me into your bedroom?" Mandy winked, admiring the slight shift Lucien made in his stance.

"Just need images of a few paintings." Lucien keyed a code into a security panel next to a second stout metal door that looked like it belonged on a bank vault instead of a warehouse.

"This does not look like your bedroom," Mandy teased.

"Obviously." Lucien's bright eyes followed her every move. Heat rolled off him, striking her skin, even with a foot of space separating them. "Though you have an open invitation to my bedroom any time you want to accept."

"What if I accept right now?" Mandy stepped closer to Lucien. She slipped her hand under his shirt, trailing her fingers across his tightened abs until his body shivered under her touch. Another moment of this electricity and she might lead him right up those spiral stairs and the bedroom she hoped to find at the top. His body emanated heat so warm her hand burned, but she refused to pull away. "You really prepared to extend that invite?"

Lucien cleared his throat. Or tried to reply, Mandy couldn't tell. *Band guy. You sure you want to take that path again?* She stepped back, smiling when Lucien just stood there. She held up her camera. "So where are these paintings?"

"Um, they're..." He took a deep breath. Mandy admired the broad swell of his chest, regretting her decision to remove her hand. "This way."

Wandering through stacks of wooden crates, she followed Lucien as close as she could. Each crate labeled with a list of titles and an address. Several of the addresses were in Romania, others destined for Italy, Germany and France. A few displayed the address of the warehouse with markings in foreign languages as if they'd just returned from some far off destination.

"These are all paintings. A few haven't been packed and I'd love to get images for the *Demon Dogs* show. God, I hate that name." He shook his head and Mandy laughed. She'd never been particularly fond of the band name but she could tell Lucien downright detested it. "I have this idea for the stage show but it'll only work if you take the pictures."

"I have this idea for an article to endorse the band." Mandy ran one finger over Lucien's chest. "But it'll only work if you let me take *your* picture."

Lucien grabbed her hand, his fingers wrapping tight around her wrist. She stared up into his big beautiful eyes and for a moment, his returning gaze glowed as hot as hers. He lifted her hand to his face, inhaled deeply, bringing his lips to the skin on the palm of her hand. She had to place her other hand on his waist to steady herself as the simple kiss nearly stole her ability to stand upright. But before the intensity pouring out of Lucien wrapped her completely, he let his hold drop and turned away with a deep sigh.

"Jeeze, do you ever loosen up?" Mandy asked, following Lucien into the darkness. "I mean Mr. Control Freak about the band is bad enough, and all the prim and proper manners are fine, kind of sexy, but being so freaking reserved has got to be exhausting. I'm tired just thinking about your control issues."

"Mr. Control Freak?" Lucien laughed. He stopped in front of a smaller set of crates, still open in the front, and paintings lining the wall behind him. "You haven't met a control freak until you've met Robert."

"And when will I meet this Robert?" She hoisted herself up on a nearby crate to get a better view of the maze they'd just traveled. "I'll be sure to bring my best chaos to that meeting and let it loose just for him."

"You won't," Lucien said. She caught his eyes watch her move as she lowered herself to take a seat in front of him. "Not as long as I want to keep my head."

"Whatever that's supposed to mean." Mandy adjusted herself atop the wooden crate, lengthening one of her long legs along the edge, letting the other dangle just within Lucien's view. How did he so easily resist what so few before him could keep their hands off? Especially since she made it more available to him than she ever had anyone else. Fuck her rules. Lucien was now a challenge, with a capitol C, that she wanted to conquer. Now.

"It means..." Lucien paused then shook his head. "Never mind."

"I know you want me." Mandy teased. How far would she have to push before he surrendered? "You can't stop peeking up at me under those fucking sexy lashes of yours. I see you checking out my legs and ass in this tiny little skirt. And I don't blame you. They are pretty fantastic." She smoothed her hand down her leg, hoping the move would break whatever resolve he seemed to be holding onto.

"You have no idea," Lucien mumbled.

She did have an idea, a few of them and they all involved cracking this guy's barriers so that he would fucking touch her. Lucien took two steps closer to where Mandy was perched. He seemed to hesitate a moment before closing the gap even more. He hovered inches away from her, just outside her reach. She needed him closer.

"Then take me," she said. Lifting her leg, she guided him closer, letting him catch her foot. She wrapped her leg around his waist, forcing him up against her. "Right here, right now."

"You are one dangerous temptress," Lucien whispered, his lips within centimeters of brushing against hers. He slid his hand up Mandy's leg, chills following the touch. "But if my boss finds us here, he may ship me to Romania in one of these crates."

"Your boss is the last thing on my mind right now." She admired the deep gulp of his throat when she entwined her fingers in his shirt. No way was she letting this moment pass without at least a kiss and not on her hand this time. Hell, she'd let Lucien Solvak do a lot more than kiss her right now, in this dark warehouse, on top this wooden crate, or anywhere else he wanted to take her. "Now kiss me."

The brief moment of hesitation that waited between them couldn't possibly last. He'd managed to keep her at arm's length for so long. She could almost see the willpower drifting away until Lucien's eyes flashed, hand inching further up her leg. And then further.

Her heart pumped faster. The mixture of warmth and the cool press of his fingers against her thighs sent electric pulses all over her body. Mandy gasped. If he stopped now she'd be the one packing his ass up in this crate and shipping him wherever the already addressed label took him without giving the location a second thought.

"Dangerous temptress," he muttered. His other hand grabbed her waist, pulling her as close to his hard body as she could get. She wanted to be closer. Sliding a hand under her shirt, his touch sent shivers up her spine.

"I like this kind of danger," she whispered. She tightened her legs around his waist, his fingers still resting on the edge of her black lace panties. Only one place left to go if he didn't stop—over the edge, and Mandy was ready to jump.

"I'm starting to see why." Lucien's smile widened slightly before his lips finally crashed onto hers, exactly where she wanted them.

CHAPTER TWENTY-EIGHT

Gone was the control. Only the soft skin of Mandy's thigh beneath his finger mattered now. Hiking her skirt up to her waist, Lucien stroked her ass, squeezing the curves that had haunted his dreams for days. With her legs locked around his waist, he lifted Mandy from the crate in one quick motion and pushed her against the wall of the warehouse.

Balanced against the cold metal, Lucien reached up to cup one delicious breast. His mouth teased at the nipple through the fabric of the tight pink sweater. It wasn't enough. Stretching the low cut neckline down further, followed quickly by the lacy bra underneath, the peaked nipple appeared only for a moment before Lucien devoured it with his mouth. He wasn't sure who moaned louder.

"Oh my god you taste so good." He looked up into dark smoldering eyes. Mandy's gaze destroyed any control he might have regained. Fingers twisted in his hair and yanked him towards her. The rough kiss swallowed his next words. Tongues tangled in a dance of lust and desire until he had to break off to gasp for breath.

God what is she doing to me?

"Don't stop the taste testing now." Her heavy breathing on his neck set every nerve ending firing simultaneously. Guiding the hand on her ass lower, the lacy edging of her thong caught on his roughened fingertips. He stroked her through the material. The dampness of her panties evoked another groan as his own arousal strained against his jeans.

How far dare he go? He teased at the edge of the lace, slipping it to the side. Licking his lips, he pulled back far enough to see her face and judge Mandy's reaction.

"God yes," she cried out, tilting her hips for him.

He plunged one finger into her wetness, following with a second when she arched against him hard. He buried his face in her neck, kissing, nipping, devouring. Everything he had, he focused on Mandy, letting loose the demons of control. Letting loose everything.

He pressed his hips harder against her body. The material of his jeans a damned barrier he cursed and thanked at the same time. With a squeal, a shudder enveloped Mandy, hands tightening in his hair painfully.

"Oh my god!" Mandy cried out. It was the sweetest sound he'd ever heard and he couldn't stop his own release from exploding.

Lucien pulled out at her cry. "M...Mandy," Lucien stammered. "I...we...shouldn't." He fought for control over his body. "Oh god. I'm sorry."

She clung to him. Moving carefully, he placed her back on the crate. Her head remained buried in his shoulder, her breathing ragged on his neck. His body shook, pent up tension twisted into regret. Stroking her hair, Lucien fought the panic threatening to overwhelm him. His body ignored him, awash in charged emotional energy. A low hum vibrated still, dissipating with each pound of his heart against his ribs.

The Paintings.

Surrounded on all sides by paintings Robert imbued with so much emotional power a demon hungered for them, Lucien would never be certain Mandy's reaction was purely driven by him. He should have known better than to bring her here.

"When you let go," Mandy raised her hands to caress his face. "Wow. Absolutely freaking amazing."

"Shit. That wasn't supposed to happen." Lucien's head spun. Not that he ever imagined this outcome.

"Really?" She touched her kiss-bruised lips. "Personally, I think you really need to let go like that more often." She tugged at the waistband of his jeans. "And you should most definitely let me return the favor."

"Not necessary." He grabbed her wrists, hoping to deflect her attentions. Heat flushed his face. Lucien stepped back, thankful for the darkened warehouse. "The paintings—"

"Fine," Mandy chuckled. "After that enticement, I'll photograph anything you want. Or don't want. Either way." She hopped off the crate and straightened her skirt and sweater. The right side sagged a bit where Lucien had partially torn the material. "Now which painting do you want me to take pictures of?"

"Those. Leaning against the wall." Lucien pointed to the open crates and the three paintings still hanging waiting for crating. Grabbing her camera off the box where she left it, Mandy wandered over to the paintings, the click of her camera already echoing in the darkness.

Lucien grabbed a wall for support. What the hell just happened? Either he had the best almost sex of his life, or he just made a horrible mistake.

CHAPTER TWENTY-NINE

Mandy tossed around in her bed wishing it wasn't quite so big and empty. Thoughts of Lucien's hand between her legs, his fingers circling in areas they had no business being near, still occupied her mind hours later, destroying any hope of going to sleep. Pulling out her laptop, she uploaded the images from the club. *Ninth Dimension.* Right. That's how her evening had started. She could only think about how it ended.

She quickly organized the *new* images according to Lucien's *new* rules for her database. She saved each with the labels he'd constructed, realizing how accurate his choices had been before she understood what they meant. Now they made sense and allowed her to pull any image she needed for whatever use she had for it, within a few seconds.

Then the picture of Lucien appeared on her screen. A thin white t-shirt hinted at the black lines that trailed across his chest. There hadn't been time last night to take off his shirt before he slammed her up against the wall. She almost regretted not being able to trace the intricate pattern, until she remembered what followed. No regrets there.

His chest, arms stretched out wide like he was throwing himself at her, appeared in the image on her screen. God, she wished he was throwing his arms around her right now.

Shit. Mandy never thought about a guy the morning

after, especially when they hadn't even had sex.

By nine am, Mandy had already done two loads of laundry, written and deleted three attempts of a review for *Ninth Dimension*'s set last night, and thought about texting Lucien approximately five hundred times to thank him.

"You look like you've been awake for hours," Kyrissa said emerging from her bedroom still wearing rumpled pajama pants and tank top, her hair pulled up in a sloppy bun.

"I have been," Mandy admitted. "Couldn't sleep."

"Hmmm," Kyrissa hummed. "I'm normally the one with sleep trouble around here."

Mandy laughed. Sleep trouble was an understatement where Kyrissa was concerned. At least three nights a week Kyrissa would forego sleep altogether to keep painting until the sun rose, or wake up in the middle of the night with nightmares that caused her to crawl into bed with Mandy. Not that Mandy blamed her. Kyrissa had witnessed one horrific scene that would haunt anyone. She doubted there would ever come a time that Kyrissa wouldn't close her eyes and see the flames engulf her mother's car or hear her mother's screams. It still haunted Mandy on occasion and she hadn't witnessed it firsthand. She was, however, there to pick up the pieces of Kyrissa's sanity and would be right beside her best friend whenever she needed a hand to hold or a shoulder to cry on.

"I guess you didn't have trouble sleeping last night." Mandy closed her laptop, no closer to writing a review of the show she'd promised herself she'd post today. Without any more information about Lucien's plan to debut *Demon Dogs,* or whatever the new band name he chose, she had nothing else to post. "You look rather rested."

"I painted all day yesterday. During the day," Kyrissa emphasized. "Finished another commission.

Can you take pictures of it today so I can deliver it? I hate to say it, but the sooner that piece is out of my studio, the better."

"Why do you even paint these things? You've hated every one of them."

"It's not hate, it's discomfort. Professor C pushes my talents, sometimes farther than I thought I'd be willing to go. But every time I finish whatever piece his clients have requested, I know I can push myself just a little bit further so I'm even more willing to keep pushing. I'm just not sure how without him, if that makes any sense."

"Perfectly." Mandy had been doing the same thing with her photography for years just to see how much further she could go. And people were finally starting to take notice of the complexity of the images she captured, the layers of emotions that hid amongst the subjects. She was just waiting for someone to hear the songs each one sang.

"So, all the pictures you have of my work, how can I get them printed? I'm thinking I need to put together an updated portfolio before next semester, start looking for opportunities to show my work. Maybe even secure a few commissions on my own."

Mandy approved of that idea so much she'd help secure the commissions herself if it meant less time with the professor.

"Ah, that's easy actually. Lucien's been helping me organize all the images on my laptop. He's created this database with all these labels." She motioned at the computer. "There's a Kyrissa label. I could probably get him to show me how to put your paintings in their own database, and create labels that make sense to you."

"You do know that I have no idea what you're talking about, right?"

"I didn't either before Lucien."

"Ah, you've started separating life into before

Lucien and anything that came after. Interesting," Kyrissa smirked.

"It's not like that." Mandy couldn't help but defend her relationship with Lucien, whatever that relationship consisted of. "I'm just trying to get enough info for an endorsement article. I think they have the potential to blow the local music scene out of the water and land a big record deal. I'm helping them, that's all."

"And how did that translate into him creating some data whatever you call it and spending hours, if not days, organizing the millions of images you have on your laptop?" She eyed Mandy suspiciously.

Mandy had to think about it far longer than seemed necessary but she couldn't remember how, exactly, the arrangement surfaced.

"He offered," she finally told Kyrissa. *Through bribery and coercion.* "I accepted."

"Well," Kyrissa said. "If he offers to make you smile every time you say his name again, tell him I said thanks."

"Funny." Mandy raised an eyebrow. "I don't smile every time I say his name."

"No? Because you just smiled thinking about saying his name."

His name didn't cause the smile, but in a rare moment of possessiveness, Mandy decided to keep the real reason—his hands, his mouth, the hard lines of his chest pressed against hers—to herself. At least for today.

"When do you see him again?"

"He has rehearsal tonight at six. If I finish this article by four, then I'll be able to get there early and I can—" Mandy stopped flat, Kyrissa's knowing smirk taunting her.

Not only was she still thinking of a guy the day after, her mind started rearranging her schedule to calculate how soon she could get away to see him again. Strings reached out for Mandy, strings she swore she'd never again embrace.

CHAPTER THIRTY

"What part of your duties do you not understand?" Robert's voice sliced through the quiet of the warehouse.

Lucien jumped. Robert sat on the very crate that a different body occupied last night. Arms crossed over his pristine white shirt, his suit jacket folded neatly next to him on the wooden box, Robert's intense stare bore into Lucien. Could he tell Mandy had been here?

Running his hands through his hair, he prayed he didn't look as disheveled as he felt. He fought the urge to check to see if his black t-shirt was straight. Instead of sleeping, he'd spent the whole night composing. Only the dawn's light breaking through his window reminded him he still had paintings to package for shipping. Hell, he hadn't even showered yet. The hint of Mandy's fruit scented perfume lingered on his shirt. God, what if he wasn't the only one who could smell it? Grabbing a hammer, he moved away from where Robert perched like a king on his throne.

"I thought you and Carmen were meeting the German curator's lawyers this morning. Your meeting with the studio must have gone well. I didn't expect you back until this afternoon." The silence grew; the air thickening until it threatened to clog Lucien's ability to breathe.

"How can I trust you to protect me if you cannot complete a simple job on time?"

Lucien spun. "God you really are a control freak," he lashed out, echoing Mandy's description. "I'll get the job done. Forgive me if my timetable doesn't match yours exactly. It's not like the fucking truck is here right this second."

"Unlike last time."

Teeth clenched, Lucien forced himself to take several deep breaths. Robert was pushing his buttons on purpose. But why? He wasn't normally this biting. Disquiet nagged in the back of his brain, but anger and exhaustion overwhelmed the warning. Lucien reined in his temper before he did something really stupid. Even more stupid than what he had already done.

Thoughts of Mandy gave him the anchor he needed. She did what she wanted with her self-confident and no-fear attitude. Everything Lucien embraced when he sang. He just needed to learn how to adopt that approach outside of his music.

"Look, these are the last paintings I have to crate." Lucien gestured to the few open boxes and the three paintings still waiting for packaging. "All the travel arrangements are confirmed, the paperwork done. The truck won't be here for another two hours and I can have this done in thirty minutes." His hand began to ache from his tight grip on the hammer.

"I schedule events for a reason." Robert rubbed at his temples, whipping away the slick sheen of sweat on his brow. "Chaos...too much of my life has been destroyed by chaos. Order—" A grimace cut off whatever words would have come next.

"Robert?" Lucien narrowed his eyes. All the color drained from Robert's face. Pain lanced up the lines on Lucien's arms. Dropping the hammer, he lunged forward to catch Robert before he toppled to the concrete floor.

Robert's curse.

Lucien fumbled for his phone while cradling the

form now writhing in agony. "Carmen. In the warehouse. Robert. He's...he's." A loud groan cut him off and Lucien dropped the phone. He was supposed to be able to stop the pain of Robert's curse. Too bad he had no idea how. Shared pain coursed through him, making him nauseous and this was only a portion of what Robert felt.

"Tell me what to do?" he begged.

Carmen's pounding footfalls running down the stairs and the heavy tread of his Grandmother rushed towards him. Carmen's hands on his shoulders steadied him, but all he could do was watch helpless as Mama T soothed Robert's agony. Something *he* should have done. Instead, he panicked.

It was his fault Robert spun out of control. His irresponsibility triggered the pain of the curse, yet Robert endured the consequences. What force in the cosmos thought he would ever be an acceptable Guardian to someone with a curse as powerful as Robert's? Maybe Christophe should have been the Guardian, not him. The consuming pain subsided, but the weight of Lucien's guilt only grew. By the time Mama T pushed Robert into a deep, healing sleep, Lucien could barely contain the shakes ravaging his body.

"Help me get him to room." The rich Romani accent of Mama T broke through the fog smothering his brain. That and a soothing hand patting his cheek. "You no worry."

Shouldering the limp form of Robert Shoalman, Lucien didn't think it would ever be the right time for him. Being a Guardian was a choice—one he willingly accepted two years ago. The Spirits granted him gifts for a reason she told him that day. Right now, Lucien believed the Spirits, or demons, or whatever offered this choice, made a horrible mistake.

CHAPTER THIRTY-ONE

One person reserved the first Sunday of every month on Mandy's calendar. Her father. She may get to select the location, even have some room to choose the time, but he dictated everything else, including restricting her camera on the premises. So naturally, today she chose the one restaurant she thought would throw the man completely out of whack. Casa D' Angelos.

"Amanda," her father cooed the moment Anthony escorted Mandy into the private dining room close to the kitchen. Alexander Hayworth hated an audience. Mandy hated the cramped room. "You look lovely as always, sweetheart." He leaned down and kissed her forehead then held out her chair.

"Daddy," Mandy said. She took a seat, folding a napkin over her lap before her father took his seat.

"I took the liberty of ordering." The table filled with all of Mandy's favorites. "I hope that's alright."

"Of course." She didn't point out that her father also ordered a dish that wasn't her favorite at all. It was her mother's. Mandy scooted her chair in closer. The sooner this meal was over with, the sooner Mandy could go back to her fantasy world where her birth father only existed in a distant memory. Not the truth where her parents lied about her adoption for the first twelve years of her life and her real father sitting across from her refused to tell her why.

Anthony plated mozzarella caprese onto her plate without asking. He filled her glass with a wine her father selected. Probably some amazing vintage at some ridiculous cost. With one sip, she knew it wasn't nearly as good as the wine Lucien chose for her.

"I had hoped you would be able to convince Kyrissa to join us this month." He pointed at an empty plate next to him. "You know she is always invited to have dinner with us."

"I tried," Mandy admitted. Kyrissa was always a great buffer between Mandy and her father. "She's working on a new series of paintings. I don't think she even heard me ask." Mandy shrugged. "You know how she gets."

"Obsessed," her father stated. "Just like her mother."

Mandy could only nod. "Mothers tend to extend lots of skills to their daughters. Kyrissa's gave her painting. Mine—" Mandy began.

Clearing his throat, he gazed at her across a bouquet of daisies, flowers he'd obviously requested especially for her. "Can we not do this tonight, honey?" He sat back in his chair and drank the entire glass of wine Anthony just refilled. It normally took Mandy until the entrees arrived before she pushed her father far enough to resign himself to drowning the lies that still existed between them.

"Whatever you want, Daddy." She finished her first course and downed her own glass of wine. Anthony was hovering and she knew he'd never let two glasses go empty at their table for too long.

"How's the apartment?" He asked.

"Fine. How's business?"

"Good." He nodded along with the single word. "How about the social scene? Any guys I should worry about? That I need to threaten?" Not that he'd ever actually intimidate anyone, he'd have one of his associates do that dirty work.

"No."

"So, have you found any new bands? Your blog hasn't mentioned any lately."

"You've done your homework," Mandy replied. She'd expect no less from the man who always had an answer unless she was the one asking the questions. She raised her glass towards Anthony who was obviously attempting not to let either of the Hayworth's drown their feelings. Anthony raised an eyebrow giving Mandy a run for her warning glare.

"I always do my homework where you are concerned."

"You're right." Mandy placed the still empty wine glass on the table before folding her napkin on the table. "Let's not do this tonight. I've kinda had a rough day and the last thing I want to do is sit here and pretend that everything is alright with you sitting across the table from me." She stood to leave, signaling for Anthony to grab her jacket from the coat check.

"Amanda, wait," her father warned. "Just give me a chance. You don't always have to put up such walls around yourself, especially around me."

"Hmm," Mandy huffed. "You erected those walls with your lies. Until you're ready to tell me everything about mom, I don't see a point in removing a single brick."

Heart racing, Mandy never looked back. She'd never walked out on her father before.

Even when she was twelve, the day her mother gave her the angel necklace and she took that first picture. With a single click of her camera, a confession slipped out.

Why would they lie about her adoption when they were her birth parents?

Her father promised to tell her the truth...later. Every day since, Mandy waited. She waited for answers, for truths that neither of her parents were ready to admit. She stuck around and waited, until she only had one person left to wait for.

Even after her mother died, Mandy kept the first Sunday of every month reserved for her father. Still waiting for the truth. Maybe it was time she changed her calendar and gave the date to someone who wasn't lying to her. Someone who made her feel alive and sang songs just for her.

Maybe Lucien had the first Sunday of every month free.

CHAPTER THIRTY-TWO

The guitar picked out soft notes of the haunting new melody. Strong, complex harmonies that excited and made Lucien's heart race. Just like the person who inspired them.

The window for the recording software on his laptop lay surrounded by images on a constant loop. Mandy's pictures. She originally hesitated when he asked for a few when setting up the database, but eventually relented—at the cost of another picture, one she chose not to take that night. The photographs depicted a beauty of sight and sound. Pictures that sung a song that Lucien attempted to capture into music and words. Specifically, the self-portrait that mirrored the one of her mother.

A halo of lights surrounded the dark locks of hair, Mandy's face haunted, yet a serenity reached out from the image to twist at Lucien's heart. An angel stared back at him. One he couldn't get out of his head. Yet couldn't face either.

As if on cue, his phone vibrated with another incoming text. He didn't need to look to know the sender. Desire yelled at him to answer. Fear and embarrassment stayed his hand. How many late night texts had he typed and then deleted? Lucien stopped counting. He had even blown off the band for two days, claiming work emergencies, just in case she showed up, as she had the propensity to do. Accidentally running into Mandy would bring more guilt than he could deal with right now.

"You no answer?" The comforting voice of his grandmother asked, as she entered his apartment. Plump by social standards, healthy by hers, Mama T moved without a sound when she wanted too. Gathering her brightly colored skirts in one hand, she plopped down on the couch next to him. "Or you still hiding and worry 'bout building doghouse?"

"Building doghouse?" Lucien chuckled, shaking his head. His grandmother's broken English and continued attempts at slang were a source of amusement for the entire family. "In the doghouse, Mama, not building."

"Da. That." She patted his cheek. "You no worry. You still learning."

"I wish Robert would figure that out," Lucien mused. He missed the warning signs and because of his inattention, the curse overtook Robert, forcing him to paint the violence he hated so much to relieve the agony. Robert recovered, but it didn't stop him from chewing Lucien into the ground for creating the chaos that triggered the episode. It left him doubting everything in his life. If Robert ever learned what happened in the warehouse with Mandy, that he had risked an unprotected stranger near his art, he had no doubt he'd be on a plane to Romania right now, chosen Guardian or not.

Lucien sighed. He retreated to his music to avoid facing both Mandy and Robert. And still couldn't get completely away from either. "I know. I just...what good am I to Robert? I can't heal him or even seem to reduce his pain. In fact, I cause it more than I ease it." He slumped back into the overstuffed leather cushions, wanting nothing more than to run and hide.

"You no cause his pain." Mama T growled, poking him in the shoulder. "Robert have own issues. You no borrow his." Carmen would have smacked him and made sure it hurt far worse. Neither woman allowed wallowing in self-pity.

Pulling his guitar to his chest, his finger stroked out random notes, some purposely off-key and lost sounding. He had no direction, or at least not the one he expected two years ago. Doubt about Robert's choice, roiled in his gut. His gaze fell on the pictures rotating across his screen. Mandy knew exactly what she wanted and went after it. Lyrics coalesced in Lucien's mind. The hidden song broke through the barrier just as the picture of Mandy surfaced on the screen.

Words melded around the notes, transforming the harshness into passionate fire. Heat settled into his core, spreading outward until every nerve burned with yearning. Just as it had the other day for a woman Lucien would gladly grant his soul to—and so much more.

"Trust your angel," Mama T whispered next to him. She pointed to the pictures on his laptop. "She lead you right."

Lucien jumped. "What?" He closed the lid quickly, hiding Mandy's pictures. "Those are just some pictures from a friend." Mama T interlaced her fingers over her ample middle and smiled. Dark hair almost completely streaked with grey, framed a face lined with creases, the trials of her years and her gifts. Her dark eyes glinted, deep wells to visions gifted to some Romani.

The Second Sight.

"You've seen her." It wasn't a question as much as a statement from Lucien.

"Go to her. No more hiding." The callused fingers patted his cheek once more, before Mama T pushed off the couch. She paused at the door, tossing his jacket at him. "You see. Spirits know. Your angel will show you way."

The door hadn't finished closing before Lucien scrambled to untangle himself from his guitar. He thought about calling Mandy, apologizing. But that he had to do in person. He raced down the back stairs, his black motorcycle boots thumping almost as loud as his heart. Thoughts of seeing her again brought a grin that no matter how hard he tried, he couldn't erase.

Pulling onto her street, Lucien found a parking place a block away near a coffee shop and post office. The patter of rain on his windshield increased from a light sprinkle to an outright downpour. Figures. He'd probably be drenched by the time he got to her apartment. He didn't care. To see her, be near her, nothing else mattered.

It took two tries to open the driver door. God is this what stage fright felt like? Nerves like nothing he'd ever experienced before made his hands shake and his insides twist into knots. Nearly falling out of his truck, the seatbelt turned into an octopus hell-bent on faceplanting him onto the street. He managed to untangle himself and keep most of his dignity intact in front of the coffee shop patrons staring at him through rain-streaked windows.

Consumed by thoughts of how to apologize, how he hoped she'd give him the chance to apologize, Lucien wasn't prepared for the stiff thrust of a hand against his chest, slamming him against a building wall. The breath knocked out of him, he grabbed the hand now twisted in his shirt, prepared to fight.

"Jay?" Fist reared back, he paused, blinking the rain out of his vision. "What the fuck man?"

"I shoulda known," Jay snapped. "Can't make rehearsals because of work, but you can bloody well find time to come see *her*."

Lucien shoved Jay away from him. "I did have to work." He yanked his shirt straight from where Jay had mangled it. Brushing his now rain soaked hair out of his face, he tried to still his racing heartbeat. He didn't have the time or patience for Jay's issues right now, whatever they were. "I missed two practices. It's not the end of the damn world. I'll be there tonight."

"I oughta kick you out of the band." Jay attempted to light a cigarette, throwing the offending object away as the rain drenched it.

"Like you'd even have a shot without me," Lucien scoffed. His hands fisted. He'd done all the work for the band. Wrote new songs, taught the guys to make them perfect, managed the hype, all to make this relaunch of *Demon Dogs* a success. And Jay threatened to kick him out.

"I'd rather take my chances with a mediocre singer who shows up, then one who's never around." Jay paced. The stomp of his boots on the pavement, pounding into Lucien's skull. "We have a week to get *Demon Dogs* ready. You need to decide what you want and commit to it."

This didn't make any sense to Lucien. They had done the hard work already. The songs were set, the stage show just needed some final tweaks, and he had finished the marketing campaign yesterday, provided Mandy would still help him.

"Son of a bitch," Lucien muttered. All the puzzle pieces clicked into place. "This isn't about the band at all. It's about Mandy." Jay stiffened in front of him. Rain poured down around them, the staccato beat on nearby cars a counterpoint to the drumroll of thunder echoing in the background. Neither moved.

"Amanda Hayworth doesn't do strings. How many times do I have to tell you that?" Jay took a step forward. Lucien held his ground. "She'll pull you in, squeeze real tight, then cut the ties and leave you lying at her feet to bleed to death. She's not worth throwing your career away."

"Just because you blew your shot with her doesn't mean I don't have one." Jealousy pulsed through Lucien. If Jay wanted Mandy back, he'd have to go through him first. "You have no idea what Mandy is worth to me."

"You dumb kid. If you won't listen to me, maybe she will." Jay turned towards the apartment. He never got the chance to take a step.

The impact against his knuckles traveled up Lucien's entire arm. Jay stumbled and fell backwards onto the sidewalk. Cocked back and ready for another shot, Lucien yelled, "Stay away from her."

Slowly gaining his feet, Jay wiped the blood off his lip. "That's twice she's made me bleed. I'm done. Do what you want. Hell, take the night off from rehearsal, 'cause I sure as hell ain't sharing a stage with you tonight." Still nursing his lip, Jay pulled the collar of his jacket up and walked away.

Red streaked Lucien's knuckles, fading as the rain washed away the sign of his failure like turpentine to paint. First Robert, now Jay. Rooted to the spot, his body shook as the wash of adrenaline ebbed. Ten feet to his right, the door to Mandy's apartment. In the other direction, Jay, each plodding step taking him, and possibly Lucien's music dream with him. Demon or Angel. There was only one choice Lucien could make. With heavy footsteps, Lucien made his decision, praying it was the right one.

CHAPTER THIRTY-THREE

Mandy tried to ignore the buzzer sounding behind her until she finished photographing the last of Kyrissa's newest paintings. She hated this new series of her best friend's work, not because the images were flat or Kyrissa's techniques lacked. Instead, Mandy's hatred seemed to emanate directly from the paint itself as if Kyrissa had managed to bottle the emotion and squeezed it onto her paintbrush. Mandy's skin crawled with every glance. Her chest seized tight and her mood swung into depths Mandy couldn't explain. Yet every picture she took of this last painting was mediocre at best. She'd finally set it up against a corner in her bedroom, letting the light from the moon outside her window hit it in such a way that Mandy finally captured all the emotion Kyrissa had painted.

And still she hated the painting.

She would have continued to ignore the buzzing if Lucien Solvak's face hadn't filled the security scanner. A soft rain fell around him, water dripping off his cheeks, but he did nothing to shield himself so Mandy took her time letting him into the apartment building. She grabbed a towel from her bathroom and pretended she wasn't counting the seconds before he appeared outside her apartment door.

"What are you doing here?" She asked, throwing the towel in his general direction. Leaving the door open, she turned her back and left him standing there.

For three days, Lucien ignored her texts and didn't return her calls. And for three days, she pretended she didn't care. Showing up tonight on her doorstep, looking as if he'd just been rung through a puddle and hung out to dry, did little to soften her mood towards him.

"I owe you a few days of pictures," he murmured. Dropping the towel, Lucien slipped his hands into the pockets of his jeans and followed her into her bedroom.

"Yeah, well, not sure I need them anymore." She stopped considering endorsing *Demon Dogs* two days ago, though she wasn't sure why. So what if he'd given her the most intense orgasm she'd ever had in a dark warehouse? Or ever. It's not like she intended for that night to tie any strings between them.

"How about you not make any rash decisions right this moment?" Lucien suggested. "I'll sit here nice and still and give you whatever fucking pictures you want. All the pictures you could possibly take." Dejection rolled off his form like the rivulets of water falling from his hair and clothes. "Not hiding from you anymore."

Lucien sat on the edge of her bed, rubbing at the knuckles of his right hand.

"Take your shirt off," she demanded.

"Excuse me?"

"And...your boots. You're dripping water all over my wood floors." Mandy pointed at the water pooling. "They've lasted nearly a century and I'm not going to let you ruin them with a puddle of rain at your feet."

"Sorry." He lifted the t-shirt over his head.

Lucien shirtless. Chest exposed. Tattoos glowing like beacons in the night. Mandy sighed.

Like she actually gave a damn about the floors.

The tight abs glistened and shone in the dull light. Her fingers ached to run over the smooth muscles, follow the white lines she wanted so desperately to trace. Hell, she wanted to lick every last drop of water off his skin.

Clearing her throat, she threw another dry towel in his direction. He needed to cover that shit up fast or he'd have trouble keeping her away from him tonight. Control be damned.

Sitting on the edge of her bed, Lucien kicked off his boots, and wrung what he could from the cuffs of his jeans. With a towel draped over his bare shoulders, he ran his hands over his head through his damp hair. The flex of his muscles, each move an image in grace and innocence. For the first time, the effects Mandy always saw in her camera hovered at the edges of her vision.

Without thinking, she snapped a picture of the way his head hung, wet hair hanging in front of his face. The lighting was soft and gray, water still clinging to his body in a few spots. Something in the air around him shifted. He hadn't argued, hadn't tried to stop her. The sodden mess in front of her hadn't even looked up.

"Hey," Mandy said, placing her camera on the dresser beside her. She'd never seen Lucien look so tormented, like demons were gnawing away at his soul. She didn't need her camera to see his mood. "You okay?"

"Yeah," Lucien said. He nodded a little too confidently for Mandy to believe him.

"Liar."

"Fine, no." Lucien exhaled hard. "I don't know. I'm just stressed with work. The band." He stilled, his gaze locking onto hers. "And I can't stop thinking about you."

"That's not exactly the worst problem in the world to have," Mandy said. She didn't want to admit that every one of her thoughts in the past three days had been about him.

"It is in my world," he said. He scrubbed at his forehead, as if in pain. "I obviously want this more than you do and honestly, I can't risk distractions right now. Yet, you're the first thing I think about every morning and the last face I see when I go to sleep and practically every moment in between."

Mandy pushed his hands away from his face, cupping his cheeks. She tilted his face up to hers. He wore innocence like a second skin to hide the vulnerability that lay beneath. Exposing those layers to her was enough to do her in, crushing any resolve she made to keep her feelings from developing any deeper. It was already too late.

"Maybe I don't want you to stop thinking about me." In fact, she wanted him to think of nothing else. "And maybe I am exactly the kind of distraction you need."

She didn't wait for his response. Leaning down, her lips drew closer to his. He didn't move away from her, staring at her mouth like he was about to devour it. She'd let him.

His hands grabbed her waist, pulling her closer before moving up to her neck and drawing her mouth to his. She let her tongue tell him exactly how much she'd been thinking about him.

Pushing him back slightly, she climbed onto his lap, straddling his legs between hers. This was where she'd been thinking about being since that night in the warehouse, what she wanted to think about every time Lucien appeared. The curl of his lips around her jaw, the hard way his fingers pressed into her hips, how his hand cupped the back of her neck, powerful yet tender.

She slipped the towel off his shoulders, glad he didn't try to stop her. Instead, he greedily removed her tank top and slipped her bra off her body like it was never there to begin with. Trails of wetness slicked her skin where Lucien kissed, sucked and nipped along her neck and atop her shoulder. Her warm skin, pushed up against his cool, hard body, made the combination the hottest thing Mandy had ever felt.

"Fuck," she muttered the deeper he pushed his teeth, taking bites out of her as though she was his to consume. "Whatever you do," she gasped. "Do not stop."

"You wanted me to lose control?" Lucien asked. A darkness flashed across his glare. "This is me losing control." He growled, flipping her onto her back in the middle of her oversized bed. Furiously undoing her jeans, she didn't have time to miss the coverage before Lucien hovered over her.

"Maybe," Mandy spoke softly, "you're finally taking the right kind of control." And she couldn't be happier about the change.

Lucien's fingers worked feverishly between her legs. Through his jeans, his arousal pressed against her thigh. Mandy needed to feel the pressure somewhere else.

She unbuckled his leather belt, yanked at the waistband of his jeans, doing everything in her power short of ripping the material. For two seconds Lucien stopped touching her. The longest two seconds of Mandy's life. She ached for his return, almost begged him to push her further down this road that neither of them seemed ready to stop traveling. A simple tear of foil, another brief hesitation and Lucien was back where he belonged, naked and hovering over her.

She lined herself up to his body, arching her hips, his tip met wetness and he pushed into her so deep she wanted to cry. Or laugh. Maybe both. The mixture of sweetness in his kisses, the roughness of his thrusts, intoxicated her more and more with each moment.

"You feel amazing," Lucien said slipping his hand under her back that exposed her to him at a different angle.

Mandy dug her nails into his back, not even letting go when he winced. It only seemed to push him deeper and harder and there was no way she could let up now, no amount of effort could ebb the flow of emotions flooding her body. Pleasure. Pain. Desire that she'd never experienced before.

His breath ragged in her ear, his body shuddered. Arms crushed her to the point of pain, yet Mandy didn't care. Lucien was all she needed. All she wanted. His muscle bunched taut under her touch. Three more thrusts and the primal growl he let loose sent her crashing over the edge.

He rolled to his back, eyes closed, pulling her on top of him. Bodies still entwined, he struggled to catch his breath, as did she. Neither of them said a word. Maybe it was just the sheen of his sweat, but Lucien's white tattoos glowed in the dim candlelight of her room. She traced the intricate patterns on his chest and arms. His eyes opened and Mandy lost herself in the innocence that was Lucien all over again.

Lifting her hand in his, he kissed the palm and laid it across his chest. "Thank you," he whispered.

"Anytime," Mandy answered with a smile. And she meant it.

Three nights ago didn't tie any strings between them. It had merely created the holes for the laces. Tonight laced the ties through those holes, pulled them tight and bonded Mandy Hayworth to Lucien Solvak whether she intended it to or not.

CHAPTER THIRTY-FOUR

The early morning sunbeam traveled up her body hidden under the light blanket, kissing the skin where Mandy had wrapped a leg over the top of the sheet. Skin he wanted to touch and stroke with fingers and mouth. Just like he had for most of last night.

Lucien should be exhausted, yet his body hummed, the warmth of Mandy's figure curled against his an infusion of energy. She drifted off to sleep just before dawn, her hair cascading over his chest like a warm blanket. He feared if he fell asleep, this would all end up as some unreal fantasy. So he watched and dreamed while awake. The new song kept him occupied and relaxed. The chords played clearer in his head now, the lyrics finally starting to arrange themselves.

Mandy. His angel.

Lucien couldn't help himself. Ever so gently, he stroked the glossy strands of her hair through his fingers. Mandy smiled, a soft sigh exhaled in warm breath against his chest. His body awoke as though that single sound connected directly to his core. The hand resting on his hip slipped lower when Mandy shifted. Her eyes snapped open.

"Sorry," he whispered. "Some parts of me wake up earlier than others." Lucien didn't know whether to shift away from her or not. Mandy let him know her choice. Sucking in a quick breath, he struggled not to push further into her hand. A low moan that started at his toes burned up through every part of him, settling into a haze of pleasure in his brain.

"I think I owe you a return favor for the other night in the warehouse." Mandy kissed her way across Lucien's chest; nipping, licking, taunting.

Already on edge, the sensations, pain mixed with pleasure, the warm licks cooled by her light breath, strained at Lucien's control. His free hand tried to yank her mouth to his. She pulled back.

"Please," his voice rough and gravelly. He wasn't above begging.

"Not yet." Her hooded gaze engulfed him. "I want to watch you."

Desire and passion flooded through Lucien in a new wave. He groaned, arching his back. Hips now thrusting of their own accord, her assault continued, one he hoped would continue for eternity. Twisting his hand into the sheets, his control eroded with each passing second. Body and mind no longer his to command. He belonged to Mandy.

"Let go," she urged.

The visceral growl curled his toes. Wave after wave of ecstasy washed over and through him. Mandy's voice whispered in his ear, soft kisses caressed his cheek, hair, lips. Breathe, she told him. He could do that. In and out. The simple mechanics of filling his lungs grounded him, returning him to earth. He opened his eyes. Deep pools of brown smiled at him.

Lucien groaned. "You're going to kill me. Not that this would be a bad way to go, mind you." Chuckling, he pulled Mandy on top of him. The sharp piercing ring of his phone alarm brought another growl from him. This one of irritation. Reluctantly, Lucien released Mandy and rolled over to dig his phone out of the pocket of his jeans on the floor.

Mandy moved to curl around his back where he sat on the edge of the bed. Her chin on his shoulder, her hands roamed his chest. "Tell me that was just a wake up alarm."

"Unfortunately, no. I've got a rehearsal early this morning." Turning his head, Mandy rewarded him with a deep sensual kiss. "Keep that up and I might not leave."

"Hmm. Can't imagine that would be a bad idea." Mandy nipped at his bottom lip.

"Normally it wouldn't, but I have this new song for the band. The guys almost have the music perfect. I just have to finish the lyrics. I would love to have it ready for the re-launch." In a quick twist, Lucien pulled Mandy around him to land in his lap. Her light musical laugher recharged him. His body started to respond to the sight and sound of her in his arms.

"You are positively glowing talking about this song," Mandy teased, reaching for her camera on the nightstand. He didn't stop her. "What's it about?"

"An angel." He burned to tell her she inspired the song, inspired him, but he couldn't. Not yet. Maybe at the debut she'd understand without him having to say a word.

She raised a single brow. "Maybe you should go practice then. I like the idea of a song about an angel."

"You do make it hard to choose." He rubbed his thumb over her bottom lip, chuckling when she tried to bite it. "Angel my ass. You're a demon temptress."

"So stay," Mandy said, biting her lip. "I still haven't taken any real photos since you've finally agreed to let me."

Lucien had never seen that look on Mandy's face before. Almost as if she was at war with her own request. He wasn't sure which side she wanted to win. After his fight with Jay, ditching rehearsal probably wasn't a good idea.

Decide what you want, that's what Jay told him.

Holding Mandy in his arms, right here, right now, Lucien couldn't imagine being anywhere else. He smiled and the brightness in Mandy's eyes grew tenfold. The angry buzz of the phone in his hand brought his intended kiss to an abrupt halt.

"You need to chuck that thing out the window," Mandy complained. "It's really cramping my style."

"You'll get used to it." Lucien chuckled. "Just like I'll get used to the camera." But the sound of his relaxed vibe faded when he saw the text.

WAREHOUSE. NOW.

"I have to go." He turned to explain. "Robert—"

Mandy had already retreated from him. The walls back in place once more, her face emotionless, guarded. The sensation hurt more than Lucien expected. He wished he could tell her, tell Robert, but secrets blocked the way.

"I've seen that look before." She covered herself with the sheet, leaning back against the headboard. "Go. Deal with whatever emergency your controlling boss demands. However." She pointed a finger at him, one brow arched. "You *will* meet me at Paddy's Club tonight at seven to check out *Spiral*. I need to do a follow-up article for my blog, without your interference this time, thank you." She mock glared at him. "We can both check out the competition. And I wouldn't mind hanging out after. Maybe have a little fun." She winked. "If you're there with me, I have a better chance of accomplishing both." She ran a finger down his arm, smiling when he stiffened in more ways than one.

"Deal." Lucien grabbed her hand, placing a soft kiss on her palm. She couldn't stop the quick inhale. "And this time when you ask me to stay, I will." He'd do whatever he had to in order to keep Mandy in his life. Even if it meant losing everything else.

CHAPTER THIRTY-FIVE

Mandy kissed Lucien good-bye and managed to keep her hands from twisting into his shirt for a second time. Leaning against the doorframe, she eyed his ass while he jogged down the first flight of steps. Truth be told, she wanted to drag him back inside, directly to her bedroom without passing go, and spend the rest of the day doing whatever one did when you spent the entire day in bed with someone. She wouldn't know because that had never seemed appealing before.

Until Lucien.

"Um, hey." Lucien's voice filled the foyer at the bottom of the four-story building.

"Hey yourself," the voice of her roommate replied.

Hearing the footsteps accelerate up the steps, Mandy held her breath waiting for her best friend. She didn't bring guys back to the apartment she shared with Kyrissa. Letting Lucien come to work on the database was one thing. Letting him stay last night was something entirely different. Mandy just didn't know what and couldn't explain it to Ky if she tried.

"I thought you were still sleeping?" Mandy held the door open for Kyrissa.

"Haven't slept yet. Studio. Painting. You know how it is." Kyrissa set her bag of brushes on the counter. "Was that..." Kyrissa started to ask when Mandy closed the door. "Did Lucien spend the night?"

"Uh, yeah." No point in denying what Kyrissa had

obviously already seen. A guy leaving their apartment in the hours too early for any respectable visit to occur.

"Wow, must be serious if you let him sleep over." Kyrissa poured herself a glass of water. "Next thing you know you'll be making him breakfast."

"Not likely." Mandy smiled. She had very different things in mind for Lucien this morning and none of them included food. "You know I only make breakfast for you the morning after."

"Very funny," Kyrissa laughed pulling out the waffle maker. Mandy had already started mixing the ingredients for almond banana waffles. It was Kyrissa's mom's recipe and Mandy learned it since Kyrissa was such a terrible cook. Mandy admired Kyrissa for a lot of things: her ability to paint with more emotion than most people ever dreamed of holding, her resiliency to follow her dreams even after living through the tragedy of how she lost her mother. But her cooking was not one of those things.

"Why didn't you call me to come pick you up? You know I hate when you walk home so late."

"Which is why I waited till the sun came up." Kyrissa smiled. "So when do I get to meet him? Other than an awkward morning-after hello."

"Come with me tonight to see *Spiral.* Lucien will be there." Mandy bit her lip. Introducing her best friend to Lucien held more meaning than when her and Kyrissa accidentally ran into Jay at a show scouting the competition. Not introducing them was more awkward than making the intros.

"Sorry. Wish I could, but one more night in the studio and I think this new series will be finished."

"Didn't you just pull an all nighter?"

"Yeah." Kyrissa drank half the glass of water. "But this series is kind of special. I really want to get it finished. Maybe try to sell it on my own."

"Oh that's awesome, Ky. I can't wait to see it then. Maybe I'll drop you off on my way to Paddy's so I can take a few sneak peek pics and then I could pick you up when the bar closes."

"That'd be great." Kyrissa cleared her plate. "That reminds me. Professor C stopped by my studio and asked about my latest commissions. Have you photographed them yet?"

"Uh, no," Mandy lied. If she admitted to finally photographing the paintings, Kyrissa would insist on delivering them to her professor right now. "I'll do it today before the *Spiral* show tonight. Then I can help you deliver them tomorrow."

"I may have to take the pictures myself. His patron wants the paintings ASAP and I could really use the money." Kyrissa smeared jelly across the first waffles out of the iron. "I truly can't wait till these paintings are gone." She nudged her head towards the corner of the room. Mandy couldn't agree more. She just didn't want to ruin her Lucien high with a brush of walking death that surrounded Professor C every time Mandy ever met the man.

"Go get some sleep. I'll work on photographing them this morning." Mandy clutched her camera on the edge of the counter. Not that she planned to use it to take one more picture of those paintings. What she planned to do was something she should have done months ago—photograph Professor Creeptastic and see what secrets he hid.

"Thanks for the waffles." Kyrissa scrubbed at a patch of paint on her cheek. "I'm shower bound, then to bed. I am exhausted." She turned and walked into her room.

Mandy raised her camera and took a picture of her best friend.

Kyrissa paused at her doorway and just shook her head. "You better delete that picture."

"Never." Mandy grinned. She had thousands of pictures of Kyrissa and each one of them revealed the same truth. Kyrissa's safety would always come before everything else in Mandy's world. Even her own love life.

CHAPTER THIRTY-SIX

"So, you do actually know where you live and work." Robert walked out of his studio. "Live at least. The verdict about working is debatable right now."

Robert's apartment usually gave off an air of clear, sharp energy. Bright track lights highlighted the art hung on the stark white walls. The exposed brick wall along the seating area gave an artistic contrast of old-world to the rest of the apartment. Dark, antique wooden furniture merged with modernistic stainless-steel amenities. A true home of an immortal; the past, present and future blended into one peaceful existence.

Except to Lucien.

The pungent linseed oil and turpentine from Robert's studio overpowered the crisp fresh scent of an outside breeze flowing through the open window. A smothering presence pervaded the entire place. The hair on the back of Lucien's neck stood up. His skin itched to the point where he checked his tattoos to see if they glowed.

"What's going on?" Walking further into the apartment, every nerve on edge, Lucien searched for the attack that loomed. Irritation at the summons, as though some pet dog died the moment Mama T stepped out from Robert's studio. Cold fear grabbed and twisted.

Oh god no. Not another abomination painting. The more times Robert painted for the demon and not for himself, the greater chance the demon would find them. "Did he—"

"No." Mama T's clipped speech spoke more in a single word about Robert's state; he hadn't succumbed to the curse, but he was close. And Lucien wasn't there to help him. Again.

Haggard looking, hair disorderly and sticking up in various angles, hands and shirt covered in paint, nothing of the control Robert routinely commanded existed.

"Did you forget that international tours required permits to be paid *before* the government released them?"

Lucien's heart skipped a beat. Pressing his hand against the breast pocket of his jacket, the stiff folds of the envelopes inside rippled against his chest. He planned to overnight the payments three days ago. No sleep, Robert's attack and Lucien's subsequent retreat into his music knocked the errand out of his head. Then Mandy...

Robert stumbled and Lucien rushed to support him to the nearest chair. His Guardian marks sparked the moment he touched Robert. Lucien inhaled sharply, as a wave of dizziness washed over him. Life. Pain. The two mixed and combined. Agony reached claws of burning fire into every part of his mind and body. But the third emotion gut punched Lucien.

Longing.

The sensation overpowered him until he couldn't breathe. Blackness crowded closer, leaving a metallic taste in Lucien's throat. Blood. A sharp stinging slap across his cheek, hard enough to rock his head to the side, sent the darkness crawling back to the shadows.

Air scraped into his lungs through ragged gasps. Lucien blinked. Fuzzy images focused into wooden beams crisscrossing the ceiling. Robert's loft. He was on his back. Why? Propping up on one elbow, Lucien shook his head, fog still surrounding his mind. What the hell just happened? As oxygen flushed through his system, his vision cleared. The round face of Mama T appeared and grabbed his face in a vice grip.

"Never touch him if mind not shielded." Deep brown pools captured his. The depth of her eyes ancient beyond imagine, but within them, Lucien found himself again. He nodded. "Da. You better now." Mama T grunted as she pushed to her feet. "You heed me and it keep you both alive."

If he had any idea what she was talking about, Lucien would gladly follow his Grandmother's directions. He looked around trying to get his bearings. Sunlight poured in from the floor to ceiling windows of Robert's apartment, dust motes dancing in the sunbeams. A grandfather clock in the study chimed the eleventh hour. Eleven? That can't be right. He arrived at the warehouse at eight-thirty.

Robert. Lucien shoved to his feet, weaving as another wave of dizziness hit him. The back of a chair loomed and he grabbed the stabilizing support. Passing out wasn't an option. He needed to find Robert.

"Drink." Mama T appeared at his shoulder with a glass of orange juice.

"Where's Robert?" Lucien croaked. His throat raw and dry. Mama T waited for him to drink before answering him.

"Dere." She waved to the couch in the studio. A pale figure slept wrapped in one of Mama T's afghans. "He be fine when he wake if you fix problem." His grandmother fixed a narrow-eyed glare at him.

"What did I do?" The stiff envelopes came to mind with painful acuity. Lucien groaned. "Oh sh—" Mama T swelled like a bear, her hand raised to cuff him. "I forgot to mail the payments." Lucien slid into the chair. If the German tour fell through it would be his fault. He'd fail Robert's trial with his music, and his chance with Mandy would be forever gone.

"Da."

"I'll square things with the German curator."

"Idea good." Patting his cheek, Mama T left, closing the studio door to give Lucien some privacy.

Lucien fumbled for his phone. As it rang, he punched the answer button without even looking at the caller. "Hello?"

"'Bout time you answered your bloody phone. Where the fuck are you?" Jay's voice snarled at the other end. "So help me, if you're where I think you are—"

"I'm at work," Lucien stated, trying to keep the annoyance out of his voice. He couldn't deal with Jay's jealousy right now. Nor was he going to tell him he had planned to blow off the band for Mandy. Robert was a much safer excuse at least where Jay was concerned. "I didn't get a chance to call you about rehearsal because of an emergency situation." Losing two and a half hours to whatever hit him hadn't help matters either.

"There's always something. Work." Jay ground out the silence. "Some band follower."

Lucien surged to his feet. "Don't you *ever* refer to her like that again!"

"I thought I got through to you. Don't you fucking get it?" Jay yelled. "Mandy doesn't do strings. You have the opportunity of a lifetime standing in front of you, waiting for you to run with it. Are you seriously going to throw that away for a one-night stand?"

"You have no idea what you're talking about. There is more than a one-night stand between us. Something more powerful than a mediocre band and a pipe dream." Muscles taut, Lucien's entire body vibrated as the words resonated within him. Mandy offered a future he didn't understand but felt deep in his core. It was more than sex. A connection existed between them he couldn't deny. Didn't want to. One he saw open up in her this morning.

"I need to know whether or not you're committed to

this band." When Jay spoke, his voice was controlled, yet the tenor of anger hovered just below the surface.

Lucien fought to uncurl his fists. His head pounded and he knew he was reacting, not thinking straight. Laying his hands flat on the tabletop, he took a deep breath. Chords from the new song sung their sweet melody through his mind. Mandy's song.

"What will convince you that I am?"

"Choose."

The simple word from Jay had Lucien staring at his phone. The harder he held on, the more his music dream slipped away. Anger. Resentment. Each brewed their poison into his dreams. Why was wanting Mandy so bad?

"You are seriously giving me an ultimatum?"

"Her or the band, Lucien. Two members can't be in love with the same woman."

"Then I quit."

Lucien stabbed the end button. The phone clattered to the table from nerveless fingers. Sinking into the chair, he now understood the waiting presence, the attack poised to smother him when he first entered the room. Burying his head in his hands, he stared at nothing. Gone. The music. The band. He threw it all away without a thought.

For her.

Checking the time, Lucien knew fixing the German tour would take all day and probably into the night. He'd call Mandy first. Cancel their date. Except, how in the hell was he going to explain to Mandy that he just quit the band?

CHAPTER THIRTY-SEVEN

Mandy stared at the text.
Can't make it. Work. Raincheck. L.
What promised to be a pulse pounding evening lay in ruins in the form of five tiny digital words. She allowed herself to look forward to seeing him again, regardless of whether she intended to get excited about it or not. It's not like there was anything tying them together. So not seeing him shouldn't disappoint her.

Who was she kidding? They had nothing but the hottest freaking sex she'd had in, well, maybe ever. Disappointment sang a song locked on repeat. At least Kyrissa wasn't here to witness the occasion. And at least the band on stage improved tenfold since the last time they played in a local venue. A year ago, they were good enough to receive Mandy's endorsement. Tonight they earned a lot more.

Mandy sighed.

She smiled up at the lead singer, not too flirtatious but just enough to let him know she approved of their new sound. The tall burly guy, stretching well above six foot, didn't even grin until Mandy lifted her camera and pointed it in his direction. Then he put on the best show Mandy ever witnessed him perform.

To date, *Spiral* held the title of best local band to ever hit the bigger venues and carry their own tours across the country. Small tours, but tours in their own right. Tonight's performance, billed as the last stop before they headed overseas for their first set of international shows, called for a celebration. Mandy couldn't be happier for their success, but she had to admit she thought Jay would a part of it when she created buzz about the local band in the first place. In fact, she was often considered the contributing factor for their being discovered by one of the hottest talent scouts in the music industry. Mandy hoped to line up the same scout to catch another show in few days, and this time Jay and Lucien would benefit. With Jay behind his kit and Lucien at the lead, Mandy knew that *Demon Dogs* would be even bigger.

"We have a problem," Jay whispered in her ear. Mandy didn't jump at the sound of his gruff voice or back away when he ran his hand along her arm. The touch did nothing compared to one finger of Lucien Solvak coming in contact with her skin.

"I have zero problems," Mandy assured him. She expected to run into Jay tonight. He once auditioned to replace *Spiral's* drummer. Together, they scoped the competition. Again.

"Lucien just quit the band." Jay stepped back, crossing his arms over his chest. He waited patiently for Mandy to respond, which took much longer than it should for her to form a coherent thought. "Did you hear me?"

"I heard you. I'm just waiting for the punch line," Mandy joked.

Jay didn't laugh.

"I wish I was kidding. But I'm not. I'm also not deluding myself in thinking the sole reason Claire Masterson agreed to come hear us play just fucking backed out. And it's all your fault." Jay pointed his finger at Mandy but obviously knew better than to poke it into her chest. She would break it before he had time to retreat.

"My fault?" Mandy asked. Everything she'd done

recently was an attempt to get Lucien to loosen up and embrace the role of lead singer. She could only do so much. Lucien needed to do some of the work too.

"Officially he blamed work and an overly demanding boss for his lack of commitment to a band that, and I quote, didn't need him anyway." Jay cleared his throat before guzzling half a beer.

"Excuse me?" She knew about problems with his boss but Lucien was definitely committed to the band and seemed so focused last night. Even this morning, his energy vibrated when he talked about the new song he'd been working on. She'd only ever seen him that animated on stage—and in bed.

Mandy glared down at the buzzing of her phone. She didn't usually ignore Kyrissa's calls, but she wouldn't be able to hear in this room and she was still trying to piece together whatever puzzle Jay was trying to lay out for her. Forcing the call to voicemail, Mandy refocused on Jay.

"How is Lucien threatening to quit my fault?" She asked again.

"He didn't threaten to quit. He actually quit. Used a few choice words to drive the point home if you know what I mean." Jay winced. "Seems he's under the impression there's something brewing between the two of you, something more important than a mediocre band. His words, not mine."

"More important?" Mandy clarified. "Mediocre?" With Jay's supporting talent, Lucien's lyrics and his dynamic vocals, there was nothing mediocre about *Demon Dogs*. Mandy didn't even joke about endorsing mediocrity.

"You need to set him straight before he makes the biggest fucking mistake of his life." Jay glared at the stage.

"I'll talk to him." Unsure what she'd say since she wasn't sure what thoughts crowded Lucien's mind, Mandy nodded. Regardless, she wouldn't let him walk away from an opportunity like this, not when she knew playing music lit his soul on fire the way hers went ablaze every time she snapped a photo.

Jay growled beside her.

"Their new sound isn't bad," Mandy said, not sure how to be tactful about Jay's missed opportunity. "But they're in need of a phenomenal drummer. Too bad they missed their chance on getting one."

"They sound great." Jay shook his head, a low groan emanating from deep in his throat. "But you're right, that should be me up there, only they aren't the ones who missed out. I threw it away."

"Am I supposed to know what that means?" Mandy asked.

After a few awkward moments, Jay turned towards Mandy. He wrapped his fingers around her upper arm, squeezing slightly too tight. "It means, don't let Lucien throw *Demon Dogs* away because he fell for the wrong chick." Jay stared pointedly at her. So pointed that the glare made her uncomfortable, turning the moment more awkward than it already was.

Her phone rang again. Kyrissa. Right now, she couldn't tear her attention away from Jay.

"That kid is so blinded by what he thinks he feels for you, he's prepared to let the band slip away." Jay tapped out the beat to the next song on the side of his empty beer bottle. "I was that kid once and when I got my shot, I didn't just let it slip, I fucking threw it against the brick wall and ran from it." Jay locked gazes with her. "Right into the closed arms of a girl who didn't want any strings."

Mandy paused. She tried to remember the last time her and Jay were together, the night he attempted to confess his feelings. Mandy cut him off before he had the chance to make any declarations she wasn't prepared to hear, much less return. At the time, she thought she was doing him a favor. Now, she wasn't so sure.

"What do I have to show for it now?" he asked. "No record deal, a band that's barely holding it together tight enough to stay visible on the local scene, and the only girl I've ever loved, I suspect is in love with someone else." Jay huffed, trailing a single finger down her cheek.

"Jay," she whispered. Nothing about her relationship with Jay had ever hinted at anything more than lust, at least on her part. "I had no idea," she choked out. "You turned down *Spiral*? For me?"

"This is the first time they've been home in a year. I knew you wouldn't come with me and I was under the mistaken impression you and I had something more than we did. I see my fatal mistake now and I'll be damned if I'll let Lucien make the same one."

Cupping her cheeks for a few seconds, Mandy stood completely still until Jay spoke again. "If you care about Lucien at all, don't let him throw away his dreams, not unless you are one hundred percent into whatever it is that's happening between the two of you." Jay dropped his hands to his side. Each step he took away from Mandy, she considered the distance a relief, but also filled with so much grief she wanted to beg him to stay. "One hundred percent," he repeated.

Far enough now that Mandy hadn't heard the actual words, only the shape of his mouth saying them, her heart dropped when the truth sunk in. She couldn't be sure she was one hundred percent ready for Lucien. At best, she'd only just this morning admitted she liked the way her pillow smelled like leather and his shampoo.

Letting him go before she could figure out what she wanted from him would be the hardest thing she'd ever had to do before. But she certainly wouldn't be the reason anyone threw away their dreams again, especially not Lucien. She'd sacrifice her own heart before she let that happen.

CHAPTER THIRTY-EIGHT

"Never thought I'd see the day where my son sat behind a desk."

Lucien snapped his head up, massaging his temples. The headache pounding across his skull jumped two notches when he recognized his father's voice.

Leaning against the doorframe of Robert's office, tie pulled loose, suit coat trailing over one shoulder, the casual appearance should disarm. Lucien knew better. Christophe Solvak could be just as demanding as Robert and more ruthless. As one who put business before family, the exact opposite of Lucien's belief, their relationship had never been easy. It took a dive when he was marked as Robert's new Guardian.

"Come to chastise me too?" Five hours of multiple re-sent documents, numerous calls to customs agents and conversations that strained his German to the limit, Lucien had no patience for his father. Not to mention missing a date with Mandy, nor the numerous text messages he had to ignore from her. "With all due respect sir, now is not a good time."

"I won't keep you." Christophe clenched his jaw.

The silence lingered along with his father. The antique clock behind Lucien ticked away. Unless the curator contacted him by nine o'clock, the whole German tour was sunk. If Lucien could just talk to the man directly, the last ditch effort might salvage his screw up.

Tick. Tick. Tick.

Still, his father stood in the doorway. Lucien tore his gaze from his father to check the clock. Five minutes left. Each click announced another notch of his life slipping away. Trapped between two forces—Robert and Christophe—Lucien dug his nails into his palms.

TICK. TICK. TICK.

"What?" Lucien snapped. Would his father never forgive him for taking his place?

"Robert can be difficult and spirits know, he and I have had our differences." His father struggled. Lucien frowned. Christophe always presented himself with a self-assured air, almost arrogant at times. Mannerisms that made working for Robert seem normal. "We have come to an agreement where you are concerned."

"An agreement? Since when did I become a bartering chip between the two of you?" This could not bode well. His life was falling apart around him. His music was gone, his reputation in shambles and his relationship with Mandy suffering before it even started.

Lucien pushed to his feet. His body shook. Over the last twelve hours, the stress threatened to snap him in two like a too tight guitar string. The last thing he needed was for his father and Robert to gang up on him.

His heartbeat sounded between his ears in time with the clock. Lucien snapped. "And who gave you the right to decide anything about—"

"I was never Robert's choice for his Guardian," Christophe said softly. "You always were. It took your grandmother's Second Sight to explain that to me and several more arguments for me to accept it."

The clock faded into silence. *Robert chose him, not Christophe.* Lucien stared at his father.

"Don't worry," Christophe said. "We were told to

butt out. Threatened, actually."

"What exactly does that mean?" The list of people who would have the balls to threaten his father *and* Robert was short. Tension drained out of him and he uncurled his hands, leaning on the ancient cherry-wood desktop. Lucien snorted. Mama T topped that list, but somehow, Lucien put his money on Carmen actually saying it. The phone chose that moment to ring.

"It means, it's your life, your choice."

Lucien grabbed the phone. "Mr. Solvak speaking." The German accent sounded over the phone line. Lucien covered the receiver. "I need to take this," he whispered. Christophe nodded, turning to leave. "*Tata*," Lucian called out. "Thanks for telling me."

His life. His choice.

"Mr. Solvak?" The German curator called.

"Mr. Kappel. Forgive me." Confidence filled Lucien. "Thank you for returning my call. As your associate told you, we have finalized all the paperwork for the loan of the artwork. There should be no further barriers to the tour happening as scheduled."

"I appreciate all your hard work, Mr. Solvak. I simply feel now might not be a good time to—"

"Mr. Kappel, please. Do not let my short-sightedness keep you and your patrons from experiencing *The Shoalman Collection*." Lucien let instincts guide him. "You were impressed with the collection from the first time you saw pictures of it, yes?"

"*Ja*," the curator conceded. Lucien heard the hesitation.

"And I believe you have a certain fondness for one of the German artists in the collection. What if I was to add the entire section of Rasner to the tour? Would that entice you to reconsider?" A muffled conversation, sharp gruff words, strained Lucien's hearing.

"Would I be able to see these pieces in person before

making a final decision?"

It wasn't the paintings the curator wanted to see. Robert would speak with clients on the phone, but left the face-to-face meetings to Carmen. Meeting Robert Shoalman in person was almost as rare as his collection. "I'm sure I can arrange a meeting with Mr. Shoalman to show you the pieces in question."

"Then we are in agreement."

"Excellent. Mr. Shoalman and I will meet you here at the office tomorrow at—" Lucien checked the schedule on the computer. "Three o'clock. Thank you, Mr. Kappel."

Lucien hung up the phone with a rough exhale, only to have his breath catch once more. Robert stood in the doorway. Pale, but dressed in a crisp button down shirt and clean jeans, he once more presented his normal controlled and formal appearance. Dark circles under Robert's almost black eyes the only remaining sign of Robert's recent trial.

"Since when did I become a bargaining chip?" Robert peered at Lucien with an intensity that contradicted the fatigue radiating from his form.

"Since you told me to make this tour happen no matter what I had to do." If he couldn't stand up to Robert about this one meeting, Lucien would never be able to convince Robert to let him bring Mandy into their world.

Strains of music teased him. The white lines crisscrossing his forearms stood out against his skin. Lines Mandy had seen. New melodies, counter harmonies, the driving beat of drums, echoed in his head. He had chosen this life with Robert. No one forced him to take the oaths. He had chosen. Just like he chose Mandy.

"You want me to manage your collection, your clients. Learn the business so you don't have to be so involved in the day to day operations." He raised his chin and returned Robert's intense gaze. "You can't have it both ways. Either let me do my job and don't interfere or..." Lucien swallowed. "Or release me."

Robert raised a single brow, understanding Lucien's demand wasn't only about the warehouse management.

"Agreed."

Fear parked itself on Lucien's chest like a ten-ton truck. What had he just done? "You agree on which part?" he managed to force out before the pressure smothered his ability to speak.

"I will take the meeting tomorrow." Robert stated. "You will be there as well, as the collection's manager."

Lucien dragged air into his lungs as the weight on his chest released him from the folly of his impulsive demand. That was twice today he tried to throw away his dreams. At least this one was safe. For now.

Lucien nodded, acknowledging Robert's decision. "Thank you."

Surrendering the office, Lucien headed towards his apartment. The antique clock struck the half-hour mark. Nine-thirty. Thoughts of the missed date with Mandy filled his head.

She'll be at the show by now.

A pang twisted in his chest. Music. Taking a deep breath, Lucien buried that dream. Maybe someday he'd revisit the possibility, but right now, he needed to focus on Robert. And Mandy.

"And, Lucien," Robert said. Lucien paused in the doorway. "You'll need a suit. My tailor is waiting for you at the shop."

Son of a... It might be his life, but Robert wasn't above making it a living hell.

CHAPTER THIRTY-NINE

"What are you doing here?" Mandy tensed the moment she walked in her door and saw her father resting on a chaise lounge that had been her mother's favorite reading chair.

"Waiting for you, obviously." He waved towards Kyrissa's bedroom door.

"She gave you the new pass code?" Mandy had changed the security code on the door to the apartment building after her father's second attempt to see her without an invitation. He owned the building, but she owned the security system. An arrangement that had worked just fine until now.

"She didn't have much choice when you added her to the list of calls that you send straight to voicemail." Mandy's father stood. He swiped down his pants, flattening any wrinkles that could have formed while he sat. She didn't see any. "An incident on campus left her feeling insecure about her safety and in need of a ride."

"What happened?" Every hair on Mandy's body rose as if a chill had just swept through the room. Kyrissa was her best friend, closer than a sister, and if anything ever happened to her, Mandy couldn't be certain she'd ever forgive herself for it, regardless who took the blame. "She was supposed to wait for me to come pick her up."

"After delivering a few paintings she felt as though

someone followed her."

Mandy gasped. She told Kyrissa to wait until tomorrow to deliver those damn paintings so Mandy could go with her. She obviously chose not to wait.

"Luckily, she thought to duck into a diner and wait to see if anyone passed. Then she called you."

"And I didn't answer." Mandy exhaled. Kyrissa was the reason Mandy had remained so focused all these years. Since Mandy had lost her mother first, she felt a protectiveness about Kyrissa's own grief because they shared that one feeling like no one else. Only sometimes, it felt deeper than that, as if the universe knew the bonds between the two existed and expected Mandy to ensure their stability.

"I convinced her to take a sleeping pill to ease her mind and promised I wouldn't leave until you arrived home." Her father checked his expensive watch, the last gift her mother had ever bought him. "I had no idea I'd be waiting so long."

Just past two in the morning, Mandy wished she'd come straight home after talking to Jay. Instead, she wandered a few well-lit streets, snapping pictures at random, and contemplating what she learned tonight. Lucien, not Kyrissa, consumed her thoughts.

"I'm here now." Mandy sighed, giving into the heaviness in her chest that had stalked her all night.

"For how long? Until the next band is playing? Or the next rock star comes along who you want to endorse, or whatever it is that you do." Her father stilled. In the light that peeked through the front window, his strong, square jaw clenched tighter. Even in his later years, he was one of the most handsome men she knew, rivaled only by a guy who barely was a man.

"That's not fair." Setting her camera on the island, she crossed her arms over her chest.

Her father cleared his throat. "Your first responsibility is to that girl in there," he said, pointing towards Kyrissa. "She needs you to protect her. If her gifts are used by the wrong person, there is no telling who might be harmed."

"I know that," Mandy bit back. They'd had this discussion more times than she could count or wished to relive. Every time, her father shut down just before he exposed the one secret he guarded so tightly and Mandy walked away no closer to answers than before they talked.

"Then act like it." His glare consumed her, but she wouldn't look away. "What do you know about this professor of hers? She seems to spend an awful lot of time in his presence."

"There's not much to know," Mandy admitted, curious at the turn of conversation. "No criminal record, hell, there's barely any mention in any public records. Just a birth, some college graduations, a few teaching awards. Nothing alarming, nothing out of place."

"You have to dig deeper."

"I've dug as deep as I can," Mandy countered. She didn't mention that she spent that very afternoon trying to dig up whatever she could on the man, only to finally admit to herself that he was spotless. And somehow the man was more elusive to her camera than Lucien. The one clear opportunity to take a picture of the professor showed nothing. It was completely blank, as if he didn't exist at all or else was a master at hiding, even from her camera.

"I know what it's like to be torn between two worlds. To have someone counting on you to protect them and the one time you look away is the one time they need you most." He sighed, lowering himself back down onto the chaise. "And you're not there," he whispered.

Not tonight. Mandy couldn't have the Guardian conversation tonight, not after Jay. It was late, exhaustion owned her, and quite frankly, she simply wasn't up for the fight.

"The way I needed the truth from you and mom?" Mandy threw a punch below the belt regardless of his exacerbated state. She didn't care.

"You want to know why we lied?" Her father didn't look up to meet her eyes. "Because you weren't supposed to happen. For two people who had sworn oaths to protect others, falling in love was bad enough. A baby?" He finally lifted his gaze to meet hers. "Your existence severed those oaths and everyone involved suffered for it. We didn't want anyone to blame you for our mistakes."

"A mistake." Mandy snorted. The skin around her tattoo itched and burned. "My only mistake was thinking that you would ever be half the man mom thought you were."

"I didn't mean that the way it sounded." He tried to correct his words but Mandy had already heard them. "We wanted you. More than anything either of us ever wanted. But we weren't supposed to have you. It put too many people at risk. So we fled to Romania before you were born and started over there. We left our charges, our oaths, ignored our responsibilities, so that we could bring you into our world even though it wasn't safe for you to be there."

Mandy didn't move. Her father had never opened up this much before and she wasn't sure he ever would again. It didn't matter that his words were harsh or difficult to hear. She asked for the truth and he finally gave her what she wanted, whether she was prepared for it or not.

"And after you were born, we couldn't risk anyone learning the truth." He looked up. Pain radiated from his gaze. "Not even you."

"Well." Mandy adjusted her footing. She held onto the island countertop, barely able to keep her feet grounded. As it was, the air in her lungs thickened, making every breath she took feel like breathing in a thick poisoned fog that stung her lungs. After a moment of hesitation, she composed herself the best she could manage. "I am not ignoring my responsibilities. I can enjoy music, take pictures of bands, and still make sure Kyrissa isn't impaled by the universe. She's like a sister to me and I will protect her for as long as she lets me."

"That's just it, sweetheart." Her father stepped closer and took both hands in his. "You have to protect her even when she thinks she doesn't need it."

Behind her friend's closed door, Mandy heard the familiar groans of a nightmare. Sounds she heard more and more frequently. It seemed sleeping pills actually made Kyrissa's sleep more restless.

"Thank you for bringing her home tonight." Mandy inhaled as deep as her lungs allowed. "I have to go check on her."

"Of course." Her father pulled her into a big protective hug. "You know I love you both dearly. You are my only daughter and she is..." her father's words trailed when Kyrissa's scream filled the apartment.

Mandy didn't wait to hear her father finish his speech, tearing out of his arms and rushing to Kyrissa's room.

"Shh," she whispered into her best friend's ear. "I'm here now."

Kyrissa stirred only slightly, the sleeping pills stronger than her petite frame, but she calmed as soon as Mandy touched her. Mandy curled up beside her and only barely heard the sound of the front door closing.

Mandy wanted the truth. She got it from both Jay and her father. She hadn't even needed her camera this time. Unlike her photographs, these truths held no beauty. Only pain and disappointment. Mandy blinked against the sting at the back her eyes.

Tomorrow she'd set Lucien free to follow his dreams and focus on protecting her best friend so that Kyrissa could live to dream another day. The universe had an odd sense of humor and way of showing that sometimes, you can't have it all. Tonight was one of those nights. Mandy wished she could wake up tomorrow morning and pretend today never happened.

CHAPTER FORTY

"Stop fidgeting," Carmen whispered out of the corner of her mouth.

"I can't help it." Lucien pulled at the tie around his neck, swearing the knot got tighter with each passing moment. Sitting on a carved wooden bench against the side wall of the small paneled meeting room, Carmen jabbed him in the ribs.

Meetings with art clients wasn't his gig. Normally, Carmen handled that end of the business. And suits definitely were not his thing. The new dark blue material itched, the white shirt starched hard as a board, and a lock of his hair insisted on falling into his eyes every time he shifted in his seat.

"Why exactly am I here?" He questioned Carmen once more. A quick glance towards Robert and the German art dealer sitting in the leather chairs of the reception area, the hum of their low conversation unbroken, assured Lucien he hadn't been overheard. "Things are back on track. All the paperwork filed. My job is done."

"You're now officially the managing art director of *The Shoalman Collection*." Carmen raised a single eyebrow at him. "In order to do your job properly, you *need* to understand the process from the start of the request discussions, through the contract negotiations, and ending with the show arrangements." Carmen fixed him with an intense stare.

Lucien rolled his eyes. What he really needed was to be composing all the music that had exploded in his head since his night with Mandy. What a night. And the morning after... He grabbed at his tie again. Had the room gotten hotter? Lucien barely contained his squirm as certain parts reacted stronger than others to the memory. He didn't dare look at Carmen, but he heard a stifled snicker.

Opening her portfolio, Carmen jotted down a quick note before tilting it for him to see. *"Robert's forcing you to stay here because he knows it makes you uncomfortable. Don't let him see you sweat."*

Great. It wasn't Robert causing the perspiration but his sister didn't need to know that. He reached over and made a note under hers *"I hate you so much right now."*

Carmen smiled at him. She loved this crap. The tension, the challenge. She thrived on it. He'd rather be standing in some loud, smelly bar with Mandy checking out his competition. Lucien grimaced. Well, what *would* have been his competition. He still wasn't sure how he was going to explain quitting the band to Mandy. Avoiding her texts and calls would only work for so long.

"Mr. Solvak." Robert's voice was quiet, but the burr in the inflection made every hair on the back of his neck stand on end. Shit. He hadn't been paying attention again.

"Forgive me, Mr. Shoalman, Mr. Kappel. I was contemplating some of the logistics of the tour," Lucien said, improvising. Glad Robert didn't actually know how to use the Romani evil eye, or else more than his skin might be crawling right now. At least the client bought the explanation.

"*Güt.*" Mr. Kappel exclaimed. "I like that you are already planning the tour."

"There is still the contract additions to negotiate and complete, Mr. Kappel." Robert glared at Lucien.

"I leave that to my lawyer." He gestured to the small man standing at attention behind him. "He knows my terms. As do you, Mr. Shoalman."

"Then perhaps Mr. Solvak can show you our warehouse operations and provide a tour of the mini studio we have here on the premise while *my* lawyer," Carmen stood at Robert's introduction, "hashes out the details with yours." Robert gestured to the office door and Lucien jumped to his feet.

"Right this way, Mr. Kappel." Lucien launched into the speech that he had given to so many managers before. Logistics, shipping and receiving requirements, all the details of a tour that anyone could even possibly think of and a few they didn't know to ask. The past twenty-four hours had ingrained those details forever. Ending his presentation just as they reached the gallery Robert maintained within the warehouse, Lucien allowed the two artists to peruse the pieces alone. With his part of the presentation complete, Lucien let his thoughts wander. They immediately went to Mandy.

A smile crept out. Just thinking about her and the night they spent together brought the shit-eating grin to his face no matter how hard he tried to hide it. The muted lighting of the warehouse reminded him of the candles burning in her room. His first time had been nothing like he expected and more than he ever dreamed. His angel had showed him how to fly.

Lucien sighed. He should have just stayed with Mandy like she asked. His world didn't seem so fucked up when he was around her. The new song played over and over in his head. He shoved it away.

"Excuse me, Mr. Shoalman." Carmen intruded. "I need to borrow Mr. Solvak for a moment to go over some security questions." When Robert nodded, Carmen grabbed him painfully by the arm.

"Ow. What's your problem?" Lucien rubbed at the spot where his sister had pinched him.

"My problem is that your girlfriend is outside the freaking warehouse." Harsh whispers boomed in Lucien's ears in time with the pounding of his heart.

"Mandy is here?" Lucien stiffened. If Robert found out, he was dead.

"I managed to catch her before she rang the buzzer and tried to get her to come back later. She wasn't having any of it. Had to talk to you, she said. Something about you ignoring her calls. Damn near challenged me to make her go away. Feisty." Carmen smirked. "Cute too."

"Not now." He checked where Robert and the client stood, a frown marring Robert's face. "Can you cover for me for a little bit?"

"Hurry up. And, Lucien." Carmen paused in her interception of Robert. "You owe me big."

Lucien waved her off. Carmen invited Robert and Mr. Kappel to come get some refreshments. Her arm linked through Robert's, she visibly dragged him away. Yeah he was going to pay for that. As soon as they were out of sight, Lucien ran to the warehouse door.

Mandy was here.

His body sang with the thought, even as the more rational part of his brain knew she couldn't stay. It didn't matter. Mandy was worth the risk, even worth losing his dreams with the band. As long as he had Mandy, he could find a way to live without the music. He hoped.

CHAPTER FORTY-ONE

The effervescent look on Lucien's face when he came to the door almost made Mandy lose her resolve. Something about his naivety and innocence shot arrows straight through her chest, plunging deeper and deeper with each passing moment.

Or maybe the suit he wore caused the sudden ache. The way his shoulders filled the jacket, imagining the buttons of the crisp white shirt undone to reveal the sculpted chest beneath. How easy it would be to twirl the tie on his neck around her fist and pull him close enough to... *to what?* To do nothing. Setting Lucien free was the only way he'd ever live his dream. She needed to snip the tie and let him loose.

She spent the rest of the *Spiral's* show trying to ignore every word Jay told her. Whatever else Lucien did last night, he spent it ignoring every one of her texts. If he quit the band for her, evading her questions confirmed the truth more than any explanation he could have attempted to give her.

Each time the audience cheered for a song she knew Jay could play a hundred times better in his sleep, Mandy became even more convinced she had to walk away from Lucien before it was too late.

Rock star could be Lucien's middle name. He had unbelievable good looks, the physique of a god, and the panty melting voice to go along with them. With the right opportunity, he was destined to win over any agent that heard him sing, to command any crowd lucky enough to watch him perform. Hell, he'd almost stolen the heart of the girl who had no intention of ever giving it up. Almost.

Now she just needed to get this over.

"We need to talk." She tried to push her way inside but Lucien blocked the doorway.

"This isn't a good time," Lucien said, his voice strained. "You can't be here now."

He led Mandy away from the warehouse, into the dark alley on the side of the brick building, away from the bright lights that hung over the warehouse door. Here, she could only see him through the light of cars passing on the street at the end of the alley.

"Here's just as fine a place as any." For Mandy, it was better than inside the building where memories of the night Lucien pushed her up against the wall and gave her the hottest orgasm she'd ever had persisted.

"You can't quit *Demon Dogs*," she spit out.

"How did you—" Lucien shook his head. "Fucking Jay."

"I don't care if you won't let me take pictures, if you don't want my endorsement. I don't even care if I have zero part in your debut," Mandy continued. If she didn't get this out now, she never would. "But you can't quit, not now."

"Jay didn't exactly give me any options."

"So it's true. You're throwing away your dreams? For what?"

"Jay is jealous that I'm with you," Lucien huffed. "He claimed I had to choose between you and the band. Said two members of a band can't be in love with the same girl."

"That word's getting a lot of use recently, and not by me," Mandy stated. Love? If one more person threw that word at her, she would start punching first and apologize later. She wasn't in love with anyone. Where Lucien was concerned, Mandy admitted only to lust.

And one hundred percent? Mandy wasn't one hundred percent anything unless it involved her photography and so far, no photograph Lucien let her take had shown love, hers or his. No way was she in love with Lucien Solvak. She didn't do strings. Ever. They just tangled you up inside until they strangled you.

"I told him to get over himself. He had his chance and blew it."

Lucien tried to reach for her hand. Mandy stepped back, crossing her arms in front of her. Brows furrowed, his hand lingered between them. Mandy prayed he wouldn't touch her. So close, she need only lean forward... *No.* She shifted another half step out of his reach.

His hand dropped to his thigh, to tap out a nervous rhythm against his leg. "Jay said choose. I did."

"Jay has nothing to be jealous of where you and I are concerned," Mandy said flatly. She looked away, but not before she heard him inhale too deeply. "It's not like we're an item for him to worry about. I am not the reason you should even be considering dropping the band."

"Wait," Lucien paused. "You'd want me to pick the band over you? What about this?" Lucien waved between them. "What about us?" he asked.

Mandy ached to grab his hand and press it against her cheek. She wanted to feel the warmth that radiated from Lucien the way the sun warmed her skin on the coldest day of the year. She wished she could beg him to pull her closer, hold her to his body. But she couldn't. Where Lucien always pulled, Mandy always pushed. This time, she needed to push harder.

"There is no us." Mandy hated the contradiction between her words and thoughts. She hated how convincing the words sounded when she hadn't meant them at all.

"But I thought," Lucien stammered, the hope fading quickly from his eyes, replaced only with confusion.

"What did I think?" He shook his head, running his hand over his scruffy jaw.

"You thought just because I let you get me off a couple of times, fucked you on my bed, that it meant more than it did." Mandy winced at the harshness spewing from her lips when all she wanted was to wrap her mouth around Lucien's jaw, lick his neck and then further. "Common mistake," she lied. "Sex, Lucien. That's all. Nothing more, nothing less."

"It wasn't just sex for me." Lucien crossed his hands over his heart. "It was the first time I..."

The silence that lingered haunted the air. *It was his first time what?*

Mandy clenched her eyes shut. Looking into his baby blue eyes, so full of innocence, would only confirm her worst nightmare.

Please dear God do not make me Lucien Solvak's first.

"Never mind. Obviously, it's not like you'd care."

"You want me to care?" Mandy tempted fate. "Tell me your secret. What are you so desperate to hide?"

His shoulders slumped, fists tight at his sides. Shadows swallowed the bright energy that always infused Mandy when she was around Lucien, leaving a black emptiness behind. That blackness didn't exist before Mandy. If she didn't let him go now, he'd turn darker the longer he was with her. Just like everyone else who'd gotten close.

"You know I can't do that." Lucien sank lower.

"And you know I can't live with secrets."

"You should just go."

"Look. It's not like I didn't tell you from the beginning that there would be no strings," Mandy reminded him. In fact, she had even heard Jay mention it to Lucien on several occasions.

"Right. No secrets, no strings," Lucien repeated, his voice flat. Lifeless. He stared off into the darkness of the warehouse. "You've made yourself pretty clear on the subject. Now go. I have a band rehearsal to attend, if they still want me." Lucien shuffled back towards the warehouse. He stopped with his hand on the door handle and called over his shoulder. "By the way, the band's new name... I wanted something that would last." He locked his gaze on her. "It's Eternity."

Mandy didn't think the knife could sink any deeper or twist any harder. With a single word, she'd been wrong.

CHAPTER FORTY-TWO

The warehouse door clicked closed severing any connect from Mandy. *"It was just sex."* He staggered sideways, the wall behind him the only thing keeping him on his feet. Lucien slammed his head backwards into the corrugated metal. The pain nothing compared to the agony ripping apart his heart. "I am such a fucking idiot."

"You're eighteen, that's a given fact," Carmen quipped from the corner. "Is she gone?"

"Don't worry." His shoulders slumped forward. "She won't be back."

"Too bad. Under other circumstances, like not showing up uninvited, she looks like she could be a lot of fun."

"You have no idea," Lucien mumbled. Visions of their night together intruded no matter how hard he screwed his eyes shut. At least if he had Mandy, the loss of his music might have been bearable. The ache inside twisted. Now he had neither.

"You didn't!" Carmen squawked. Lucien snapped his head up to see his sister staring at him open mouthed. "Holy crap. You did."

Pushing off the wall, Lucien attempted to sneak past. Heat flushed his face and neck. He was so not going to discuss his sex life with his sister. "I have to finish the inventory before Robert finds another reason to yell at me." The hard grip on his arm stopped him.

"Oh no you don't. There is no way you are going to drop that bombshell and think I'm letting it go."

"Carmen, I am *not* discussing my...we are not having this conversation." He tried to disengage his arm, but Carmen didn't let go. "You're my sister for crying out loud. Just. No."

"And who exactly were you going to talk to? Robert?" She smirked. Lucien blanched white. "Or better yet, Mama T? I'm not sure if she would disown you or start planning your wedding."

Lucien groaned and collapsed onto a nearby crate. Dropping his face into his hands, the weight of what he had done crashed down on him like an overloaded pallet of crates. He thought Mandy cared. How stupid could he be? Now everything was fucked up. His Guardianship, his music, even Mandy. He ripped off his tie in one motion, gasping like a drowning man. "Oh god. I'm so screwed."

"I hope so, if you did it right."

"Okay, we're done." Lucien shoved to his feet but Carmen pulled him back.

"I'm sorry," she chuckled. "Couldn't resist. I was beginning to wonder—"

"Carmen!" Lucien snapped.

"Look, this is not as bad as you are making it out to be." Carmen paused. "Unless what I overheard was true. You didn't actually quit the band did you?"

"You were listening?" He glared at her.

"Only for part of the time." Carmen laid a hand on his arm. "You're not seriously contemplating giving up your music are you?"

"What am I supposed to do?" Lucien ran his hands through his hair. Pushing to his feet, he paced back and forth in the narrow receiving area. "Robert needs me here, although for what I have no idea and according to him, I'm never going to understand." Tension built inside of him like a volcano waiting to erupt. "The band was a dream. I should've known better. And Mandy..." The pain in his chest twisted harder. Jay had been right. Sharp. Painful. Like he said—a wound that didn't heal. "I never should have let her get close. Never should have—Fuck." Throwing all his weight forward, his fist connected with the wall. Pain radiated up his arm.

"Lucien, stop!" Carmen grabbed his hand, examining it for damage. "You break your hand and the band *will* be a dream with the opening only three days away."

Lucien let her drag him into Robert's empty office. His knuckles throbbed, the skin torn and painful. But nothing compared to the ache in his chest at the thought of losing his music. And Mandy. "What do I do, Carmen? I've screwed up everything. Lost it all."

"First, you need to stop feeling sorry for yourself."

"I'm not—" He stopped with one glaring look from his sister. Okay, well maybe he was being a bit overdramatic. Mandy said Jay wanted him back and that she'd write the article about the band, endorsing them. He still had three days until their re-launch. The marketing was ready to go. The songs and stage show set. He even had the name now. Still he balked.

"Second, you admit the real reason you're holding back."

"The real reason?" On the edge of the cliff, an abyss beckoned. Lucien wasn't sure he wanted to acknowledge that hollowness yet.

Carmen huffed and propped her hands on her hips. "Is music just a hobby?"

Lucien ground his teeth. The cold harsh emptiness erupted like a raging volcano.

"That. Right there." Carmen poked him in the chest. "Even thinking about your music in those terms pisses you off."

And the lawyer gets right to the heart of the matter. Music. *Your life. Your choice,* his father had said. Lucien ran his hand over a crate. One of thousands.

Centuries of the past surrounded him in the warehouse. Robert's past. It was time to leave his own legacy. Or at least start one.

"What do you want?" Carmen asked.

"I want the dream," he whispered. "The band." Carmen finished bandaging his hand. He flexed the fingers. Less than forty-eight hours ago he had caressed skin so soft and warm, it seemed a different kind a dream. One he wasn't willing to let go without a fight. Lucien snorted. "And the girl. I want her too. So fucking bad it hurts."

"Then fight for both of them. And not by punching walls." His sister's smile radiated understanding and support. "Only you can decide if the dream, the whole dream, is worth the sacrifice."

"I have to tell Robert this isn't just a hobby. That music is part of my life." Lucien swallowed. Carmen nodded. He took a slow, deep breath. Confronting Robert meant admitting everything. All Lucien's secrets. Including Mandy. "Where is he?"

"If *he* means me, then I am right here." Robert walked into his office. Seating himself behind his antique wooden desk, he waited, formal...controlled. Everything Lucien wasn't right now.

"Is Mr. Kappel gone? The tour..."

"Everything is finalized and Mr. Kappel appeased. He and his lawyer left to catch their flight." Robert steepled his fingers. "Did you have something further to discuss?"

Lucien's mind blanked. How did he explain to someone who had lived for five hundred years that he wanted to *start* living? Carmen nudged him from behind. Her hands crossed over her heart; the Romani gesture to give completely of oneself. Except it meant so much more. Lucien straightened his entire six-foot-one frame and faced the waiting stare of Robert.

"I'm debuting in a band called *Eternity* in three days. There will be an article and an entire marketing plan to promote the band." Lucien clenched his fists. "This isn't a one-time gig either. I love music. I love writing lyrics. I love to perform. I need it, just like you need to paint. Well, when you paint for yourself, that is, not for the curse." Lucien faltered until a poke from behind redirected him. "What I'm saying is, music is a part of my life. I can handle both the band and my duties to protect you. I know I can. Maybe not perfectly at first. But I'm learning. I'm gonna make mistakes." Lucien cringed, "Probably big ones at first, but the point is, it's my life too. I want to start living it." Lucien held his breath.

"Anything else?" Robert hadn't moved from the high back leather chair behind his desk during Lucien's entire rambling explanation.

"Yeah. There's this girl." A cold sweat crept down his back. Bringing a stranger into their world didn't affect just Lucien. Her presence could put everyone at risk, including her and her family. "I think she can handle being in our world, safely. There's something about her, I don't know, I just..." He didn't want to mention that Mandy saw his white ink tattoos if he didn't have to. Nor her unique ability with a camera. Not yet. "My gut tells me she'll be okay. That she belongs."

"I should have known there was a woman involved." Robert shook his head. "No wonder you have been acting like such a fool." He looked pointedly at Lucien's bandage before he could tuck it out of sight. "So what do you need from me?"

Lucien stood with his mouth open. No shouting. No rants about strangers invading their secret world. He sank into the worn leather seat behind him, the chair creaking beneath his weight. "That's it?"

"Would you rather I yelled?"

"No." Maybe he did need to hear Robert raise his voice, anything that would make Lucien realize how crazy he sounded right now. "Wait, you're okay with all this?"

"When I agreed to your demands, I accepted all of them."

Lucien sat a little taller in the chair. Was it possible? Had Robert really accepted his choices? Even though he feared to break this newfound approval, Lucien pressed for confirmation. "So you have no issues with my music debut?"

"I have looked over your marketing plan. Thorough. Complete. Well thought out. You have done your homework for the market and on how to protect yourself, and me, from discovery from outside sources." Dark creases framed Robert's eyes. Lucien braced for the impending 'but'. "We will, however, discuss the use of certain photos in your stage show."

"That wasn't a no..." Lucien wasn't surprised the paintings were a contention point. The silence crackled with anticipation. With each passing second, building energy from the pending answer washed over Lucien until he vibrated. He held Robert's gaze. This was his moment. He refused to shy away from the choices he made. Not now. Not after he fought so hard to get here.

"I always knew you had interests outside the art world and beyond protecting me. I respect the professionalism you have displayed in connecting those interests."

"So I can use them?" Once Robert saw how he planned to stage Mandy's photos, Lucien was sure he could convince him to allow them.

Robert sighed. "We can discuss the prospect, *if* you can prove to me the paintings will not cause anyone harm."

It took all of Lucien's willpower not to whoop with joy, but one other item needed clarification. "And Mandy? What about her?"

"She will require further investigation before I am willing to trust her with my secret." Robert fixed him with a look that would wither most people into dust. Lucien nodded. This wasn't a negotiable point. "Her full name would be a good place to start."

"Amanda Hayworth." Lucien blinked. Did Robert just flinch?

"Keep your mouth shut around Ms. Hayworth, Lucien," Robert said. "If you can, then we may avoid having to pack up and move. *Again.* I would rather stay here, at least long enough to give your Grandmother's vision time to play out."

This time, Lucien did whoop. Grabbing Carmen, he spun her in a circle, her laughter echoing in his ear. He dropped her to the ground as plans raced through his head.

"I need to call Jay and get the guys together. See if they'll take me back." He paced. There had to be a way to have both the band and Mandy. Never did he expect Jay to be a harder sell than Robert. "We'll have to practice. Tonight. Non-stop. And the final press releases have to go out." Lucien stopped. Robert still watched him. "You never planned on stopping me from my music, did you?"

"We all have our talents, Lucien. You just needed to figure out what you wanted to do when you grew up." A corner of Robert's mouth quirked upwards. "I am still waiting for you to grow up."

"Thanks. I think." He kissed his sister on the cheek preparing to leave and she whispered into his ear.

"You have one part of the dream. Now go get the other one."

"I plan on it," Lucien replied. Mandy awoke a new level in his music, one he wasn't sure he could reach without her. Now Lucien needed to convince her to be part of his picture in spite of herself.

CHAPTER FORTY-THREE

It wasn't often that Mandy stared at a grouping of her own photographs and wanted to rip them to shreds. Her nails dug into the palms of her hands, Mandy held her fists tight against her body to avoid punching something. Anything.

Looking at the images of Lucien Solvak made her want to do exactly that. Too blurry, partially hidden, one was only a close up of his ear, none were even remotely usable for her article.

"These are all crap." Pushing the photographs off the table, Mandy prevented only one of the images from falling to the floor, one where the corner of Lucien's mouth was curled in a smile.

"I disagree," Kyrissa said. She stood over the images scattered on the floor, rearranging them like a puzzle. Mandy thought about which ones she could light on fire without her roommate getting burned.

"Sometimes, you have to look at things from a different perspective," Kyrissa said. "Look how these lines would match up if this picture was larger." She took the very first image Mandy captured of Lucien and overlapped one that showed only his shoulder. At an odd angle, the second image appeared as if Lucien just leaned down and she snapped the picture from above him.

Mandy took a step back. In the haze surrounding Lucien that first time she saw him, a subtle orange-red band of color streaked across the brick wall behind where Lucien stood. His shoulders squared, head held high, confidence ebbed and flowed, filling the blurry image in a way Mandy hadn't noticed before now.

Kyrissa aligned another image with the two photographs on the ground. A close up of the left side of his face, Lucien's hair fell in front of his eyes. Mandy remembered cursing that piece of hair for covering the deep blue, but now she wanted to stroke the dark strand of hair. The blue that stared out between the strands was softer than Mandy remembered. Peacefulness resonated out from a glare so intense Mandy could hardly look away. Blue. The color shimmered from the photo with a depth that couldn't exist in real life.

"You might be onto something." Mandy grabbed another image, laying it over the section of the blurry image that contained Lucien's arm. The new image showed an exposed forearm where Lucien had pushed up his shirtsleeve, letting the white line tattoos shine over his skin. From each line, gold hovered in the lighting above his arm. The color of enlightenment and divine protection.

"Of course," Mandy muttered. She wasn't speaking to Kyrissa, or anyone else. "Why didn't I see this before?" She kept arranging the images on the ground until she was certain she had an entire portrait of Lucien Solvak.

In those few moments when he relaxed enough to let her in, it left him unguarded. He showed her truths ingrained so deeply within himself, so protected, this was the only way he dared to share, to let his real self be known to her. This was her Lucien. The Lucien she wanted to share with the world without giving him entirely away.

"Because you were too busy looking at the partial images to see the whole picture." Kyrissa placed a hand on Mandy's shoulder. "It's not to scale, but that is the most amazing portrait of anyone I've ever seen."

"Everyone's a puzzle." Mandy smiled. The mystery of Lucien was much deeper than she imagined the first time she met him, but unraveling it just became more satisfying than she ever dreamed. "Until you put together the pieces."

"And you put together the pieces all right." Kyrissa nodded. "Uh, now what do you intend to do with them?"

"My article." Mandy quickly grabbed the images from the floor. She shoved them into her favorite portfolio case. "I have to get to the printer and enlarge a few of these," she said, slamming her laptop shut. She didn't take the time to put the photos into any sort of order, knowing which images she needed to reprint and exactly where each one belonged in the larger picture that would make the image of Lucien sing.

Then she'd share it with whoever wanted to listen.

CHAPTER FORTY-FOUR

Lucien rang the security box buzzer for the third time. Stepping back, he looked up at the top floor. If he started to yell, or maybe sing, that might get Mandy to answer. He tried her phone. Straight to voicemail, just as it had been for the past three days. Guess he understood how that felt now.

Running a hand through his hair, Lucien checked the time. Thirty minutes left before he met with the band. Jay agreed to let him back in the band, but at a cost. Discussion of Mandy was off limits. At least until after the re-launch tonight.

About to press the buzzer again, Mandy's roommate opened the outside foyer door.

"You must be Lucien."

"She's mentioned me?" Lucien's pulse doubled. If Mandy's friend knew about him, then maybe there was hope.

"She kinda had to after I saw you leaving the apartment the other morning."

Blood rushed to his face. Oh shit. He had forgotten about that little meeting. "Oh, yeah. Right." What the hell did he say now? Scuffing his boot along the marble step, the silence dragged on. He didn't have time for this. "Look, I really need to see her."

"She's not here," Kyrissa stated. Arms crossed over a beat-up old sweatshirt and wrinkled pair of pajama pants, Lucien got a sense he must have woke her up.

The pillow creases on her cheek confirmed his hunch.

"If she's just avoiding me, I'll take the heat." Not normally pushy, Lucien prepared to barge into the building if necessary. "I'll tell her you tried to stop me."

"Seriously." Kyrissa planted herself firmly in front of him, arms baring his way. "She's off printing a few pictures for the blog post on your band."

"She's writing the article?" Lucien took a step back.

"Provided you're still in the band." She glared at him with a look Lucien was certain she learned from Mandy. "So are you?"

"It's complicated." Lucien sunk to sit on the top of the stone steps. "Yes, for now. I guess." Lucien sighed. "I don't know exactly where I stand. Or how long the band will keep me around. Hell, I barely know what day it is right now. The last few days have been a blur." All of them filled with songs and images of Mandy. "I don't know anything anymore. Especially where Mandy Hayworth is concerned." A light touch settled on his shoulder as Kyrissa sat beside him.

"Mandy is complicated."

Lucien snorted. "Now there's an understatement." He studied the petite blonde sitting next to him, bare feet tucked under her. A quiet intensity pulsed from Kyrissa, familiar somehow. Comforting. "You know her better than me. What do I do? How can I get her to give me, us, a chance?"

Kyrissa picked at the paint flecks on her nails. Her face contorted, smoothed out, and then scrunched up once more. Every passing second coiled his muscles tighter, his body ready to spring forth from the tension—or break under it. Lucien forced himself to stillness, afraid he'd break the fragile thread of hope he saw forming. *Please* his mind begged.

"Be yourself."

"Myself?" Which self, Lucien wondered. The rock star she expected? The guy who was head over heels for her? Or the Guardian she could never know?

"Mandy has a knack for seeing the things people don't want her to. Don't lie to her." She smiled. "She'll know if you do."

Lucien stared at his hands. What Kyrissa wanted was impossible. A sundering of his two worlds settled into a stabbing ache, chilling him to his core. He could never tell Mandy about his life as a Guardian. His oaths forbade it. "Some secrets are not mine to tell," Lucien mumbled. He pushed to his feet, holding out his hand to help Kyrissa to hers.

"I'll tell Mandy you were looking for her. That the two of you need to talk."

"Thanks." He turned to walk down the street.

"Lucien," she called, standing in the doorway. "Don't give up on Mandy. She understands more than you think. She can be stubborn and pigheaded, and sometimes a bit bossy." Kyrissa opened and closed her mouth several times as if arguing with herself before finally coming to a decision. "She's also completely devoted when she cares about someone. And she cares about you more than she's ready to admit." Snapping her mouth shut, she went inside.

Lucien wasn't sure how long he stared after Kyrissa, but people started to give him strange looks. He walked towards Gallery and his last practice with the band, the city passing by unnoticed. His eyes open, yet he didn't see. People talking, cars passing, life happening all around him—all of it faded into the haze of nothingness.

Mandy understands.

White tattoos, marks Mandy should never be able to see, separated him from her greater than any abyss. The intricate lines wrapped his arms yet his oaths marked him even deeper. A side he could never share with her. Lucien never regretted his choice to become Robert's Guardian, still didn't, but he regretted the secrets his choice created.

Now he needed to talk to Mandy more than ever. To tell her goodbye.

CHAPTER FORTY-FIVE

"Amanda Hayworth?"

Mandy turned on the front step of her apartment building just before her hand reached to press in the security code. A guy about her age hovered much closer than comfortable for Mandy to let down her guard. His eyes darted over her shoulder into the foyer of her apartment building. If he wasn't dressed formally in a crisp white shirt and pressed black pants, Mandy would have already pulled out her pepper spray.

That his dark brooding looks were kinda hot helped, too.

"That depends." With the images finally printed for the picture she intended to use in her article, she didn't exactly have time to entertain the smiles of a stranger or the questions of an eager fan, even a good-looking one. She had two hours to compile the images into one that would capture the essence of Lucien well enough to show everyone else what she saw in him. In eight hours, he'd perform for the first time in the local scene. Mandy intended he did it in front of the perfect crowd, a crowd prepared to fall so hard for him, they would never recover.

"I am looking for the Amanda Hayworth who is friends with one Lucien Solvak. Perhaps you know him?"

Mandy paused, her fingers clutched an oversized

folder of images tucked under her arm. The longer she stood still, the more it threatened to slip from her grasp. At her side, the metal body of her camera slapped against her hip and the strap of her laptop bag fell from her shoulder.

"I know Lucien." She knew him well and missed him more than she cared to admit.

"My name is Robert Shoalman and I wish for a moment of your time to discuss our Lucien."

Robert Shoalman. "You're Lucien's boss?" Lucien worked for the heir apparent of an art collection that spanned centuries. Kyrissa had been yammering about that collection for years but even more so when they announced a showing of the works nearby. Mandy had even agreed to go. "No wonder he's so afraid of you. I for one, don't care who you are."

"Hmm," Robert sighed. "I certainly wish we had met under different circumstances. I think you would find that working together would greatly benefit our mutual friend, if not be an asset to us both."

"Lucien is not mine to discuss," Mandy huffed. Why hadn't Lucien told her he worked with *The Shoalman Collection*? She might have been slightly more understanding of his work load, or at least pretended to understand. Turning to enter the code into the security pad, the envelope slid further from under her arm.

"Allow me," Robert said behind her, grabbing the photographs before they ended up scattered across the city sidewalk. He pulled the door open at the sound of the latch releasing.

Normally she wouldn't allow a strange man into her building, but his mention of Lucien piqued her curiosity. She'd seen him jumped at a simple text from this man. Kyrissa practically worshipped him.

"Thank you," Mandy said, grateful her computer bag waited until she was inside the foyer before it dropped to the floor. Fingers repositioning the camera at her side, she briefly considered taking Robert's picture. The intensity of the stare focused on her stalled the air around her. Of their own volition, Mandy's fingers reversed their movement, sliding away from the button that would lay all this man's secrets bare. She wondered what he hid. Unfortunately, she didn't have time for that mystery.

"Whatever you have to say about Lucien, please say it. I'm late."

"Direct." Robert smiled. "A trait I appreciate."

"Well, I have a picture to create, an article to finish writing and post ASAP, and not enough time to do it." Mandy reached for the envelope just as Robert placed the images on an antique credenza in the foyer. The two motions collided, scattering various photographs all over the marble floor.

Robert sighed, reaching down to collect a photograph. Eyes narrowing, he scanned the images Mandy planned to use in her final exclusive. "Are all of these of Lucien?" he asked.

"Yes," Mandy said piling the pictures on top of each other.

"I will admit, I do not recall this part of Lucien's marketing plan."

"Not sure it was a part of anyone's plan. Funny story though." Lucien was right. He had no claim to the title of control freak with Robert Shoalman around. But there was no way this arrogant artist was going to stop her plans. Each second that passed was one less moment her blog followers had access to Lucien's marketing. "He wouldn't sit for a photograph and only let me take one candid picture every day, none of which turned out usable on their own, due to unforeseen circumstances. Some he moved and blurred the image. A couple I'd taken up close on purpose a few were too far away and the angle off. So I've cropped them to suit my needs." Mandy laughed, the memories of Lucien always made her smile. Until she remembered she pushed him away. "Now this is what I have to work with."

"Individually, these are more interesting than I would expect." Robert said holding up a picture of Lucien's scruff covered jaw line. It was Mandy's favorite amongst the pictures and brought back memories she wished it hadn't. "But I am not certain what these will accomplish."

Mandy snagged the photo in a quick yank and threw it on the floor again. She placed a second one beside it and lined yet another up under those two. After a few seconds, Robert gasped over her shoulder as the larger picture took shape. What had appeared as blurry backgrounds before now silhouetted Lucien's entire form in a way even Mandy had never seen. Distinct. It entrapped his very essence.

"Impressive." Robert took a step back. "You have managed to capture every element of our young friend, as well as some elements Lucien usually manages to hide from most people."

"Despite whatever secrets he thinks I can't handle, he wasn't trying too hard to hide from me," Mandy admitted. "I was just too blind to see it." She may not know everything about Lucien Solvak, but she knew enough to trust whatever reason he had to withhold information from her.

Mandy laid the final image in place. His eyes. Blue so intense it filled her dreams at night.

Robert's sharp inhale echoed in the silence of the foyer.

"That boy could not hide himself from you if he *had* tried." Robert crouched down. Tracing the faint white lines that covered Lucien's forearm, Robert sighed. "This mosaic of Lucien is remarkable. But your photography is rather... inspiring."

"Look, I don't know what you're doing here, but if you think you have a chance in hell of stopping—"

Robert held up a hand, cutting her rant short. Such

a simple gesture, but it brought her up cold. She pulled her camera closer. The mystery of Lucien's boss grew.

"The stubbornness of a true Hayworth for sure," Robert mumbled.

"Excuse me?"

"I have no intention of stopping you. Or him," Robert stated. "I merely came to inquire about your intentions to assist with the marketing of the band's launch. What I have learned in this meeting is worth far more. I now understand why Lucien feels so compelled by you."

"It doesn't matter." Mandy gathered the stack, shoving them back into the oversized envelope. She burned that bridge. Freaking dynamited the sucker. Hefting her laptop bag and camera once more, she headed up the steps. At the first landing, she turned to say goodbye. "I'll help launch his career and make sure Lucien doesn't walk away from his dreams. Beyond that, I won't make promises." Saying the words aloud picked at a wound still raw and painful. "Lucien has his secrets. I have mine."

"His secrets are not his own." Robert stood at the bottom of the steps, running a finger along the wooden banister. Mandy loved that banister so much that during the renovations, she scraped a hundred years of paint off the wood herself. Robert caressed the wood like a long lost lover. When he turned his gaze back to her, longing haunted his ageless dark eyes. "They are mine and if you would allow for a more private discussion, I am willing to share them with you today."

"Your secrets?" Truth rang in his words, a truth she felt deep in her core. She held her camera up towards him and smiled. Would he allow her one picture to expose what he guarded so close?

With a simple nod from this man she did not know, Mandy raised her arm, pulling back the lens until it captured all of Robert Shoalman. But Mandy couldn't bring herself to look. Not yet. "I assure you this is one of the safest buildings in the city and no one else is in it but us."

"Very well," Robert continued. "The things he has been unable to share with you are because of me, to protect me." Robert straightened. His presence filled the foyer as though suddenly there was more of him. Mandy found herself descending the steps. The same sense of revelation from the night with her father engulfed her. Her white ink tattoo burned on her shoulder.

"I have lived many lives, and in each one I am pursued by a demon. Lucien protects me."

"Many lives?" Two other words repeated themselves in Mandy's head. *Protects me.* Her gaze darted to the ceiling towards the apartment she and Kyrissa shared before returning to stare open mouthed at the man in front of her.

"He's your Guardian." Mandy sighed. The truth had been all over his images but was so outrageous she didn't think to see it.

"Yes, as I suspect you are Guardian to another."

Mandy shifted silently before nodding.

"I am cursed to imprison painful emotions into paint for all eternity, no matter the destruction it causes to myself and those around me." Robert spoke as nonchalantly as she ordered her coffee every morning. "Lucien's protection is the sole reason I am able to stand here before you and ask you not to walk away from him."

He didn't wait for her to respond, staring up at her only briefly before turning. In that moment, the pain in Robert's eyes was unmistakable. She'd seen it the night her father told her a truth twenty-one years in the making. Or maybe, she recognized the same sense of guilt between the two men.

Mandy chanced a glance at the display of her camera. Robert's form was bright white and so clear, she could almost see right through him, just as every image of Kyrissa had ever appeared.

Truth.

This was Robert's truth. He trusted her with a secret so profound and life changing for them both, that she wasn't entirely sure what to do with the knowledge. All she knew was that this information no longer wedged itself in between her and Lucien.

Mandy hugged the folder of photographs tighter to her chest. She cut her ties to Lucien to free him. The remnants currently twisted around her heart, harsh reminders of what might have been. Lucien would have his music, his dream. She'd make sure of it and that's all that mattered. Perhaps, what she saw in Robert's pain mirrored her own. Understanding the sacrifices people made to protect the people they cared about.

CHAPTER FORTY-SIX

"You fucking did it!" Jay pounded Lucien on his shoulder.

Lucien looked up from his laptop screen and Mandy's blog post. The article posted six hours ago and already the hits on the band's site skyrocketed a hundred fold. He checked her site obsessively since finding out Mandy still intended to endorse them, waiting to see which picture she used of him. Worry that the Guardian tattoos would show and lead the demon chasing them directly to him and Robert tore at him until he saw her post. Only a hint of the white ink showed in the final picture. Mandy had protected him. What he didn't expect was a picture so complete. The collage of images showed him the way she saw him. The way he wanted her to see him. All of him.

"It's a good article. Mandy did a great job." He couldn't have done a better marketing spread himself.

"Good? It's bloody fantastic." Jay bounced on top of a table to reach the high small window in the green room that looked out on the front of the building. "The gig doesn't start for another two hours, and people are already lined up to get into the venue." Jumping from furniture to furniture piece, Jay whooped like a twelve year old. Rusty and Adam egged him on.

A smile crept out from the gloom surrounding Lucien. Since his return two nights ago, both he and Jay had been overly controlled around each other.

Only when the music started did either of them let go. Despite Mandy's decision not to be with him, she had shared L.J. Slone and *Eternity* with the world in a way no one else ever would. Just so he could have his dream. Lucien looked at Jay. Their dream.

Jay slammed down on the leather couch next to him. "This is it, Lucien. All the hard work." he grinned. "Even the split lip was worth the pain." Jay crooked his head towards the other two members. Rusty nodded, dragging Adam out the door.

Lucien swallowed. He and Jay had an understanding now. New Band Rule – they didn't mention Mandy around each other. Jay was already straddling that rule and getting ready to break it entirely. Pushing to his feet, Lucien grabbed a bottle of water from the fridge. Jay stayed silent, not speaking until the door clicked shut.

"In all my years in the local scene, I never read an article of hers quite like this one." Jay leaned forward to scroll down the blog.

Well he hadn't said her name, so technically he hadn't broken the Band Rule. Lucien twisted at the plastic top, not tight enough to open it, just enough to feel the ridges of the cap against his palm. Was Jay going to stir this up now, right before the show?

"Thought we agreed not to talk about...this."

"That was before I saw her article, the pictures." Jay rubbed his hand along his bottom lip where Lucien had clocked him. "Before I saw more of Mandy Hayworth in a collection of images than I ever have. And the pictures aren't even of her."

"We don't have to do this, Jay. You were right. Mandy doesn't do strings."

Jay exhaled sharply. "Boy, that girl is so tied up in strings where you're concerned, she's made bloody knots."

"No. She—" Lucien clenched his jaw until his teeth hurt. The air in his lungs smothered him, heavy with the memory of her words. He had given her everything. The new song started singing in his head once more. "She was quite clear on the matter," Lucien forced out.

"She lied." Jay stood in front of him. He pulled the mangled bottle out of Lucien's hands. "Cause I told her to."

"You what?"

"I couldn't let you throw your dream away. Not like I did."

"But you love her. You said two band members—"

"I know what I said," Jay snapped. Blowing out a breath, he placed the bottle on the counter in a slow, controlled motion. "Problem is I had no right to say it. I have no claim to Mandy. Never did. Never will." He snorted. "I was just too stupid to realize that earlier."

Lucien scrubbed at his face. Head pounding, he grappled with the puzzle pieces thrown at him. Robert, Jay and now supposedly Mandy. Nothing made sense. Looking up, Mandy's blog caught his attention. Multiple pictures, some clear, some blurry. By themselves, confused and unrelated. But together, Mandy's gift beckoned. Passion, desire, and yes, love surrounded the collage in a bright aura, stringing it all together into a single image. Him. The image sang, harmonizing with the song now clear in his head. With all his flaws and strengths displayed, she loved him enough to share him with his music.

"You see it now, don't ya?" Jay sat on the back of the sofa, arms crossed over his chest. "And you are seriously gone on her."

"Where do we go from here?" Lucien asked. "I told you I'm committed to making this band, our dream, a reality."

"We take *Eternity* from Heaven to Hell and back again."

Lucien nodded.

"Then you fucking find a way to tell that woman ya

love her. Sex her brains out." Jay snorted and Lucien fought the rush of heat the thought evoked. "And never let her go."

"I know exactly how to tell her." Lucien paused. He couldn't do it alone, but wasn't sure he had the right to ask for Jay's help.

"You've finally got the lyrics." Jay's gaze never left Lucien's face. "Fucking hell."

"Do you guys trust me?" They had practiced the music, but never with the lyrics. Their re-launch depended on a good show. An untried song could destroy everything they'd spent weeks preparing. Each breath Lucien took seemed shallower, slower than the last, while his heart beat twice its pace, as though to compensate for the time crawl.

"Guess we're gonna find out."

Jay walked over to the door and yanked it open. Adam stumbled before catching himself on the doorframe. Lucien laughed. So much for secrets. Rusty cuffed Jay on the arm and saluted Lucien. All three settled in front of Lucien. Waiting. Lucien wondered when exactly he became the de facto leader.

"Alright master marketeer," Jay urged. "Beguile us with your new idea to take us to the top."

No matter what happened afterwards, Mandy would know how Lucien felt about her. He owed her that much. She set him free to pursue his music by sacrificing her own spot at his side. Rubbing at his forearms, Lucien knew the cost of some choices, of the pain they inflicted. He'd make sure her choice wasn't in vain. Now it was time to soar.

Eternity lay in front of him. Lucien charged headlong into his choice. "Here's what we're going to do…"

CHAPTER FORTY-SEVEN

Staying back at the bar, Mandy stood much further away from the stage than her usual position. She liked to be up close, right in the middle of the action, where she could feel the music through the people dancing around her. Let the energy of the room filter through her and her camera. Those nights always produced the best images.

Tonight, she distanced herself from it all, or rather, she kept her distance from Lucien.

"Thanks for coming with me tonight," Mandy said to Kyrissa. Mandy hadn't been sure how she'd convince her best friend to come out with her, but since her article released, Kyrissa didn't seem to need convincing. Kyrissa glared when she heard all the late night phone calls it took to convince Claire Masterson to be at the show. She witnessed the hoops Mandy had to jump through to get her article on *The Scene* website on such short notice. Kyrissa had even bit her tongue while Mandy threw her father's name around to make sure the piece would run in time for the performance.

"I wouldn't dream of being anywhere else." Kyrissa squeezed her hand lightly, offering the support Mandy wasn't able to ask for.

"You've got to be kidding." Looking over Kyrissa's shoulder, the last person she expected strode towards the end of the bar. Dressed in a suit and tie, her father stuck out like three-day-old fish in a buffet.

"Amanda," Alexander Hayworth greeted them. He leaned back against the bar and folded his arms over his chest. "It's good to see you again, Kyrissa."

Mandy didn't move to greet her father. She wasn't sure what she'd say to him if she did. They had only talked briefly since her father's confession. Her fingers tightened on her best friend's, pleading for help.

"It's good to see you too, Mr. Hayworth," she said to Mandy's father. She cleared her throat. "If you'll excuse me, I'm going to go check out the art." Kyrissa pointed to the back of the room. She squeezed Mandy's fingers before removing what little buffer Mandy and her father had.

"What are you doing here?" Mandy asked. Acid burned in her stomach, hating that his mere presence made her doubt her ability to protect her best friend. She'd be lying if she said she was happy to see him. It was bad enough he'd inserted himself into her friendship with Kyrissa. Music and photography were her life and she didn't want him intruding in either of those.

"My homework." Her father turned towards her, one eyebrow raised. "I needed to see the guy who inspired this." A printed copy of her article about *Eternity* slapped atop the bar. Even on the cheap paper, with poor quality ink, the image of Lucien nearly jumped out at her. Her heart clenched tighter in her chest.

"It's about a band," Mandy tried to correct him. "Not a guy." She knew from the moment the words formed in her head, they were a lie. Hearing herself say them out loud only solidified how wrong she was.

"I have read every blog entry and article you have ever posted. Never have I read anything with as much passion as this one." He held the paper up, clearing his throat. "If you think you have to die before you hear an angel sing," he quoted, "you're wrong. The new lead singer of *Eternity*, the band formerly known as *Demon*

Dogs, is part rock god, part man, but L.J. Slone's voice is so powerful it'll make angels weep."

"Not a lie," Mandy said, lifting a finger in the air. *Eternity* prepped the stage. Rusty and Adam picked up their instruments, Jay lingered near the back. Another man fiddled with the sound board. But Lucien still hadn't made an appearance. He didn't seem to be the make an entrance kind of guy.

"None of those guys are angels," her father stated with such confidence no one would doubt his ability to tell the difference between man and angelic beast.

"None of them are Lucien," she agreed. Jay moved offstage, twirling his drumsticks in the air. Mandy frowned, moving closer to the crowded floor.

What if Lucien was getting cold feet?

"It would help if he showed up for his own debut," Alexander commented.

Mandy held up her finger. Why was it so hard for him to trust her? "He'll be here." But a hard knot formed in the pit of her stomach.

What if he was going to throw his own career away and hadn't needed her help to do it?

"Guys like Lucien are a rare breed, sweetheart. When you manage to catch one, you have to hold on and never let go." Her father lifted the silver necklace off the skin of her neck. His thumb rubbed the worn metal as if he could stroke the nostalgia right off of the pendant.

In his eyes, a shadow lingered, one she tried to look past. Mandy inhaled. The shadow no longer stopped her. As though the truth had unlocked a door, her father no longer held back, letting his pain and regret show for the first time since Mandy discovered the truth about her parents.

"Mine was taken from me too soon. I've struggled for breath every day since, and you've suffered the most for it."

She couldn't disagree but no argument would erase

the pain in his eyes. She'd spent so much time harboring resentment for what her parents had taken away from her, yet the very thing she had missed was standing here now. Lucien was right. She'd spent so much time looking at images through her camera, she had forgotten how to see the people right in front of her.

"I've managed. You're my dad. We share a lot of memories, a history, and genes neither one of us could deny, even if we tried." She lifted herself up and kissed her father's cheek. "And despite what I wanted you to think, I never stopped loving you."

"Now that is music to my ears." He pulled her tight to his chest. Mandy inhaled his scent, smiling. She forgot how much she hated his aftershave. The hug was brief, but no longer awkward.

"But I honestly did not come here to win back your good graces. I owe you more than that. Besides, I'm here to meet this guy of yours." Her father glanced around the room.

"What about my responsibilities?" Mandy tried not to let the sarcasm seep through. This forgiveness crap was going to take some practice.

Her father glanced over his shoulder. Two minutes ago, Kyrissa had moved to the other side of the room to check out the art that graced the perimeter wall. Mandy hadn't lost sight of her once.

"Who am I to judge how you handle your life or your responsibilities? If you say you can handle both, I'm the last person to say otherwise." Her father sighed, a sound weighted with years of regret. "I gave up that right a long time ago. Besides," he said pointing toward where Kyrissa stood on the other side of a glass wall staring at a painting. "How much trouble could find her in a glass encased hallway?"

"You'd be surprised," Mandy chuckled. Her father laughed, a sound she missed for too long, as if he knew from experience how true her words rang.

Not looking at the same man Mandy walked out on last Sunday, she raised her camera. The shutter clicked. Her father straightened his spine, eyes narrowing, but for once, he didn't protest. Mandy didn't need to see the image to know it had changed. The shadows that usually blurred his likeness had dissipated, as if finally telling his truth had done more than lift a weight from his shoulders, it cleared his conscious. For that, Mandy would be eternally thankful, even if the truth hadn't been easy to hear.

Her father cleared his throat, searching the stage once more. "So where is this Lucien character? I need to meet anyone worthy of reaching into your soul like this." He lifted the article again. In the rolled up paper, all she could see was the slight smile of Lucien Solvak peeking out.

"You'll meet him," she assured. She couldn't be certain under what pretense, just a friend who happened to be a singer, or a guy she wanted a whole lot more from. "But first he needs to get on stage and shine."

"Looks like he's about to do just that," her father whispered.

The room darkened, only a few lights left on stage and a few along the floor. Conversations buzzed and people surged towards the stage, each vying to be the first to see the new lead singer. Even before the music started, an instant calm fell over the crowd. Without seeing his face, or hearing his voice, Lucien's presence claimed the room. And tugged on a few strings attached to Mandy's heart.

CHAPTER FORTY-EIGHT

Never before had Lucien been nervous stepping onto a stage. The stage was his escape, his music the release from all the weight of the world threatening to drag him into oblivion. The darkness held no fear for him.

Except this time.

As the lights in the club dimmed, the stage black, members of the band slipped past Lucien to their places. Each one offered an encouraging nod in the dim blue backstage lighting. This song, his song, could make or break them. Lucien rubbed the sticky sweat from his palms against his black jeans. The smooth wood of his guitar lay across his spine, chilling the skin beneath his shirt. Did he have the right to risk everything they worked to achieve? Lucien jumped as a hand fell on his shoulder.

"Let go and sing from your heart." Jay squeezed his shoulder lightly. "She'll bloody love it. So will the crowd." Jay moved to his drum kit just as the sound tech pointed at Lucien.

Show time.

The bass drum started with a soft double beat, echoing into the quieting club. Lucien's own blood pounded in time with the sound. The rhythm built slowly, drawing the crowd into the heart of the music. He smiled in Jay's direction. Despite their differences where Mandy was concerned, music flowed through both their veins.

Rusty's bass guitar picked up the pattern, enhancing the melody as though adding its breath to the pounding of the heartbeat. Backlit, the silhouettes of the band members began to appear in muted reds and blues, both the music and the band coming to life. *Eternity* reborn from the ashes of the death of demons.

Standing in the dark, Lucien searched for Mandy, but the dimly lit bar offered only blurred figures. Was she looking for him? Was she even here? What would she see if she took his picture right now? The coward trembling inside, or the rock star she believed him to be?

Adam's mournful rift on guitar kicked the intro of the song into full gear. The crowd cheered. Lucien couldn't breathe. His chest caved in like he had exhaled too deep and the air grew thick, sitting on his chest instead of letting him breathe in.

Choking. He was literally choking on the side of the stage on what could possibly be the biggest night of his life. A sharp crack of wood against his ribs had him sucking in air, the rattle of the drumstick against the floor lost in the music. Jay pointed at Lucien with his second drumstick, then mimed Lucien's obvious choking, followed by rubbing his fingers together.

Lucien hadn't lost the bet to Jay at his initial tryout for the band. He sure as hell wasn't losing it now. Clicking his wireless mic on, his voice filled the darkness right on cue. The spotlight waited for him to move to the front of the stage. He moved forward, the cheer of the crowd reverberated over him the moment he gained the light. Faces came into focus. So did Mandy.

Their gazes locked. She didn't lift her camera, didn't even try to take his picture, as if he could stop her tonight. He wouldn't. He needed her to see him clearly because when he sang, it was the only time he felt whole.

Letting the music fill every sense, Lucien released all his worries, giving his voice wings. Mandy. Only she existed. Nothing else mattered. His music could tell her the things he never could. It should be impossible, but her perfume surrounded him, stirring memories of a gift freely given. His skin warmed from remembered kisses and gentle touches. What he'd give for one of those touches now. Passion burned bright, giving form to his words.

Misguided hope, impossible dream.
Yet through it all, you believed in me.
The darkness shatters, death has no hold.
You helped me see, Eternity.

Music. The band. Each had been a dream, one he fought for, but in some ways never believed he could ever achieve. From the moment they met, Mandy never doubted him. Her take-on-the-world attitude—a perspective he only obtained when he sang—gave him strength to embrace that emotion outside his music. To challenge himself to succeed, not only with music, but with her as well.

Gifted wings to reach new heights.
Made me dizzy, you shined so bright.
The darkness shatters, death has no hold.
You helped me find, Eternity.

In her arms, arms he ached to have around him forever, Lucien found a peace he never knew existed. Staring at him across the club, hair curled over one shoulder, a glow surrounded her. Guys were supposed to be obsessed with the physical act of sex. Mandy shared with him a night of passion and desire. His choice to be with her had been pure emotion. One that swelled within him once more. A fire he was determined to share with her again.

Oh dark Angel who guides my night,
The darkness shatters, death has no hold.
When I'm with you, it feels so right.
You helped me love, Eternity.

His fingers flew over the guitar strings in harmony with Adam's driving lead. Every brooding sound Rusty's bass made lent support to Lucien's lyrics as if they'd rehearsed them relentlessly instead of playing them together for the first time tonight. And Jay. No matter what differences still existed between him and Lucien, it was Jay who was bringing the song together in ways Lucien never imagined possible. Cohesive. Strong. If Lucien was the voice of *Eternity*, Jay was the lifeblood. Together, their love of music, the need to create and share the pure energy of song, coalesced into something bigger than either of them imagined. Power to escape the constricting bonds and let others soar.

Lucien held nothing back. This was the life he wanted. The life he needed. The band. The stage. His music. And Mandy looking on with adoring eyes. He wanted it all and just had to convince Mandy she wanted to be a part of it. That she could no more walk away from him than he could let her go.

The stage blacked out on the last beat of the song. The crowd exploded.

Eternity had arrived at last.

CHAPTER FORTY-NINE

Watching Lucien perform, only one word came to Mandy's mind—magical. Or mesmerizing. Rock God definitely fit. Even out of body experience applied, but that was four words.

Motionless, the weight of her camera hung at her side for the entire set. For once, her fingers hadn't twitched to pick it up or lift it to her eye. For the first time in forever, she hadn't ached to take a picture of the person standing in front of her. She didn't need to. Every word Lucien sang plucked the strings of her heart as if he sang only for her. Every glimmer in his eye tugged on those ties. And whenever their gazes met, knots formed and squeezed a little tighter.

The staging worked better than she imagined when Lucien showed her the design sketches. The way the guys were lit only from behind at first added a layer of mystery that the crowd couldn't wait to peel away. With every new light source that lit the stage, the band peeled away the layers like masters. Definite rock stars. Rock stars that grabbed the crowd around their necks and commanded the attention of every single person in the room. And they had gotten it. No one looked away, an entire room of people that swayed along to songs they didn't know yet, worshipping at the altar of a Rock God they hadn't known they'd be meeting tonight. And now that they did, minus Kyrissa of course who was still enjoying the art,

Mandy had no doubt *Eternity* had just gained devoted followers of their own making.

The guys deserved the success. Jay deserved the success. He deserved to be playing in a bigger band than this scene, bigger than them all. And Lucien, no way of denying he lived for the challenge of leading them all through whatever eternity he could take them. No denying she wanted to be the first in line to follow.

"You were right." Mandy's father tapped her shoulder. Mandy had forgotten he was in the room, absorbed completely in the witness of *Eternity*. "That boy is all angel," he said, inclining his head towards the stage.

"Yes he is," Mandy whispered. When she turned, her father already started walking away. "I thought you wanted to meet him," Mandy called.

"Oh, I will." Her father smiled, a knowing look crossed his face. "But not tonight. Tonight is your night, honey. Go congratulate Lucien on a great debut." He swept his hand across the crowd who still screamed for an encore. "Just not too much celebrating," he said raising a single brow. Her father turned and disappeared into the crowd before Mandy had a chance to process the words she'd just heard, much less respond.

She laughed, shaking her head. That conversation she never intended to have with her father.

Checking over her shoulder, she assured herself that Kyrissa was still protected in the glass gallery before Mandy pushed her way through the crowd. A few people pushed back. Just so happened the door that led backstage was at the front of the stage. It was also protected.

"Mikhail?" Mandy let the name linger on her lips. "I didn't expect to see you tonight. This is your family business?"

"It is. My Uncle Christophe asked me to run a

security detail around this place after a recent break in."

"Wow. You're Lucien's cousin." Mandy chuckled. He hadn't been lying about a complicated family. "Your Uncle won't be sorry. That live feed you set up for me has been a godsend. Thanks."

"You are very welcome." Mikhail winked, clipboard held out in front of him. If Mandy had to guess, he had strict orders. No one gets past him, no one got backstage unless they were on the guest list. Would she find her name on that list?

"Her name's on the list." Carl nodded from behind Mikhail. His arm was in a cast, stitches over his left eye and a bandage wrapped around the back of his neck.

"Carl. What happened?"

"Casualty of working security and stopping an attempted break in." Carl shrugged, his sling pulled tight around his neck. "It's good to see you here though. That article you wrote is the reason ninety percent of these people came to check out the band."

"Thanks." Mandy smiled. "The guys put on an great show."

"That they did. But your boy did amazing. He had the audience eating out of the palm of his hand." Carl glared at her. Was he waiting on her confirmation that Lucien was hers? Or waiting for her to deny it?

"He was incredible." Mandy's cheeks ached from a smile she didn't realize she'd been sporting since the first note had come out of Lucien's mouth.

"That he was," Carl agreed. He stepped aside and let Mandy pass. Mandy was definitely someone. But was she Lucien's someone?

CHAPTER FIFTY

"Holy fucking hell! Did you hear that crowd?" Rusty exclaimed. "Two encores and they're still screaming for more." Rusty mussed Lucien's hair with both hands.

Lucien pushed Rusty off laughing so hard his sides hurt. So much for the Band Rule. Riding high off the energy feedback from the crowd, nothing could upset him. He wanted to yell at the top of his lungs. It worked. The lyrics, the songs, the stage show. Everything had gone flawlessly.

"I assume this means I have to share you with this rag-tag bunch of misfits now?"

"Robert!" Lucien exclaimed. Tailored suit, pressed white shirt and perfectly straight tie contrasted against the jeans and t-shirts the band sported. Lucien moved quickly to grasp the outstretched hand, caught off guard when Robert pulled him into a quick embrace. Not one prone to public displays, the gesture told Lucien more than words ever would.

"Guys, I'd like to introduce you to my boss, Robert..." Lucien flipped his gaze, unsure whether to introduce his full name. Robert nodded, a rare smile on his face. "Robert Shoalman. His images were the ones we used in the stage show."

A low whistle sounded. "*The* Robert Shoalman?" Jay walked over to shake hands with the painter, before shoving Lucien with his shoulder. "You've been holding out on us. No wonder you're such a fucking marketing genius if you have Robert Shoalman teaching you."

"This was all Lucien. The marketing skills are his own and he has taught me far more on the subject than I have him." Robert chuckled. "Besides, I was told this was his life and not to interfere."

Lucien cringed, but Robert's wink put him at ease. Before Lucien could say anything else, Robert turned towards the other members of *Eternity*.

"Can we have a moment?" Robert asked. "Alone." None of the guys questioned Robert's command disguised in a question, leaving without another word. Robert had that effect on everyone, even his band.

"What's wrong?" Lucien eyed Robert's relaxed stance, the way his shoulders rested peacefully and his usual tension didn't fill the air around him. If Lucien dared, he'd say Robert seemed more comfortable than he'd ever seen him.

"You were right." Robert faced the entrance of the room, staring at the closed door. "Mandy is more a part of our world then I could have anticipated." Turning, their eyes locked. "She knows who I am. *What* I am."

Lucien gasped. *No!* His mind raced over every conversation. He was careful. Oh god, had he slipped? "I didn't tell her. On my oaths, Robert, I would never—"

"I told her."

"You?" Lucien grabbed the rail of a high-backed bar stool to keep from falling. In all the different scenarios he came up with, Robert telling Mandy his secret flat out never occurred to him. But one question remained that he couldn't answer. "Why?"

"There is no reason my secrets must come between you and Miss Hayworth."

"I don't know what to say." Lucien contemplated running to Mandy, swooping her up in his arms and never letting go. Except she'd already pushed him away. "Thank you," he finally said even though he didn't think Robert's exposure would help where Mandy was concerned.

Robert nodded.

A knock on the door echoed into the silence. "Excuse me, Mr. Shoalman," Carl interrupted. "There seems to be a young woman inside the glass art gallery."

Lucien went on alert.

"Stay." Robert raised a hand. "I will look into it."

"Are you sure you don't need me?" The band was now a part of his life, with Robert's blessing, but his first duty lay in protecting Robert.

"Enjoy your night. I can handle a woman too close to my art."

As Robert slipped out of the green room, select VIP's entered to celebrate with the band. Lucien only had eyes for one. Several reporters engaged him in conversations, which Lucien only half participated in, his attention on the dark haired beauty skirting the edge of the room.

"Go to her," Jay whispered in his ear. "I'll distract this group of vultures."

"So you can hog the limelight?" Lucien teased.

"Pfft. Only if I can bloody well get you out of it." Jay grabbed his arm as if to push him towards Mandy. "You know you want to, what's stopping you?"

"It's not enough if I want us to be together." Lucien tore his eyes from Mandy to stare at Jay—if anyone would understand. "She has to want it too."

A shadow crossed over Jay's face, but dissipated when he smiled. A pain released to the past. "Trust me. She wants it."

A light touch rested on Lucien's arm. Turning, his heart leapt. Deep brown eyes swallowed him whole. No walls, no barriers, only adoration stared back at him.

Jay cuffed him on the shoulder, holding out a fifty between his thumb and index finger.

"I'll take that," Mandy said, snatching the fifty.

Jay snickered before moving further into the room.

Mandy winked at Lucien, tucking the bill into her bra. "Hey," she whispered.

"Hey." Lucien had so much he wanted to say, to tell her. Words deserted him. Air struggled to pass his lips. He could perform in front of hundreds, yet this one woman left him speechless. He pulled her hands into his. The light fruity scent of her perfume tantalized his nose. Her rapid breath—or was that his—washed away the buzz of the voices surrounding him. He couldn't get his smile to fade. She was here. Now. With him. And he couldn't make a single sound come out of his mouth.

She reached up and straightened the strands Rusty had mussed earlier. The touch of her fingers against his scalp sent shivers down his spine.

"Mandy—"

"I was wrong," she cut him off.

Lucien forced the air in and out of his lungs, willing his heart to stop its rampant pounding against his ribs. He had made his decision, but Mandy had to make her own.

"About?"

"Us." As she said the single word, Mandy traced over the white tattoos on his forearms. Skin to skin, soothing every fear he couldn't control until she touched him. He still didn't know how she could see them, but somehow, it no longer worried him. Stepping closer, he waited to see if she would push him away again or meet him halfway. She laid a hand over his heart, the warmth seeping into every crevice of his body.

"You were right. There is something between us. Something I wanted to deny."

"Why?"

"*That* is a long story." Mandy smiled.

"I have time. All the time you want or need." Lucien licked his lips. She was so close. He wanted her closer.

"I hate when you do that," Mandy mock glared at him.

"Do what?" Lucien slowly wrapped an arm around Mandy's waist.

"Lick your lips like that."

Lucien blinked. "Why?"

"Because it makes me want to do this."

Mandy tugged on his hair, pulling his mouth to hers. The sweet taste of surrender catapulted him back to heights of passion he had almost lost. His heart sang.

Mandy had chosen.

Wrapped in his arms, Lucien crushed her against his body, claiming her lips in a deep, sensual embrace. Giddiness stole over him as the kiss ended. Scooping her up, Lucien spun her around. Her laughter echoed in the room, the greatest music of the night.

CHAPTER FIFTY ONE

Mandy Hayworth never felt more at home than when her lips were touching Lucien's. The warmth and energy they shared spread with each passing moment until it filled her completely. She didn't need her camera or any photographs to feel secure in Lucien's strong arms. As if reading her mind, he tightened her body closer to his in the safest of all embraces.

"You have no idea how much I've missed this," he whispered in her ear. Those simple words were enough to weaken her knees and set her heart racing.

"I've some idea." Mandy gently eased herself away from Lucien's chest. She wiped lipstick off his mouth. Exactly her shade. Mandy hadn't factored in the possibility that Lucien merely licking his lips would cause such a reaction that she wouldn't be able to control herself from bringing his mouth down to hers. Not that Lucien seemed to mind.

"So," Lucien began. "What did you think of the show?"

Mandy smiled. She liked the way Lucien worked for a compliment, one she didn't intend to give until later, when they were alone.

"It was alright." She shrugged and let her eyes roll.

"I'll show you I am more than alright." Lucien winked. He leaned in closer again and whispered, "Later."

"I am counting on that." Mandy sighed. Reliving the

memories of the one night they'd spent together weren't enough anymore. She needed more of him, every piece of him she'd discovered in her photographs and all the pieces she hadn't yet explored.

"Just one thing. I come with strings," Lucien said. His eyes turned the warmest shade of blue Mandy had ever seen, a cool crisp blue, but with undertones of gold radiating out of the center. She couldn't determine whether the gold existed or if her eyes were playing tricks on her. She didn't care.

Mandy lifted her hand to his cheek. "I know."

Confusion marred Lucien's good looks. "What changed?"

"Later." She leaned up and kissed him again. Quick, a light press into his lips so she wouldn't get carried away, at least not right now. "I'll explain when we're alone and I can tie myself in every string you'll let me."

"They're all yours. Exclusively." His fingers pushed hair away from her face and claimed what was already his, her mouth, her body and her heart.

Lightheaded, she cleared her throat, breaking a kiss she would rather embrace forever. "You have a few fans to greet," she said. Most of the people in the room kept their distance and attempted not to stare. But with all the sideways glances followed by wide grins, Mandy knew they were the hot topic.

"You're the only fan I need." Lucien leaned in to kiss her once more. Damn he was insatiable. Not that Mandy minded.

"You might want to rethink that." Mandy hitched her head to the side, catching Claire Masterson from the recording agency headed in their direction.

Looking over her shoulder, Lucien's eyes widened. He slipped his hand away from her face and down her arm but never lost contact with her skin, until his fingers wrapped in hers and tightened.

"L.J. Slone." Claire held out her hand. "Claire Masterson. It is a real pleasure to meet you."

"Likewise," Lucien replied.

"Mandy, we meet again."

"It's good to see you, Claire." Mandy smiled. Lucien raised a single eyebrow in her direction. She winked. "Didn't I tell you this trip would be worth it or what?"

"Honestly, it was worth much more than I imagined. Dare I say you were holding out on me? The way you can spot talent." The short redhead shook her head. "One of these days I am going to convince you to come work for me."

"I'm flattered," Mandy beamed. If Claire didn't have ties to her father, Mandy would consider the offer in a heartbeat. But those ties existed and Mandy needed to make her own way without her father's name attached to any offers. "But I'm pretty happy scouting the local scene. At least for now." Mandy squeezed Lucien's hand. "And you know I will call you the moment someone is worth your time."

"Then I will look forward to your call, Ms. Hayworth." Claire turned towards Lucien, pulling an envelope out of her oversized bag. "I don't normally do this. However, sometimes exceptional circumstances call for quick decisions." She held out a manila envelope, the recording studio logo emblazoned on the front. Mandy could barely contain her excitement.

"Is this..." Lucien couldn't finish the sentence.

Claire held up her hand. "This is for you and the guys. It's an offer to *discuss* representation." Lucien squeezed her hand in a bone-breaking grasp. Mandy flinched but didn't pull away. She never intended to pull away from him again. "Enjoy the rest of the night. We can talk business on Monday morning."

"I, wow. Thank you." Lucien took the envelope. Mandy spotted Jay on the other side of the room sporting the biggest grin she'd ever seen on him. Lucien and Jay exchanged thumbs ups across a crowd that seemed to be multiplying.

Claire laughed looking between the two guys. "I

wrote my direct line on the back. Use it." Claire turned to walk away. She looked back briefly. "Call me first thing next week," she said.

"I will." Lucien nodded. "Promise." Lucien hugged Mandy hard once Claire was out of the room. "Holy shit! How did you do this?"

"I just made a call. You guys did the rest." Mandy laughed. Lucien bounced on his feet, unable to stand still. His dream. He held it in his hand. A dream she'd gladly share with him.

"Go on," Mandy said.

"Go where?" Lucien asked.

"Go celebrate with the guys. I have to find Kyrissa." Mandy kissed his cheek, her lips nibbled at his ear. "You and I will celebrate later tonight." Against her chest, Lucien inhaled so deep she worried he wouldn't be able to exhale. His stomach muscles tensed beneath where her hand lay against his hip.

"I'm counting on that." Lucien shifted beside her, no doubt making an adjustment before he attempted to walk across the room.

"So. Am. I." Watching Lucien walk away from her shouldn't feel so right. But how could it be at all wrong when she knew, without a doubt, he'd be walking right back to her?

Raising her camera, Mandy captured the image of *Eternity*. The band and the men tied to it clear against the bright aura surrounding them. Effects Mandy could now see both with and without her camera. Lucien looked back at her, his smile permeating straight to her core. Mandy didn't need her camera to show her the strings between them. She couldn't wait to wrap herself in every last one.

Shoalman Immortal

THE SHOALMAN CHRONICLES

Book 2

TONI DECKER

CHAPTER ONE

At the end of the bar, Kyrissa Spears swirled a tiny straw in her pink drink, waiting for the moment she could make an escape to the other side of the room. She didn't care to drink the liquid in front of her. She wasn't here to listen to the music. And she feigned only half interest in whatever her best friend said beside her. Kyrissa was here for one thing.

She was here to feel death.

Kyrissa had spent her fair share of hours in crowded bars, breathing in stale air, listening to mediocre bands play music between drowning their songs in cheap beer. While her best friend Mandy may have loved these nights they hung out together, Kyrissa always counted the minutes before she could go home and paint away her frustrations. Or anger. Or whatever other feeling she could conjure up and force onto the tip of her paintbrush.

Tonight was different. Tonight, much to Kyrissa's surprise, Gallery, the hottest local music venue, had managed to attract a sampling of death to hang on its walls and Kyrissa wouldn't miss it, not even for her own death.

The Shoalman Collection was the largest collection of paintings that appreciated death as an artistic subject the way that Kyrissa thought it deserved to be appreciated, or in her case, worshipped. Every painting in the collection captured the emotions so often forgotten about during the process of dying, or those left behind. Within the paint, grief emanated from the surface, resentment swirled in the air, and the absolute feeling of nothingness culminated in the heart of every patron that witnessed the collection. The Isle of the Dead, the crown jewel of the collection, embodied the pinnacle of every one of those emotions.

There were larger spaces available in the city, some that offered far better lighting, a more astute art appreciation oriented crowd, and none of them subjected their patrons to loud thumping, hard beating rock bands. Kyrissa couldn't understand how Gallery attracted any of the pieces at all, much less tonight's show, which exclusively contained only works from the collection. Tonight would provide her an opportunity to appreciate Gallery's good fortune. And hers.

If only the most prized piece was here. But no one had laid eyes on the Isle of the Dead since it first debuted onto the art scene. Or in the case of the Isle, grabbed the art scene around the neck and tightened its grip until breathing faltered.

From her barstool, Kyrissa admired the works of art lining the perimeter of the room, protected by a glass hallway that allowed access to no one. The barrier between her and death taunted her the way a drink mocked an alcoholic. She tried to ignore the vibrations that made every hair on the back of her neck stand up. And she pretended she hadn't noticed the chill in the air tonight that she'd never witnessed so many of the hours she'd spent at Gallery before. Most of all, she paid no attention to the man standing behind the glass staring out at her. Tall, dark and handsome didn't do the man justice. More like instant lust and star of every one of her future fantasies.

And now he was all she could see.

Dark hair, clipped short enough to be completely respectable but long enough for Kyrissa to imagine running her fingers through it. Dark jeans, with a shirt tucked in above the waistline so tightly, it screamed for Kyrissa to come pull it out, scrape her nails along the sculpted abs underneath and lick the perfectly square jaw line until her tongue met his mouth. The mouth that formed into a flattened line when he caught her staring. But Kyrissa couldn't look away. His eyes, wide, had locked on hers and she didn't have the key to release the intense gaze.

"Who's that?" Kyrissa pointed to the man. He nodded slightly before leaving the enclosure.

"Don't know, don't care." Mandy didn't even lift her head to see where Kyrissa was pointing. She was here for the upcoming band, specifically the lead singer, Lucien. Mandy hadn't stopped talking about him in weeks and even though she tried to convince Kyrissa it was purely casual, if not over already as she tried to explain last night, Kyrissa could tell Mandy didn't believe her own words.

"I'll be right back," she said searching for the mysterious man behind the glass but he had disappeared down the hall at the back of the club that led to the alley. On more than one occasion, Kyrissa had followed Mandy down the same hallway to get the scoop on some band or another. Contemplating following him down the hall into the darkened alley was tempting, but not quite as tempting as standing in the spot he just vacated.

"Okay, but don't miss *Eternity.*" Mandy offered a pointed stare in her direction. "They should be on stage in twenty minutes." Convinced this band was about to be picked up and hightailed onto the larger music field, Mandy wanted the audience to support them the way she did. That's why she had given the local band her personal endorsement, offered an exclusive glimpse into the new lead singer and wrote a glowing article that was likely to make the biggest critic rethink their position. The band had apparently also given her the heart of their lead singer, even if she hadn't yet admitted that she wanted it.

"I'll be right over there." Kyrissa pointed to the glass wall that separated the art from the music. The partition framed the perimeter of the room, enclosing pieces of art both local and recognized worldwide. "Just wave me down when they come on."

Mandy didn't respond, craning her neck over the crowd, no doubt searching for Lucien amongst a room full of music lovers, even though he was probably backstage. Kyrissa shook her head, laughing as she ventured away from her lovesick best friend.

The glass hallway that protected the paintings was narrow, with just enough space between the brick wall and the glass to allow someone to change out the art periodically and pass easily within the space. At this distance, Kyrissa admired the brush strokes and she could almost count the layers of paint evident on the canvas. From two feet away, Kyrissa even respected the carnage of one painted so realistically, she could taste the coppery tang of the blood. But too much distance still existed between her and the art, as if she was standing on the wrong side of the glass. Which she absolutely was.

Kyrissa wanted nothing more than to get inside it, step up close to the paintings and breathe in the same air. And now she knew it could be done, she just needed to figure out how. Or find the man to show her how. He'd been right in the spot she stood. One minute behind the glass, the next he was on the other side walking away. Running her hand along the last pane of glass, she was surprised at the give when she pushed. Another gentle nudge and the hidden glass door released, springing open and letting Kyrissa inside.

The air changed the moment Kyrissa stepped inside the art gallery, the way a storm brings on whirling winds and takes every drop of ocean water out to sea. Every breath she took spanned two. Every heartbeat lasted the length of three. And every moment that she stood amongst this art, she wondered how she could possibly ever capture a tenth of the emotion contained in these masterpieces. The thrill of getting caught was part of it, knowing how elusive these paintings were, it was a wonder there weren't armed guards at every entrance. But Kyrissa could separate the danger from the pulse of energy emanating from the paintings. Her own blood seemed to slow to match the beats of the energy until they formed a rhythmic coupling she'd never experienced before.

It wasn't that these paintings were painted with any more skill than she possessed. She had plenty. And it wasn't that she used any less passion in her own art that these artists used; she had passion enough to go around. It was just that every painting evoked a visceral reaction, in its purest form, from whomever caught a glimpse of them, making the patron actually feel whatever emotion the depicted death contained—courage, longing, even serenity.

Kyrissa had this ability too. She was a painter who worshipped the collection like a religion because she was a practicing member. But the last time she let loose her control of her gift, she painted death. And somebody died.

CHAPTER TWO

If she touched one of his paintings, his curse could kill her.

Or worse... claim her for itself.

"You should not be in here," Robert demanded. As soon as the words left his mouth, the sensation of his error struck him. The woman spun to face him. Blond hair like multi-faceted streak of sunlight swayed around her nearly bare shoulders. Wide blue eyes stared into his and Robert found himself contemplating which pigments he could use from his collection to capture that color in paint. Whoever this woman was, she fit within his artwork as though he painted her there himself.

"I'm sorry." She pointed to the glass door now standing open behind him. "The door was unlocked." She gestured to the artwork. Robert tensed, but her hand never came close to any of the frames. Almost if she knew better than to touch them. "I've never seen so many of *The Shoalman Collection* in one place before and never up close like this."

"They are behind a glass barrier for a reason."

"But it blocks the emotions," the blond stated. "Each layer of paint conveys a different feeling. Serenity, peace, but also pain and grief. This one in particular." She gestured to the image of a grave nestled deep in the woods. A lone figure knelt by the mound of rocks, head bowed, a single hand laid flat against the headstone. "The longing emanating from it…" She hugged herself, rubbing up and down her arms. "It gives me chills. I can feel the desire that existed between these two. The regret from the one left behind. I want to comfort him. Tell him life will get better." Her fingers reached towards the paint, hovering just shy of the canvas.

Robert stared. "You feel the paintings?" Most people viewing his works sensed their impact, but never before had anyone picked up the individual emotions.

"Can't you?" She looked over her shoulder at him, a puzzled look marring her beauty.

"Of course I can." Robert pursed his lips. "That is one of the reasons my collection is protected behind the glass hallway."

"Your collection?" The woman gasped. Her hands flew to her mouth, eyes wide she stared at him. "Oh my God. You're Robert Shoalman."

"And you are?"

"Kyrissa. Kyrissa Spears." Color blossomed throughout her face. She dropped her gaze and started picking at the flecks of color on her nails.

Paint. Robert recognized the speckles on her nails, and now that he looked, on her boots as well. Whatever else Kyrissa Spears did, one thing was certain. She painted. He stepped closer to her. Her ability to see the full emotional impact of his painting intrigued him. She looked up, meeting his gaze.

Robert's body stirred. He might be over five hundred years old, but his body remained that of a twenty-two year old male. Responses he long thought dead unburied themselves from under centuries of denial. Every curved line, from her neck, past her breasts, to her full hips, made his hands ache to touch her. She was beauty waiting to be painted and Robert found himself stirring with the need to be that painter.

"I should go," Kyrissa whispered. Yet she remained frozen before him.

"Stay." Robert didn't know where that came from. As though someone else, a person from long ago took control. An entity that tired of being alone. "I mean, I could give you a personal tour."

"You'd do that?" She narrowed her eyes, her gaze raking him from head to toe and back again. Robert couldn't help but smile. No one had looked at him like that in a long time. Her blush returned. "I wouldn't want to be a bother."

The eagerness in her voice contradicted her statement and sent a charge through him. This was ridiculous. Why was he offering to show a perfect stranger paintings he kept at arm's length from everyone else? *Because she understands them.* That thought brought Robert up short.

"No bother," he answered. "You are already here after all." Smiling when Kyrissa cringed, Robert gestured to the first of his paintings. After a moment, she smiled back. The brightness of her grin lit up her whole face and sent another rush through him that chipped away at the cold hard core within him.

"I've admired your collection for years and your own work too," she added quickly. "Your debut was a smashing success. I wish I had been able to make it. Seeing the Isle of the Dead alone would have been worth the trip. Tried, but tickets were impossible to get. Not even my best friend could get them and she can get everything she wants pretty much. It must have been amazing to be among all those..." She glanced up, trailing off, but dropped her gaze again quickly. "Sorry, I ramble when I'm nervous."

"I make you nervous?" Robert was glad to know the energy vibrating through his body wasn't limited only to him. "I am just a painter. Like you." The comment casual, Robert hoped it might garner more information on this mysterious woman who understood his works.

"Pfft. Not like you. There is so much emotion in your images." She paused in front of one of the pieces he painted under his current persona of Robert Shoalman. "I painted like this once." A whisper of longing echoed in her voice. "I wish I could do it again. But it's been so long and I don't think I can."

He inhaled sharply. No one painted like him. He wouldn't wish the agony of his curse on anyone else. Without thinking, he grabbed her hand. Every emotion captured in the paintings hanging in the small cramped space amplified as though doubled. She jumped but didn't pull away. Her breath increased along with his. Fingers tightening, the heat where skin met burned like fire. Did she feel the increased power too?

"You cannot learn this kind of painting," he whispered. The thrum of his heartbeat pounded in his ears until it echoed between the walls and pulsed within the connection of their hands. Her touch, hands rough from the paints and harsh cleaning chemicals of their chosen profession, more arousing than the slide of the softest silk across his bare skin. "You either can paint emotion into the canvas or you cannot."

"I have. Once. I can show you." Her mouth took a firm line and she pulled her hand out of his. Both of them gasped as the connection severed.

His paintings. They were creating an emotional overload, one he was not sure he wanted to stop or embrace further. A hundred years passed since his last connection to another. A hundred years of solitude, of loneliness. "We need to leave."

Afraid to touch her again, Robert held open the glass door. Staring at her until she moved, he closed the door after them making sure to engage the electronic locks this time. Immediately reason returned as the pounding beat of music and smell of stale beer replaced the charged sensation between them. Robert took several deep breaths before turning to confront Kyrissa. His body and mind back under control, he took in her tense form. Picking at the flecks of paint on her nails, she gazed around searching the room. Probably looking for an escape as much as he. But her comment stuck with him.

What if she was truly gifted? He had only ever found one other with the true gift and she had been ruthlessly torn away from him. In spite of his best efforts to the contrary, the prospect of seeing Kyrissa again morphed from atypical interest to anticipation.

"So when can you show me your painting?" He locked his hands behind him. One, to hide their shaking, and two, to keep himself from reaching out to touch her again. Perhaps his body was not merely charged from the emotions within the paint, but also from the beautiful woman standing in front of him.

"You're serious?" Kyrissa stared at him like he'd sprouted wings. She shook her head and closed her mouth. "Um, tomorrow afternoon? Or maybe tonight. After the show. I should check with my roommate though, before I invite a strange man home from a bar."

"Check with me about what?" Mandy Hayworth appeared and Kyrissa grabbed on to her with the desperation of a drowning woman. "Robert? What are you doing with Kyrissa?"

"*This* is your roommate?" Robert gasped and several unanswered questions surrounding Mandy fell into place.

"You know Robert Shoalman?" Kyrissa accused Mandy in the same breath.

Kyrissa Spear's ability to sense his paintings just took a hard right turn and piqued his curiosity a hundred fold. Now he had to see her painting. As an immortal being, Robert had numerous Guardians over the past five centuries—mortals pledged to protect him from the darkness of his curse. Now he needed to find out why Kyrissa Spears required a Guardian.

WHO IS TONI DECKER?

Two authors telling one sizzling story after another about twenty-somethings getting along in their own crazy, fantastical worlds. Both women are wives and mothers, sharing brain cells and characters as if they only exist with the other.

Toni, one half of the Toni Decker brain, is an avid reader of all things Young and New Adult while Kira, the Decker half of Toni Decker brain, devours fantasy for midnight snacks.

Together, their stories are one part New Adult, one part fantasy and three parts of holy hotness. We leave it up to the readers to decide who writes which character.

You can follow our journey on
Twitter: @ToniDeckerBooks and @KiraDecker & @ToniPicker

FaceBook: Toni Decker, Kira Decker, Toni Picker

Tumbler: Toni Decker Books

Wordpress: ToniDeckerBooks.wordpress.com

Made in the USA
San Bernardino, CA
16 September 2014